Dennis K. Hausker, a 1969 graduate of the Michigan State University and a Vietnam War veteran, is now in his seventies. He married his wife, now a retired teacher, in college and lives with her in Michigan, although she is from Maine. "I'd move back there in a New York minute," she tells him, though he is not sure what that means. At this point, he is only familiar with Michigan minutes.

The couple love to travel and their last trip was to Australia and New Zealand. It was a wow moment although the plane ride was a killer. He loves sports and follows MSU Spartans closely.

Of course, I dedicate any of my books to my wife. We're 52 years into our marriage and going strong. For this book, I also want to mention Matthew Hudy who provided assistance and creative inspiration in the work. Also, he has computer knowledge that I lack, being the luddite that I am.

Dennis K. Hausker

EVANSHARD GLADE

AUSTIN MACAULEY PUBLISHERS™

LONDON * CAMBRIDGE * NEW YORK * SHARJAH

Copyright © Dennis K. Hausker (2021)

All rights reserved. No part of this publication may be reproduced, distributed, or transmitted in any form or by any means, including photocopying, recording, or other electronic or mechanical methods, without the prior written permission of the publisher, except in the case of brief quotations embodied in critical reviews and certain other non-commercial uses permitted by copyright law. For permission requests, write to the publisher.

Any person who commits any unauthorized act in relation to this publication may be liable to criminal prosecution and civil claims for damages.

This is a work of fiction. Names, characters, businesses, places, events, locales, and incidents are either the products of the author's imagination or used in a fictitious manner. Any resemblance to actual persons, living or dead, or actual events is purely coincidental.

Ordering Information
Quantity sales: Special discounts are available on quantity purchases by corporations, associations, and others. For details, contact the publisher at the address below.

Publisher's Cataloging-in-Publication data
Hausker, Dennis K.
Evanshard Glade

ISBN 9781649794550 (Paperback)
ISBN 9781649794567 (ePub e-book)

Library of Congress Control Number: 2021911144

www.austinmacauley.com/us

First Published (2021)
Austin Macauley Publishers LLC
40 Wall Street, 33rd Floor, Suite 3302
New York, NY 10005
USA

mail-usa@austinmacauley.com
+1 (646) 5125767

This is my first book with Austin Macauley, so I'm looking forward to our partnership. My other books with other publishers left a good impression and I expect the same here. Thank you for sharing in this enterprise.

Prologue

Menacing clouds filled the night sky, as if foreshadowing a great battle. Lightning arced through the roiling maelstrom of the massive approaching storm. Ground-shaking thunder boomed in response to each jagged bolt of electricity generated from the multicolored clouds. Some of those bolts struck the ground, causing fires to ignite.

There was an unnatural feel to the weather, like it was far more than a normal seasonal storm. Seething with potency, terrifying and raising the hairs on one's arms, even the wild animals scampered for cover in fright. Laced throughout the clouds was a red tinge and many of the lightning strikes were sharp red in color.

Against this backdrop stood arrayed a grim horde of savage figures. Their crude leather hides covered thickly muscled bodies with bulging necks, each wearing a scarlet ruby fastened around their necks.

At their head stood Kraga, the leader, a giant being of daunting physical power and consuming hatred. With a feral look in his eyes, he appeared to be the avatar of death preparing to do his grisly work. He, like his people, was bereft of pity, compassion, or any other redeeming emotions. They were primal, frozen in their bestial roots, incapable of anything other than brutality and mayhem.

Surveying the scene, he grinned like a demon at the thought of what they would do to the helpless innocents in the villages scattered across the valley below. However, those villages were just fodder on the way to their goal of Carngard, the great city of the King, stronghold and bastion of their enemy centered in the country of Warmark, the greatest of the nations of the world.

Gripping his rune-covered stave, it glowed with a faint pulsing aura, like the steady beat of a heart. Connected to its wielder, the weapon caused a mirroring pulse in the ruby gem around his neck. Placing the stave in a sling behind his back, he drew weapons.

At last, he paused no longer. Turning to face his army of doom, with a battle axe in one hand and a war club in the other, raising his muscular arms, he voiced a deep roar. His brethren answered with a deafening shout that echoed throughout the entire valley. Hungry for battle, they began the charge. War had come to the land of the King.

Chapter 1

The Ruby Infant

Run faster or you're dead.

The words kept repeating in his mind, over and over. Sweat poured down his furrowed brow plastering his golden hair to his face and neck. His sharp blue eyes were focused on the dark path ahead. The exertion of the flight tested him to his limits and the terror in his soul nearly throttled him but he had to persevere. Carrying an infant, and she was precious beyond words, defenseless, and only he stood between her and the nightmare that stalked them. Stumbling and falling in the dark couldn't be allowed as death would be quick to follow.

Panting heavily, he labored to maintain the grueling pace, clutching the child covered in a tattered linen wrap. Glancing at her for a moment, her slightly crimson hair protruded from under the cloth, but what always caught his attention were her bluish eyes. With her lucid facial expressions, she looked wise beyond her tender age and seemingly aware beyond the reasoning of a little child.

Around her neck, she also wore a ruby pendant glowing with a soft pulsing aura. Strangely, for as terrifying as were their dire circumstances fleeing for their lives, the calm look she wore calmed him.

He mused mentally, but it came out as a question: *Perhaps it is possible to evade certain death?* He couldn't be sure.

The sound of hunting horns behind them was too close. Nearing the end of his endurance and looking around in a panic, he hurried up a small copse to hide in a thicket of brambles. Gasping at the additional exertion of scaling the rise, he was at his physical end of strength and could only pray they would race past.

It wasn't long before a seemingly unending stream of fearsome-looking invaders sprinted along the path he'd been on only moments earlier. Holding his breath in fear, he could only wait.

Miraculously, although it took considerable time for them to pass, he and the child were safe, spared for the moment.

Calming his heavy breathing and taking time to drink deeply from his sheepskin gourd of enhanced berry wine, the magic elixir refreshed him instantly and buoyed him for his difficult next step. Munching on cheese cubes, dried meat, and a handful of berries, he filled his growling stomach and then turned to her. His heart no longer thumped against his chest wall, but his fear had not diminished.

The milk he carried in his knapsack to feed her would only last for a day at most. It was imperative to find shelter and sustenance. Getting to the city was virtually impossible with the swarming enemy army between them now.

Although near enough to see in the distance across the wide meadow, it was irrevocably beyond his grasp. Closing his eyes, he softly muttered a prayer for strength and protection. It caused the child to chortle and kick her feet. Opening his eyes, he looked down at her.

"Silence, little one, we're not safe here."

She smiled at him, warming his heart in spite of the danger. After her milk, she burped. He chuckled and hugged her.

"You're truly precious, baby girl. I will protect you."

Brave words to say, but he didn't believe them. This enemy was driven and would never stop chasing him to find her. He was but one man to stand against the onslaught. How he knew the fact she was at the heart of their feral pursuit, he didn't know. Strangely, it was a truth that was simply in his mind after her appearance.

He needed to get some sleep to gather his strength. He mused, *Racing about in the dark is no viable plan. This sparse cover is better than stumbling into an enemy patrol.*

Just as he was about to lie down, the alarms sounded in the city, deep booming tones of bells and horns that echoed across the countryside. It was frightening to hear, ominous like a portent of Armageddon.

Could this really be the end of days? Again, he had no answer to his own musings.

Thinking back to his last conversation with Tartan, the Warmark King, he wasn't encouraged. In his dotage, the man was dismissive of all warnings, more interested in his idle pursuits. His days of leadership had passed long ago, along with his ebbing mind, as he sunk down to his basest emotions with poor choices directed at his servant girls who'd quickly developed skill in avoiding him, and certainly never being alone in a room with him.

The only hope for salvation and survival of the city rested in Storak, Commander of the Royal Army. Battle-tested, savvy, and shrewd, only he could mount a viable defense. Whether that defense could stand against this seemingly invincible dark tide sweeping over the realm remained to be seen.

The deep warning bells and horns continued to toll. As much as it provoked him, he couldn't vacate his spot to join the defenders. She took precedence over all other things.

What little sleep he could steal that night failed to fully refresh him. He awoke later groggy, and only swigs from his gourd revived him. She was hungry and after her meal, he was worried at how rapidly the supply of milk was disappearing.

"I must do this," he muttered as he arose. There was no other choice but to go back to the path and into the hazard of roving enemy patrols. He'd slept some, but that didn't alleviate his abiding fear. That fear seemed to heighten his senses. Smells were sharper, sounds caught his notice, and even the colors around him seemed more vivid.

As a wizard, he was not without defenses. However, facing an overwhelming army single-handedly wasn't within his abilities. This situation required quick wits and quick decisions. Similarly, her protective amulet was untested since she was so young and had no ability to invoke any powers until she was trained. That could only happen later if he could keep her alive. He was not privy to the tale of the mystery of her parents.

Easing down the rise back onto the path, he took the first turn he found to go parallel to the distant city. Though the probability of any village surviving the rampage was slim, there were possibly hidden survivors where he might find aid. With that general thought in mind, cautiously he forged ahead.

The sun peeked over the far horizon onto a gorgeous warm day. A cloudless azure sky indicated the brief intense storm had passed completely. If not for the war, it would have been a perfect scene. Birds chirped loudly flitting about far above searching for food. They were oblivious of what men did below.

Avoiding open ground, he stayed in the deciduous forest moving as rapidly as he could. Still, the risk of betraying their presence to enemy troops was high. Having no destination was discouraging. There was no guarantee anybody was alive out there for him to find.

Traveling until late afternoon, he heard the sounds of war commencing against the city. It was deafening with the roars of troops, the clash of weapons, and the explosions of ballista hitting the protecting walls and gates.

Turning at a sound behind him, he saw two youngsters run away deeper into the forest.

"Stop," he cried. "I need your help."

Moving after them, it wasn't long before he was confronted by adults. Five men brandishing swords and bows and arrows eyed him fearfully.

"I wish you no harm. We need your help." He held up his hand to calm them.

The men eyed him uncertainly. The biggest of them spoke.

"There's no help left in the world, stranger. We're all doomed. It's just a matter of time. Once those brutes finish off the city, they'll comb the countryside until they kill every living person."

"Please, we're desperate, and standing here to be found is—"

"Alright, follow us and move quickly."

The group sprinted away into the foliage and after a short distance came to the camp of these survivors. It was skillfully hidden in the deep forest in a cave.

He counted bodies and found ten men in total with twelve women and thirteen children.

"We're all that's left of our village."

"Are you in charge?"

"I've got the biggest mouth, so maybe I speak for the others."

Several women came over to take the baby. "We'll wash and feed her, stranger," said a sharp-eyed dark-haired young woman. She had long hair, but looped around her head and fastened up to keep it from being a problem on the move. Her discerning countenance caught his attention.

"Thank you, ma'am. I can't tell you how much that means to me. It's my charge to safeguard her."

She looked at the child and then back at him with a questioning glance. The baby eyed her in return. Pondering the child for a moment, she asked him, "Are you a wizard?"

"I am."

"The child, she's not like…"

"She's special."

"She has a feel to her, an aura." The woman had a look of fascination on her face staring at the baby girl.

"She does, ma'am. Again, I thank you for your help. As you can see, her milk supply was nearly spent."

The young woman broke her stare to look back at him. "I can be her wet nurse. I just had a baby."

"Thank you, you're a lifesaver in every sense of the word."

Following them into the shallow cave, everyone gathered around for an impromptu meeting.

He pondered for a moment before speaking, "I know you have questions for me, but can I hear your story first please?"

Rather than the big man speaking, instead he looked at the young woman holding the baby. Everybody else also looked at her.

She started slowly, and sadly, "Of course, we all heard them coming, but it was deep night and we were slow to awake and rise from our beds. Our men tried to mount a defense, but it was futile. The enemy swept through our village slaying with ease. Survival was a matter of luck. Most of the villains took little time to search about for victims. Some few of them took time to, well…you know. Women know about war and the fate of innocents.

"The enemy spared virtually no one. Those of us you see here, mostly we were out of the village for various reasons. Coming back, we barely escaped capture and slaughter. We could only band together to survive. All of us lost family. We're huddled here, but we have no plan for the future."

"I'm so sorry that happened to you."

"You're a wizard." It was a rhetorical statement, not a question. It felt to him like an onus.

"I am, but let me explain. I'm not like the High Mage or the members of the High Council. I'm only recently elevated into being a full wizard, though I have nearly no field experience. I haven't fought in any battles. I have powers, but that is no guarantee I can protect us."

"What about this daughter, is she yours? Did you lose a wife?"

"No, I have no wife, and she is not my daughter. I know nothing about her. She has been with me only since yesterday. I awoke in the night to a sound and found her placed in my room. Whoever brought her left no message, other than a single note with a lone word, Selana. I don't know if that is a message, or perhaps her name? However, I had an overwhelming feeling she was now my charge to protect with my life. That amulet around her neck holds great power. I can sense it, but I have no access to use it. It may be that it's beyond the abilities of a junior wizard like me."

"Her delicate perfect facial features are angelic. Her parents must have been wonderful people. We can call her Selana and assume it's her name."

"I suppose that could be true, that they were wonderful. I'm a skeptical person by nature. I don't like to make assumptions about anything. Being attractive is no guarantee of goodness or fine character in a person."

They stared at each other for a moment before she spoke again.

"The crux of this for you, for her, and for us is what do we do next? Will you lead us?"

He frowned. "Am I the best choice for the job? I doubt it."

"Regardless, there's no doubt there are no others in this cave better suited for the job."

His eyes glazed for a moment pondering the daunting task, taking responsibility for all of these lives. Continuing the conversation, he speculated about the obvious in a reflective tone.

"There are so many questions, not the least of which is what to do next. After all of these ages where the barbarians stayed in their mountains, why did they come now? Have they become servants of dark powers? That storm was no natural event. I sensed great power being wielded and can only assume the dark mages have chosen to enact a plan."

"What can common people like us do against such might? You saw how easily they destroyed us. They will be back."

"I agree with you."

"However feeble you think you are, you were chosen to protect this precious child for a reason, and we're imminently better off with you than without."

He glanced around the group. All of the faces stared at him, some looked hopeful, and some looked worried. At that point, he had no doubts he couldn't abandon them.

"What is your name, wizard?"

"Jeren, son of Jeren. My fellow students called me Jeren the lesser. They meant it in jest, but there is truth in the taunt. My father was a great man, well-respected and significant in our community. He was formerly an officer in the Royal Army and served for most of his life."

"Did you ever consider following his path into the military?"

"Not really, it wasn't the direction I wanted to go. He never spoke openly, but I sensed he was disappointed in me, like I was a coward."

"Surely he must have been pleased you were accepted into the path of wizardry."

"I don't know. He was taken with illness and died rapidly. My mother was devastated and moved away back to her ancestral home with her family. She has since passed away also. I chose to follow my destiny here when the way opened to seek the power in magic. I worry you'll depend on me and I'll fail you."

"That's not a worry for us. It seems to be some self-doubt of yours. The facts are we're put together here in this precarious state and I believe we must all agree to trust and help each other. Think of it as you doing your part for our little band."

Jeren pondered only a moment. The option of striking out alone again seemed foolish.

"I will stay with you. Selana needs milk, for one thing. Having a group is better than the alternative, I agree."

" Thank you. My name is Arium and my baby boy is Darik. This man you called our leader is Stren. He's correct; he's the loudest of us, but we're all grateful for his size, strength, and fighting skills. He saved us on the run numerous times slaying attackers so we could escape."

"Hello, Stren."

"Jeren."

"What about your husband, Arium?"

"He was killed in the first fighting, back in the village."

"I'm sorry."

"It's done now and we can't afford to grieve our losses or we'll join them soon enough. What would you advise we do?"

"I know you would desire to gain sanctuary in the Carngard, but that isn't what I would do. Getting through the enemy army surrounding the city is impossible, much less gaining admittance. They would never open the gate, for obvious reasons.

"Also, even if we got in, there is no guarantee they will prevail. We'd be trapped inside a dying city to be slaughtered by savages. As you already know, they show no mercy to women or children. If we have a chance, we must forge our own way out here. Leaving the area going away from the war on the city increases our chances. Enemy patrols will lessen the farther away we go."

The villagers looked at each other.

"It's risky," said Stren. "However, I agree with you. Clearing enemy picket lines to avoid their noose makes absolute sense to me. Even without deciding where to go, any place is better than sitting here vulnerable in the middle of an active war zone. We can adjust as we go."

"I'd say we take a day or two hunting to build up meat and water for the journey. Once we begin our trek, we must be as swift as possible leaving this place."

Everybody nodded their heads in agreement. They now had purpose, regardless of any risk.

"I will cast a cloaking spell to shield us from discovery in the meantime."

The villagers beamed, like suddenly they were safe from all harm. Jeren almost cautioned them, but decided to let them enjoy the feeling of protection for the moment.

Going out of the cave, softly he muttered words to invoke the powerful magic.

Returning into the cave, Arium handed him little Selana, smiling warmly at him. "Thank you, Jeren,"

He shrugged, taking the little bundle into his arms. Selana smiled too. It was amazing to him, she never cried. He 'felt' like she was bonded to him, like he was her father.

How can that be in a single day, he mused in wonder? He had no conception, nor could he be sure he was correct in that idea. In truth, it was he who bonded to her.

Hunting at sunup in the morning when the animals were on the move to feeding grounds and watering holes went well. The women were well practiced dressing the kills and efficiently extracting the meat to prepare it for their travels.

Meanwhile, the men made more bows and created additional arrows. Stren explained, "Having a bow lost or broken while on the move wouldn't allow time to stop to make more. We need a redundant supply, just in case. However, additional spears are made more difficult without benefit of forges to make metal tips. The same is true of swords."

As the men discussed the preparations, Jeren spoke, "I'll probably sound foolish to you, but I think we need to arm everybody. The women must be taught to fight to defend themselves. There are so few of us."

Stren frowned. "Perhaps they can learn to shoot with bows in time, but as far as swords…"

"Again, I don't want to sound foolish, but back in your village, I suspect there are weapons lying about."

"What? Go back to the village?" asked a bewildered older man.

Stren spoke again, "I think you're right, Jeren. The enemy would never expect us to return there with everybody dead. Gathering plenty of arms is a smart move, and our horses there may be roaming around. We'd have pack animals and there's probably plenty of food to gather. I agree with the idea."

"Is it far away?"

"Traveling on foot, about half a day, I'd say."

The other men shrugged or nodded with no better ideas being suggested.

While the women were busy working on food preparation, Arium was listening close by.

She added her ideas, "Can I suggest you scout the area there first? If you can corral sufficient mounts, ride back here. All of us can then ride back to the village to scavenge what we can, pack up the spare animals with supplies, and then make a swift ride out of here. Can your concealment spell be used to hide us while we work, more than just a small bubble?"

"I have never tested the limit of how far I can extend the cloaking magic."

"Well, it must be done, even if we incur more risk. It's precarious no matter what we choose to do. Let's get to it."

The men chuckled at Arium's authoritative tone. She wasn't amused.

"Get up you louts; we have no time to waste."

"Yes ma'am," said Stren. He arose as did the other men; the smirks remained on their faces. Only Jeren didn't smirk.

Stren took the lead as they marched out heading back to their old ruined village. He was right that it took half a day to travel, even at a brisk pace. Jeren labored at the pace and was being forced to gradually tone his muscles to cope. For him, it meant frequent sore muscles. His comrades suffered few of his maladies. Their normal work kept them adequately toned for physical strains.

For a little band of survivors sorely in need of good fortune, finding and catching ample horses was surprisingly easy. It was distressing to see the dead bodies strewn about, those that hadn't been dragged away by wild animals.

Riding back to the cave took a fraction of the time and soon everybody was loaded up and the cave abandoned. Fortuitously, they were gone when a party of enemy raiders came down that same path only an hour later.

Riding into the village was emotionally charged for the women and children, particularly seeing dead family members slain in the attack. It was Arium who took charge of the moment.

"I'm sorry, but we have no time for this. They're gone and we can't bring them back. Get about our business gathering stores and weapons and let's flee before the enemy finds us here in the open."

"What about burying—"

"No," said Jeren firmly. "We can't do that. I understand the gesture, but that would alert hostiles that we passed this way, and that we're out here still alive. We don't need them tracking us."

It was a sullen group who went about the somber business of stripping away anything of use to the troop and loading the many pack animals with food, weapons, and the other useful items. Adding to the dim feelings was a gray rainy day. Dressing in heavier garb against the precipitation and wind, and to protect the children from the elements, there was some muttering in the ranks.

When everybody was remounted, they looked at Jeren. He had no problem recognizing the sour mood of his new flock. *Perhaps this isn't the best choice*, he mused mentally, but wisely said nothing. Looking confident was the only real option for him amongst strangers.

Arium asked, "Where do we go?"

"Initially, we go north."

"What, toward the mountains, their mountains?" Her incredulous look was daunting.

"Only until we clear out of the immediate area, then we'll gradually curve to head west going parallel to the mountain chain."

"What's to the west?"

"Hopefully, it's the beginning of a new life, away from this war."

Arium looked questioningly at him and then at Stren.

Stren scowled and shrugged his shoulders. "Arium, we have nothing better. None of us has done any traveling to know what's around us. Jeren can still cloak us, so I don't think where we go is the main issue."

Arium muttered something and then she shrugged. "So be it."

She'd provided Jeren with a harness to place Selana against his chest similar to what she used for carrying her own son. It made it infinitely easier having his hands free. Selana tolerated it very well and fell asleep as they rode. The warmth of her little body against him was comforting, and strangely reassuring. His own cloak he used to cover her as well as himself.

Just when they made their turn westward and started to feel optimistic, suddenly riders emerged from the nearby trees and rode to surround them. Dressed in the red uniforms of the Warmark Royal Guard, they were distinct within the King's armed forces. With shiny gold colored helmets, gold epaulets on the shoulders and gold piping, they wore black pants with a gold stripe down the side, and shiny black boots. Still, they carried the standard of the monarchy.

"Who are you?" shouted their Captain.

Nobody spoke for a moment, startled at the sudden ambush. Arium answered, annoyed.

"Who do you think we are? We're survivors from a village massacre. You've frightened the children and they don't need more frights after what they've seen. Your city is under siege, so how is it you're out here to harass your peaceful and unprotected subjects?"

The Captain bristled at her impertinent tone and defiant look.

"Captain," Jeren spoke quickly. "This is not the time or place for anything but cooperation. We've just left a cave where we were hiding to flee the area in search of a safe place to start anew. She did ask a good question."

"We were away carrying royal dispatches abroad. By the time we returned, the enemy was everywhere. We've fought every day and realize there is no chance to return into the Royal City."

"Frankly speaking, Captain, I don't know if the forces in Carngard can prevail. I suspect there is far more involved than an invasion by mountain barbarians. I sensed considerable power being wielded in that unnatural storm. My belief is the dark mages have sent the barbarians, though I know nothing more. It's my speculation, but…"

"So you're a wizard? That's a welcome boon finally. It's easy to become discouraged when facing impossible odds. I'm Captain Grakar Morstem, by the way. I have twenty troops, which is not much of an army."

"It is to us. We'd be grateful if you chose to join us, even though we'll probably ride out of the realm, perhaps for good."

The Captain eyed them for a moment and then looked at his troops. They sat impassively waiting for his decision as their leader.

Grakar nodded his head. "We will ride with you, pilgrims. We'd have no hopes of survival remaining here. There are too many enemy troops."

Subsequently, the trek westward resumed. Captain Morstem rode up to the front of the column beside Jeren, curiously eyeing the baby strapped to his chest. Then turning around to look back at Arium, he explained, "Ma'am, the man come up to ride beside you is my second-in-command, Lieutenant Brek Storig."

The Lieutenant tipped his helmet to her and spoke, "It's nice to meet you, ma'am."

He was dashing, young, muscular, ruggedly handsome, and he caught Arium's notice. She nodded in return, but seemed flustered for the first time Jeren had seen.

"This is your child," said Brek rhetorically.

"It is. This is my son, Darik."

Brek then looked at Jeren. "Is that your child you carry, wizard?"

"No, she was placed in my care recently. Honestly, I know nothing of her origins. We call her Selana, though if she was named differently by her parents, we have no way to know that."

"An interesting mystery, the origins of the child," said Captain Morstem. "Just like what you say about more being behind this sudden invasion, I would guess the same is true with your little passenger."

"She's a good little girl. I've come to cherish her in our brief time together."

Grakar replied, "That is understandable. She's a stranger to all of us, but coming around her, I feel at peace."

"She has an aura," Arium added. "I picked up on it too, the first time I held her. As Jeren said, she is special. What that will mean for her future and for ours, we'll see."

Jeren continued, "I'll try to assure she survives to grow up. I believe the enemy army is looking for her which is another reason we needed to be away from this area."

"Is this something you know, the horde searching for a single infant? It seems an unlikely reason to invade our nation."

"I can't say with certainty, but I strongly believe it. If the person or persons who brought her to me placed ideas in my mind, I don't know. I awoke to find her mysteriously in my room. That's all that I know at this point. I admit, the rest is only my speculations."

"Do you know what is ahead of us going west, Captain?" asked Arium.

"Please call me Grakar, ma'am."

"Then call me Arium."

"To answer your question, to the west is the nation of Grecia, realm of King Argost. Beyond his lands, I don't know. I've been to his capital city of Boria once. They're not a prosperous land and much of the ostentatious display you see in the palace in Carngard is not seen there in Boria. They live a Spartan existence by necessity as they don't have the natural resources of the lands around them.

"I will say they have one major asset. Their army is a very good one, and perhaps the best there is. The Field General is old, but crafty enough to appoint a genuine battle master to lead crack troops to protect their country. He's also a genius at military strategies.

"Otherwise, they would have been gobbled up long ago by their bigger neighbors. He's a relatively young man to be a general. His name is Gerak, nicknamed the beast because he trains his troops constantly to the highest level. In battle, he does fight like a beast, as do his troops. Though a general in rank, nonetheless, he personally joins his soldiers fighting the enemy, heedless of any risks."

He paused a moment, replaying some memory in his mind.

Looking over at Jeren and then back at Arium who were listening closely, he continued, "That army is more than a match for any fighting force on this planet. The bigger armies all around them do not intimidate which is why they live in peace with those greedy neighbors. Starting a war with Gerak would not have a good outcome for any invaders."

"It sounds like a good destination for our little band."

"It does, I agree."

Camping that night, Jeren cast a protection over the camp. Although the spell didn't keep out the misting rain, it put everybody at ease. Soldier and civilian alike shared freely from their supplies and chatted amicably, getting to know one another. If not for the dire circumstances occurring in the world around them, it would have seemed a perfect outing. Normal sounds of the night abounded as if nothing was amiss in the land. However, they didn't risk making any campfires in light of the war with roving barbarian patrols in the area.

Jeren sat talking with Stren, Grakar, and Brek. Arium couldn't manage to stay away. After feeding the babies, she made her way over inviting herself to join the leadership brain-trust in conversation.

The men smiled at her. She took it as smirks.

"What, am I not welcome here because I'm a woman?"

"Of course, you're welcome," Jeren replied warmly. "This is not a group to exclude anybody. Your thoughts and opinions are just as valuable as anybody else."

"Good, I'm glad you have a brain in your head, Jeren. Some men are not so wise about dealing fairly with women."

Captain Morstem replied, "I suspect if anybody were foolish enough to cross you, it would not go well and they would pay a terrible price."

All the men smiled and agreed.

She pondered them for a moment, considering if they were secretly making sport of her. Finally, she answered. "Well, I'm glad that's settled, so what are we talking about?"

Jeren replied, "Grakar was sharing some observations about our destination."

"What kind of observations?" she asked suspiciously.

Grakar frowned. "Not those kinds of things, if that's what you're implying. We were official visitors there on official business."

"That doesn't normally stop men from pursuing their kind of mischief. I'm not naïve, or stupid."

"Regardless of your pointed opinions, Arium, what we noted in our visit to Boria is what I've told you. Our interest wasn't the women, it was their military. I glimpsed Grecian army training sessions and it was brutal. They come very close to killing blows on a routine basis. Having serious injuries is not uncommon. Actually, the troops see injuries and scars like badges of honor and proof of their courage. Working always in tandem as they're trained to avoid being isolated in battle, small numbers of their soldiers are the measure of any soldiers anywhere.

"I was dazzled and could only be envious of such military skill and precision. With my unit, I've tried to incorporate their training methods and devotion to duty. It's helped keep us alive when facing those feral invaders."

"What if the enemy crosses the border?" asked Stren.

"In battle, I like their chances, even against the barbarians. They have no fear and I think the result would be many fewer barbarians left to run about."

Arium muttered, "If they wiped out every living one of those beasts, I would be very happy. They took my husband without a care or a conscience. I could never forgive such a crime. They're barely above the level of animals and are a scourge that needs to be totally eradicated from this world."

Jeren replied evenly, "I'd say that's a matter for another day. Quelling those disturbing emotions is something of a necessity for all of us, in my opinion. We can afford no mistakes of any kind."

Captain Morstem added, "Soldiers learn that lesson early. What we see in battles, losing dear friends, it ignites hatred that one must learn to control. Battle isn't forgiving of mistakes and grants no second chances."

Arium scowled, staring away into the nearby forest.

Chapter 2

Flight to Boria

Everybody agreed that going to seek refuge in Boria seemed the prudent choice, but getting there was far different than actually being there. The Grecian border was still a considerable distance away. As long as they remained in their own realm, they were subject to the perils of the war and enemy troops on the move.

Jeren worried more as he watched the developing dynamics in their newly merged group. The very thing that had concerned him before, it bothered him more so now. He was a wizard and sooner or later, they would expect miracles from him. It wasn't that the soldiers were suddenly incompetent or inattentive. It was that the edge they'd had with facing death nipping at their heels, it seemed to be gone replaced by their belief a wizard had the answers for any eventuality.

Jeren knew better than that. If he had any answers, HE would be surprised.

Riding steadily along, not looking behind because he already knew what was happening, the soldiers and people rode interspersed talking as they were settling into those feelings of safety and magical protection. Jeren felt like screaming at them, *Wake up, you're not safe.*

Coping with the strange sensation of being lonely in the midst of a crowd, it proved to be difficult. The mental weight of his burden in this situation tested him.

Selana made some baby sounds causing him to glance down at her. She cooed happily and chortled, kicking her feet and arms. If she could somehow sense his unease and stress, which seemed impossible, she had the perfect tonic. Suddenly, it seemed they were plugged in together and his angst simply drained away. His worries gone, he couldn't even remember what had troubled him only moments before.

Riding forward until the sunlight started to fade in the late afternoon, they'd avoided detection thus far. The rain clouds had passed over the horizon. It emboldened the group to imagine danger was gone and they were in the clear. Jeren knew nothing could be further from the truth.

The terrain was intermittent stands of forest mixed with open land used for farming. Normally, it would have been a peaceful and relaxing setting. There had been no further occurrences of the strange weather, for which Jeren was grateful.

Camping at the edge of the tree line kept them out of open ground, out of sight, and yet not deep enough into the forest to be subject to roving predator animal attacks. Again, Jeren established a magic to shield them from prying eyes.

Captain Morstem assigned soldiers for shifts of camp guard duty for the night.

Morning came early to a cold camp, with no fires allowed to draw notice. Even as they rode farther away from Carngard each day, the distressing sounds of battle still carried to them.

"At least the Royal Army still holds. I feel guilty being here fleeing for our lives," said Brek. He was talking to Arium while she ate a quick breakfast. Mostly, she didn't respond. Wolfing down her food and coffee, finally she muttered to him, "The babies must be fed."

Feeding the two babies had to be done in the middle of the people by putting a blanket over them and her. She felt self-conscious about it, but there was no other way. With the extra baby now, Arium was conscious of her own need for adequate food during the relocation out of the country. Privation wasn't a good predicament for a wet nurse trying to feed both children.

Packing up the camp, the troop set out westward again.

On this day, the Captain rode beside Jeren again to discuss strategy. "I've been talking with Brek and we worry about staying on this road. The enemy will be watching for travelers. Perhaps we should look to do what they don't expect."

"What did you have in mind?"

"One option is to parallel the road staying just inside the tree line. However with that plan, we could stumble onto enemy warriors in hiding, waiting and watching."

"What's the alternative?"

"Well, if I send a small unit of my riders ahead on the road; that could spring any traps waiting for us. If the attack comes from a small force, the main body can quickly rush forward to join the vanguard to slay them. If it's a large attack, they flee westward drawing the enemy away while we race after them freed to cover ground rapidly."

"Training for wizards doesn't include military plans and strategies for conventional armies. You must use your best judgment. I can offer no useful help about this."

"Have you fought before, Jeren?"

"I've neither fought with arms, nor with magic. Of course in our training we had mock magic battles, but very controlled and non-threatening. For wizards, learning actual magical fighting is something of a trauma. One must plunge in and survive or perish. Usually we're in groups with experienced wizards who can help us."

"Where are your brethren now? Why are they not defending the King and the city?"

"I don't know that they aren't. Perhaps that's why you still hear the sounds of battle."

"You got no instructions from your High Mage?"

"When I awoke in my quarters, the building was empty. The barbarians were closing in fast so I had to flee instantly to save Selana. I've been running ever since."

"That is strange. I wonder if there were other forces involved in the background. Apparently, it wasn't your own order that anointed you with responsibility for the child."

"I wonder the same thing. However, such forces would have to be as strong, or stronger, than the High Mage and the High Council to drive them away. I find that hard to believe. There were no bodies or signs of battle."

"Dark Mages, perhaps; what other force could there be capable of this?"

"I…don't know. This sweet innocent child couldn't be one of their ilk."

"Are you certain of that?"

A chill ran down his spine. Selana was sleeping peacefully. It was hard to imagine her as any threat, present or future.

Riding behind Jeren and the Captain, Brek was continuing talking to Arium. She responded to him, but seldom engaged in conversation and tended to act aloof or impatient. For Brek, who always had women chasing after him, to have a woman treat him such stoked his fires like pouring a flammable liquid on a flame. He had never lost in that arena and it irked him now she wasn't instantly dazzled and in awe of him.

Arium fussed over her son frequently, or asked Jeren about Selana as they traveled.

Jeren was slightly amused by the contest. He'd never pursued a woman before. His studies and training had allowed no time for romantic pursuits. The Captain paid no attention.

"So what are your thoughts, Jeren?" asked the Captain.

"Well, they must sort out their own…"

It dawned on him suddenly. The Captain wasn't talking about Arium and Brek.

"I mean…as I said, I defer to you about any military decisions. Guessing about what is the best choice in an area where I have no training or experience would be foolish and could lead to dire results."

The Captain narrowed his gaze for a moment and then looked back at Brek. Brek turned his head forward and he stopped talking at Arium. "Is there something you need, sir?"

"I've been talking with Jeren about our concerns about staying on the road."

Brek sat up to pay closer attention.

"He prefers we make the decisions. Such things are out of his element."

"As you wish, sir, what are your orders?"

"We've been fortunate thus far, but I don't want to tempt fate. Will you lead a small band ahead to test our theory? Remember; do not engage unless we have the clear advantage. Flee and lose the pursuit rather than draw their notice onto us in this column."

"Yes sir."

"We're vulnerable out in the open, and Brek, be very careful. We can afford no losses at all with this small band."

"I understand. I won't let you down, sir."

Turning his face to Arium, she stared at him with worry.

"Goodbye, madam."

"Brek, listen to your Captain and be safe. Those barbarians are dangerous."

"I will."

He chose four of the best troops and rode away at the gallop. Grakar started the column forward following the vanguard keeping them within eye sight. If something dire occurred it was vital to be in a position to react quickly, whether to join an attack or the race into hiding.

Stren came up to ride beside Arium. Jeren heard them talking softly.

They rode for perhaps an hour when suddenly, Selana awoke with a startled cry. Jeren looked at her in alarm.

"What is it?" asked Arium.

Ahead, they saw a dark wave of the barbarian warriors racing out from concealment in the forest toward the vanguard unit from both sides, in force. Against overwhelming numbers, it wasn't a situation where they would turn and fight. Racing ahead at full gallop, the vanguard was in no real danger. The enemy tried to give pursuit, but their army didn't ride animals. Capturing or killing Brek and his soldiers wasn't possible for them. The important issue was whether they would spot Jeren and the trailing column.

Captain Morstem rapidly led them into the cover of the forest. Riding north through the trees for a time, they gradually angled toward the west. Slowing down the pace was forced on them as the forest here was thick with undergrowth and there was no path, *per se*, for them to follow.

The women and children were very brave in handling the adversity with very little sound. Being scratched by thorns and briars left numerous bloody cuts, not to mention the pain of those injuries as there were some of the children who were very young; therefore, making it quietly with the children was an ongoing danger. The men worried a great deal about them crying out and betraying their position.

Luck held for a time as they tried to make up lost ground on the vanguard unit and escape discovery by the enemy. That luck ran out as they ran into a barbarian patrol traveling south, which intersected the path of the group.

For the first time, Jeren was forced into battle mode as this was no small force attacking them. Captain Morstem deployed his remaining soldiers into a skirmish line. The village men lined up behind them to cover any potential breakthroughs by enemy warriors. Even with the allies mounted and the enemy on foot, it was not going to be an easy fight.

The barbarians went screaming into their normal battle frenzy, ready to slaughter. However, their leader spotted Jeren, and in particular, he saw Selana strapped to his chest. For the first time, Jeren heard her cry. Glancing at her face, she was terrified. It evoked feral rage in his heart and any issues with taking life evaporated from his mind.

Starting a chant gathering power, he shouted the final word, *Flammis*, unleashing a devastating torrent of blue power. Sweeping across the enemy force from back to front, they were wasted in an instant of crackling searing blue flame. Only the warriors directly engaged in hand to hand with allied troops remained.

Instantly, the battle shifted to the favor of Grakar and his experienced troops. Dispatching the remaining marauders occurred swiftly and soon they resumed the journey, hurrying away from the carnage. Grakar opted to move back closer to the tree line to improve travel speed and to find the vanguard unit.

If significant enemy forces were nearby, it was a risk he was willing to take to increase the speed of their travel.

For Jeren, after the fright of the sudden fight forced to do battle ended, he felt the roiling emotions of first blood kills. Even with creatures so reprehensible, taking their lives bothered him. It wasn't any intellectual reasoning punishing him; it was deep in his spirit, like he had put a stain on his soul. Looking down at Selana, she eyed him closely with a look on her face he could only describe as enigmatic.

Once they rode out of the adverse forest terrain into easier sparser areas, the Captain halted the group.

"Is anybody injured?"

A number of soldiers and a couple of village men reported minor injuries. With Jeren's sudden magic attack, the group had been spared any loss of life. Grakar looked at Jeren's face in recognition of his emotions. He spoke knowingly.

"Wizard, we all go through it, that first time having to kill. It's not easy, and the memory never goes away. You gradually come to understand you do what you must. There is no other choice. From what you said about visiting these people's ravaged village, you saw what the barbarians do. Don't waste time shedding tears for them."

Arium piped in, "Jeren, I told you that first day, we're better off with you than without. Now you see the truth of my words. This was no sin for you. Their lives are the sin. What they do is the sin. I suspect this will not be the last battle we have. Toughen up."

The soldiers chuckled. Even Jeren couldn't repress a smile. "Yes, ma'am."

Briefly bandaging cuts, they rode away shortly. Skirting the tree line, Grakar scanned the highway searching for signs of his people. They were not in sight.

"Well, I assume they escaped. We've seen no bodies."

Jeren was looking at Selana who'd fallen back to sleep.

"She seemed to react just before the battle. I don't know if she can foresee what's going to happen before us. It's the first time she's cried, when we were in danger."

"She's no normal baby. What we're dealing with, I think only time will reveal the scope of it. I don't think that's a bad thing."

"I feel no threat from her. Perhaps we're all naïve about it, but I will continue to defend her, with my life if necessary."

He saw the hint of a smile on her tiny face in her sleep. His feeling of calm returned to stem the tide of his self-doubts after the battle.

Traveling until dusk, they did their usual, making camp inside the trees. Again it was a cold camp. The vanguard unit was elsewhere for the night. Whether that was by choice or necessity, they had no way to know.

On this evening, Arium chose to place her bedding beside Jeren.

"I think it wise if I'm close at hand and able to care for Selana as well as Darik. Do you have a problem with that?" It sounded more like a challenge than a request.

Jeren shrugged and smiled. "Of course not, Selana loves you as much as me. I appreciate all that you do for her. I guess I think of her as a daughter with you as a mother. I'm not saying—"

"Jeren, I know what you're saying. I don't take offense and I realize you intend no disrespect to me."

"Good, because I don't disrespect anybody. I have too little practice in dealing with women. If I cause you strife or stress, it's truly inadvertent. I claim no competence with the fairer sex."

Arium eyed him a moment. "You're right, there is a great deal with relationships that passes you by. It doesn't need to be a problem. I can teach you about this."

"Thank you, I can never learn too much about any topic."

"Jeren, I will tell you, you're a good man. Accept it as a simple statement as I'm not one to compliment."

"Eh…"

"Now is the time to be silent. That's your first lesson."

He nodded and smiled. Arium picked up Selana to bathe her before sleep time in the camp. Darik was already cleansed.

Later, when they all lay back to rest, it was difficult to sleep. Everybody felt a sense of foreboding. Much later in the darkness, the usual forest sounds went silent alerting the sentries of danger nearby. Selana suddenly awoke, which woke Jeren. He felt her fear transmitting into him as her tiny body was trembling. Glancing about, he cautiously raised his power to bolster his magic cloaking the camp, but also to carefully spread out wider in the area probing for threats. This didn't have the feel of barbarian warriors closing in. This was a far more sinister threat.

Jeren could only wonder if actual dark mages were roaming about searching for them. Alerting them with his probe was a severe risk and he wasn't practiced in confronting or fighting their deadly powers. Consequently, he decided to discontinue the probe, concentrating his full power into the concealing shield.

Selana remained stirred up for a time, but eventually, she settled down and was quickly asleep. Jeren took it as a sign the threat had moved away. Their good luck continued, at least for the time being.

He glanced over at Arium. Her eyes were open, staring at him.

"All is well, ma'am, you can sleep in safety," he whispered.

"Can I ask you about wizardry?"

"Yes."

"The power you wield, is it innate within you, or is it taught?"

"Well, it's something of both, actually. I showed both an aptitude for learning the way, and I had the necessary inner abilities to cultivate power."

"Can you tell if I have those traits?"

"I…eh…"

"It's a simple question, Jeren."

"I suppose I could check."

"I've seen the tragic result for common people in our lives. Defenseless and easy prey for evil, I will no longer tolerate that state for me, or my son. If you plan to train Selana when she is old enough, I want you to train Darik too. As for me, I want to start immediately. I will also ask the Captain to train me to fight with weapons. You can join me in that martial training. Neither of us can afford to be weak, ever again."

"I…agree, to both of your proposals."

"If we become the greatest wizard/soldiers in history, I think that is a very good goal, don't you agree?"

"How could I not? We've already established a person does not disagree with you."

"Good, now we can sleep."

Falling back to sleep at that point was difficult for him. His mind had been set in motion working out all that her plans would entail. It would not be easy for so many reasons. Not the least of which was being on the run trying to avoid death.

The dawning of the twin suns brought a stir to a sleepy camp as nobody was well rested. The sensation that true evil had passed too nearby haunted the group. The women of the camp were somber and the children fearful. Daily being forced to eat cold food took a toll in itself. It would have been easy to complain, but everyone realized death stalked them. Even the children internalized their emotions to endure hardships stone-faced.

Riding again as soon as they could muster, Grakar decided to ride back out to the highway to increase the pace. Outrunning the barbarians was less an issue since they now knew the enemy was always on foot.

Around noontime, the vanguard unit rode out from the tree line.

Brek beamed. "I'm so happy to see you. We had a fearful night and got little sleep. Something dire was in the woods." Looking at Jeren, he asked, "Do you think those evil wizards could be nearby hunting us?"

"I think that is a real possibility. I thought that very thing last night. We also felt evil pass by us."

"Captain, is it safe to ride the highway?"

"Brek, I feel haste is the better choice now. I want to put distance between us, the enemy warriors, and especially any dark mages lurking about. Stay with us now as splitting our forces is no longer the best option."

He turned to Jeren. "Do you think they search for us, or the child?"

"My thought is we wouldn't matter anymore than any other Warmark citizens and soldiers. Selana is the only explanation for why they could be chasing us. We allude to her being significant without knowing any reasons why. As time goes on being with her, the reactions I see, the feelings we all have, it points to Selana perhaps being far greater a person than we could imagine. Even as a little child, she exerts her aura."

"I can't disagree, Jeren. If she can do these things as an infant, what potential can she have when she's grown?"

"True."

"By the way, I've spoken with Arium. She expressed her wishes about her goals. What is your feeling about training her? The other women also wish to be taught to fight."

"I have no objections. She's also asked me about training in wizardry. I've agreed to test her for the proper aptitude and for that kernel of innate ability necessary to foster magical power."

"Then we are in agreement. Tonight, we will have a busy camp to start training them."

That evening, they camped far into the forest. After a quick meal, with sentries deployed, Jeren cast the concealing protection while the remainder of the group gathered around to watch when Jeren sat down with Arium.

They sat cross-legged, knees touching each other.

"Arium, my first test is the hardest. If you lack that inner flame, anything else isn't possible. What you potentially have is an ability that is dormant, like a vestige of something of our ancient past. To access it, think of it as an egg where I must crack the protective shell. It isn't easy and I must warn you not without discomfort. How people react varies widely. Even with those who cannot succeed, it is not a pleasant experience. Do you understand what I'm saying?"

"I can't understand what I've never gone through. I can only say regardless of any consequences I'm determined to try this. The goal is worth any growing pangs I must endure. How long does this take?"

"I can't answer that. It can be swift, or perhaps it requires repeated attempts. Also, you should know this can be something of an intimate process. I must enter your mind. Having a person gain access to your inner thoughts, feelings, and your deepest secrets can be distressing. It requires extending trust, that your mentor will do you no harm. At the same time I see your secrets, you will see mine also. Are you ready for such total exposure of your life?"

"Can anybody say yes to that? Regardless of any possible ramifications, I'm committed to this task. Let's do this thing."

"As you wish, Arium, now close your eyes. I must raise power to begin this. You'll feel growing warmth within your whole body and then when I come into your mind, it can be disorienting. Some people become physically ill."

Taking a deep breath to steel her emotions, she nodded. "I'm ready."

Going into another person was an experience like no other. Jeren's training in the academy had been on the receiving end most of the time. Only toward the end did the novices practice on each other, but in none of those cases was it a first time experience. This was a scary prospect for Jeren as it was possible to injure the person if he made a mistake.

Pushing through the outer husk of flesh and bone, he cautiously moved into her brain. Her body reacted immediately as she shuddered and let out an audible gasp. Jeren gave her time to adjust to their joined consciousness. The shudders calmed and he proceeded. Arium was shocked when they could communicate with their thoughts.

How are you doing, Arium?

I'm fine. You were right, it is disorienting, but gradually, it seems to be getting better.

Do you see what I was saying how all within us is laid bare?

I do. From what I see of you, I understand what you're seeing of me. We know each other like no other two people alive.

That's not really accurate. All wizards go through this. We're not alone in sharing truths.

It would be easy to judge. Knowing my missteps and foolish choices puts you in the same position to judge me.

I'm going to search for that nugget I spoke of. I can't say how long it will take, or if it is even there to be found. In the meantime, the passage of time won't affect you. You won't even be aware of it.

Proceed, Jeren, I trust you implicitly. Now that you know my secrets, you can see why I said that.

Likewise.

Beginning the process, it was consuming because what he searched for could be encased almost anywhere.

For the camp members avidly watching the strange process, there were no words spoken. However, they could see things were happening as Arium's body reacted in many different ways with more of the shudders, sometimes gasps, moans, and groans. Her body rocked occasionally while Jeren remained relatively motionless. Hours went by for the camp while Jeren and Arium remained in stasis seeking her nugget, and the answer if she was a viable candidate.

At long last, Jeren stumbled onto something. Having never done this, he couldn't be sure this was his goal. Carefully closing in to study the site, the spectators saw his hands grasp her head, his forehead pressed against hers and then Jeren directed his power to delve into her brain at the proper place.

That assault caused her to react violently, writhing in his hands and crying out. The barrier was stubborn. Jeren worried about increasing the strength of his probe, but there was no turning back now.

With a serious surge, he punctured the membrane and gained access to what was within.

Arium gasped loudly, "OH!"

Her inner blue flame ignited, surging throughout her body. Jeren remembered that feeling. Like it was a racial memory stored in her cells, she uttered words from an unknown language. It happened the same way for all acolytes, and now she'd joined their ranks, a descendant of what had been before.

For the spectators, it was an incredible scene. Both Jeren and Arium glowed with an aura of blue light. That light increased in intensity. Arium's body tried to cope, but her muscle spasms, writhing, and shudders increased sharply until she reached the pinnacle with a loud cry and collapsed limp into Jeren's grasp.

Both of them opened their eyes at the same moment.

"Wow," she said. "It was all that you said, and more. That part at the end where you opened my nugget? It was like…"

They both chuckled for a moment. She continued, "I see with different eyes now. I can feel Selana in a new way, something that was not in me before."

"I think you should rest now. It takes time to adjust to all of your changes. A good night of deep sleep will do wonders."

"Thank you for this, Jeren. I feel close to you like no other person in my life."

"I understand; let's not talk further for now. Tomorrow you'll have better control of all facets of yourself, including your emotions. This is a one-time experience like no other."

"That is so true. I would like to sleep, but I must feed the babies first."

"Yes, of course." Jeren looked embarrassed. She shook her head and smirked.

"Men," she muttered.

In a new development, when Arium fed the babies, her newly awakened blue aura encased both her and the babies.

Meanwhile, the rest of the camp had begun the combat training for the women and the older of the children. Jeren got up to join them.

His first sparring partner was Brek who smirked at him.

"Ah yes, wizard, now you are on my territory. I think it best if I school you diligently, don't you agree? You must gain competence as soon as possible."

Jeren smiled. "Do your worst, rogue. I will rise above your insults."

Brek's expression changed. "Don't misunderstand, Jeren. I wish you no harm. My making a playful jest doesn't imply enmity between us. You're the critical member of this group for our ultimate survival. The fact is Arium has feelings for you. Yes, I experience hurt feelings and jealousy, but I'll get over it. I agree with both of your goals to be supreme wizards and supreme warriors."

"Arium…" He never finished his reply as Brek began a determined attack. Jeren was immediately on the defensive with no ability to attack in return.

Brek kept him busy for hours until Jeren's arms couldn't lift the sword any longer.

"Am I hopeless, Brek?"

"Certainly not. We want to show all of the trainees what they must do toning and strengthening muscles. Enemy fighters won't care if you're too weak. It will be live or die in a fight. That's the reality of battle."

"I understand."

"I doubt it, but you will."

"Regardless of whatever you honestly feel about me, I want to say; I respect you and appreciate your taking time to tutor me. If they must be hard lessons, so be it. I must do the same with Arium. The path to wizardry is not simple or easy. It's easy to get frustrated as one strives to progress through so many steps trying to gain competence. No wizard is the same. Some stand as titans among their brethren."

"Is that true of the dark mages?"

"I would assume that. It's logical. Where we have the High Mage, I'm sure they have their equivalent. Little is known about them and their practices. They remain secret, hidden in the shadows out of scrutiny. I believe they do no good in the world."

"Based on the short time I've been around Arium, how she acts, the determination in her, the desire to overcome any hurdle, I wonder if she could become one of those titans you spoke of?"

"I wouldn't be surprised. I see what you see in her. The tragic circumstances of the destruction of her village and the killing of her husband have put focus in her thoughts and actions like I've never seen before. I think there is no limit to what she can accomplish, including becoming a titan among wizards."

Both men stood in silence pondering an exceptional woman, lost in their thoughts.

Looking over, Arium was fast asleep with the babies at her sides. She looked at peace with the world.

"I will sleep," said Jeren. "It will be a full day tomorrow."

Around the camp, the training battles had ended and sleeping rolls were laid out for the night. Sentries took their positions watching over the camp and scanning the surrounding area beyond Jeren's cloaking spell.

Getting under his blanket, Jeren glanced over at Selana. Her faint smile seemed to be permanent these days. Strangely, Arium had that same faint smile.

She was clearly in the midst of a powerful dream as hints of a blue aura flickered occasionally and he saw her lips move, like she was reciting from an ancient tome. Whatever words she mouthed, they were whispered in silence so he had no clue what was being said.

Lying back, he was spent both physically and mentally. Closing his eyes, he was asleep in moments.

A light rain started in their sleep, not enough to soak everybody, but when they awoke, the bedding needed to be dried out.

Another day's ride brought them to the border of Grecia. There were no Warmark soldiers in the Warmark station. Across the border as they approached the Grecian border station, Jeren peered with keen interest at the guards, these legendary soldiers. They were no-nonsense types, intense and fully prepared in case of trouble. Their Captain walked out to meet the travelers.

"Captain Morstem, you're back so soon?"

"Captain Tarman, it's good to be back. I'm sure you've heard about the invasion from the barbarians."

"We have. Are you here to ask us to fight your war for you?"

"No, we seek asylum, at least in the short term. I don't know that Carngard can beat these creatures. They're like a plague sweeping over everyone and everything. May we enter?"

"Since we know you, I'll say yes. However, if we get a flood of your refugees, that will be a different matter."

"Thank you."

Chapter 3

Grecia

They entered the land of King Argost, and more importantly, the realm of General Gerak Kroll, the legendary.

Traveling the main road toward the capital, the Grecian army had patrols everywhere. They eyed the refugees grimly as they passed by.

"They're taking no chances," Brek remarked.

"I'd expect nothing less from them," Grakar replied.

Jeren spoke, "Those green uniforms blend well with the background forests."

"Gerak thinks of all things and looks for any advantage. There could be no safer place for us, if we can gain asylum from his majesty."

"Will that be a problem?"

"I don't think so, but they're always cautious in Grecia. Even though they fear no invading force, at the same time, they don't court danger or intrigue. If our being here caused consequences for the King and the country, we could be sent packing back across the border. Perceptions are as important as reality to them about such things. Does that make sense?"

"It makes perfect sense."

"Does that answer your question?"

"Somewhat. We'll leave it to you to do the talking in the palace."

"I may need your dialogue too, Jeren. This is too important for me to handle alone. I'm still just a soldier, not a statesman or scholar."

"How far is it to Boria?"

"About a day I'd say, give or take. We can't go particularly fast dragging along the civilians."

"No hurry, I was just curious. The terrain seems a bit hillier and with even more forest."

"They do have flat places and they farm also. Everybody needs to eat."

Falling back to ride beside Arium, he asked, "Are you comfortable with the first exercises I gave you? Due to our circumstances, I had to go out of order to an extent. I needed something you could do mentally while we rode."

"I've had no problems. I know it's just the start of a long road, but internally I can feel my progress. It's going faster than I would have thought."

Suddenly, Jeren felt the urge to glance at Selana. She was awake and alert, like she was a part of the magical piece training Arium.

Jeren pondered, *It's not possible she could have a hand with this. She's just a baby, but what if she's somehow speeding up Arium's learning curve? That can't be possible, can it?*

That enigmatic smile was back on her face, eyeing her pseudo-father. Her pseudo-mother eyed her warmly in return.

She cooed, "You are the sweetest little thing, Selana. We love you."

The baby beamed and chortled, kicking her feet and waving her arms wildly.

Turning her face to Jeren, she continued, "I'd like to say one other thing. What you awakened in me, the power. It's palpable, I can sense it, feel it, and touch it. It's so powerful an experience surging through me I'm struggling to cope. Is that normal?"

"At the very beginning of training with no prior experience, the answer is no, not really. Normally, that would be farther down the road, much farther. As you say, you're making remarkable progress. Actually, I would say unprecedented progress. I've never seen such in my experience."

"I am truly a different person now, and to my reckoning, a much better person. Does this please you?"

"What matters is if it pleases you, Arium."

"It does please me." She continued softly, "The experience we shared, the insights we gained, should we talk about it?"

"I'd say not at this time. I'm sorry I couldn't warn you beforehand about the ramifications and implications of that union."

"I think of it more as a bonding between us." Now she had a shy look on her face.

He looked away at that point, answering in a neutral tone, "I can't disagree, but surely you can see we need to proceed with caution."

She laughed heartily. "You can no longer fool me, Jeren, oh mighty wizard. We know each other down to our cores. Though you're afraid to take some steps, I am not. That's the real truth of this."

Jeren looked around uncomfortably. No one seemed to have heard her, for which he was grateful.

"Can I ask your forbearance, please? I'd like for you to give us some time to sort things out."

"Sort things out, eh? Okay, Jeren, as you wish."

She continued to smirk at him. Reaching over, Arium lifted Selana into her arms.

"Hello, my precious little one."

Selana squealed in delight. Both Jeren and Arium felt a sudden warm inner glow.

Late in that day of riding, a day Jeren subsequently chose to ride beside Captain Morstem, they approached the gates of Boria, capital city of Grecia and seat of King Argost.

Arium rode up to beside Jeren to enter the city together with him. Both stared at every facet of the scene, from the sturdy construction of the defenses, to the rugged people who lived there. Grakar had been correct. Grecian life was geared toward function over form. There was little display of wealth and vanity in favor of a simple life free of schemes and intrigue. Palace plots, seamy episodes, such things were virtually unheard of here in this place. Some citizens were curious staring at the strangers, but most ignored them while going about their own businesses. Small shops were the norm rather than large business enterprises found in Carngard.

Wood was the main construction material used in the buildings. Stone works, or any other types of materials were virtually non-existent that they could see. Only when they got to the palace was there any variance.

Arium spoke, "I noticed the shrewd construction design for those wide protecting outer walls. It appears to me there are multiple tiers. With thick wood layers outer and inner, I'd guess they put courses of stone in the middle of the wood walls to make them impenetrable. The wood was soaked in flame retardant I would assume judging by the discoloration of the wood. I could smell the odor of the coating.

"As far as the layout inside, the palace is in the center of the city, but it seems other municipal buildings are dispersed so an invader couldn't make a quick conquest, as there are many alternate places to take key officials in an emergency. Military gear is positioned everywhere. They can be ready to fight in moments."

"That's very perceptive, Arium. I noticed the same things."

"Since my awakening, my clarity of thinking, powers of observation, and quick comprehension, they have soared."

"Good."

Eyeing him mirthfully at his pretense at aloofness, she asked, "Do I intimidate you, sir?"

"You always intimidated me. Now it happens to be intimidation in all areas rather than just certain ones."

Again, she laughed heartily. "Jeren, we're going to have our little talk much sooner than later."

"I can hardly wait."

She smacked him on his arm in mock outrage.

An official of the royal court met them at the palace entrance. He was tall, elderly, spindly, and a severe-looking man. His beard was scraggly and didn't have the effect the man intended. Rather than studious, it made him look unkempt and clownish.

"Who are you?" he snapped peevishly. His high reedy voice added to the impression of a self-important buffoon, a strange anomaly in the city of serious, skillful, and purposeful people.

Grakar was annoyed. "Cleeves, I was just here. You know exactly who I am. Stop this nonsense and take us to the King."

"But, but—"

"No buts. I'm still the emissary of Warmark; now move."

Grudgingly, a scowling Cleeves turned and led them into the palace, but muttered the whole way. Even his gait was comedic, like he listed to starboard. His face displayed a sour look the entire way.

As they walked, there were considerable courtesans come out of their rooms to gawk at the strangers. Never far away anywhere in this land were fierce looking troops at the ready. These were experienced men. Those weapons they wore were not mere ceremonial props and their hands rested on the sword hilts.

The palace itself was underwhelming as palaces go. Thick heavy wood beams provided the support for the structure, but no attempt was made to conceal them from sight. It was like the building had never been completed. Lit torches were placed in sconces mounted periodically to light the way in the evenings.

This palace was a drafty place, which was both good and bad. Moving the incessant smoke in the air was good, but keeping the rooms heated was problematic. The battle pennants of the famed military units as well as decorative tapestries along the hallways continuously wriggled from unending air currents. On the tapestries were depicted great battle scenes from Grecian history, all of which were legitimate victories.

Approaching the ornate doors into the throne room, the design of the heavy doors was clearly for defense. Mounted on levers due to their daunting weight, it took a team of huge men to swing the doors open. The great seal of the King was etched into the wood.

Cleeves led them into the chamber full of various Grecian citizens, some courtesans, a few commoners, and ample military folk. The King was seated on his throne hearing the pleas of various Grecian citizens. The throne of a Queen was empty.

King Argost looked up as Cleeves meekly sidled forward.

"Eh…sire…eh…"

"Speak up, Cleeves, I can't hear you when you sputter."

"Here is Captain Morstem, of Warmark. Returned to us to…I don't know why."

His highness smiled wryly.

"Captain Morstem, you've returned. What is it your King needs from Grecia this time? I thought I made our position very clear."

"I'm not here on behalf of my King, sire."

"Oh? Well then, what can we do for you?"

"I can only be honest with you. I'm sure you know the barbarians have invaded us from the northern mountains and have swarmed over Warmark in a dark wave of death and destruction. We attempted to journey home, but it was impossible. Fighting daily, our small unit was driven back again and again from reaching our capital city. It happened we met these village survivors fleeing for their lives and agreed to join forces…to seek sanctuary."

"I have heard about your war. You understand we don't loan out our forces and don't join in foreign wars?"

"That's not what I'm asking. Carngard will stand or fall based on their courage and skills. There's nothing to do about that. I can only plead you will show us mercy and allow us to reside here under the protection of your walls and your mighty armed forces."

"It has never been our practice to take in strays, Captain. You already know that."

"Before you make such a decision, perhaps you'll allow me to introduce us. I feel this is a time to take care with any decisions."

Nodding to Jeren, Arium, and the babies, he waved them forward.

Coming close enough for the King to see Selana, his expression changed.

"Oh my," he muttered. "What is this we have here?"

"Sire, this is Selana, a special child placed in the charge of this wizard, Jeren. The woman is Arium, a recent widow in the war, and newest apprentice to Jeren in the magic arts."

"A wizard, you say." The King perked up with keen interest. "We've never had a wizard in the realm, at least not to our knowledge. Do you claim partnership with this band of stragglers?"

"I do, and may I say, sire, we're more than strays. We're all people and have worth, as much as any of the citizens of Grecia."

There was an audible gasp amongst of onlookers. King Argost was never challenged. Jeren chose to stand his ground, even as the ranks of the Grecian troops came to the *en garde* stance with a martial shout. The King's expression became severe.

"Do you imagine a wizard has no danger here, or that you can throw about verbal barbs and insults with impunity?"

"I don't imagine anything of the sort. What I perceive is this is a society which prides itself on toughness. You respect toughness and I think you're testing us to measure our mettle. I can assure you, after what we've been through, there are no cowards here. I don't pretend I'm the High Mage, or even a wizard of great renown. What I am is the unwitting guardian for this collection of people thrown together by dire circumstances. Death has touched all of these villagers. If that makes no impact on you, we've come to the wrong place and we're happy to leave."

The King eyed him for a time pondering his words. Turning his head, he nodded. General Gerak Kroll himself walked into the room.

"What do you make of this, General?"

"I find no falsehood here. I know these Warmark soldiers, and though I don't know these others, I sense no guile. I respect this wizard for the brave words. Whether he can actually protect his flock, I wonder. The word from Warmark and from Carngard is strange; the invasion has fizzled. The unquenched blood lust that drove the barbarians mad seems to have cooled. The siege has pulled back, though they still control most of the country. The disturbing news is word of the dark mages coming into the area and moving about. That is a dire turn indeed. I would be glad to have our own wizard here in residence."

"What do you say to that, wizard?" asked the King.

"I was hoping for just such an invitation. Traipsing about the country exposed to feral designs was a recipe for disaster. I hope you can excuse my behavior if you still think me rude. It was not my intention, only to care for these people."

"Fair enough, consider the matter closed. Now tell me about this baby that draws me so."

"She was placed in my care by unknown persons. All I knew was on that day it became my mission to protect her. I have nothing more than opinions, but I feel strongly she has roots in magic folk. Beyond that I can tell you nothing. My hope would be to live here in safety to let her grow up. I could train her later to whatever extent she has abilities. Would that be a problem for you if we have a tiny community of me, Arium, Selana, and Darik following the path of magic?"

"If I grant this, would it incur risk for my country and my people?"

"Honestly, I don't know. I suspect why the barbarians pulled back from Carngard may be because Selana was not there. Who she is to them, I don't know. However, when we were accosted by a barbarian raiding party in the forest, once their leader saw Selana, he changed radically. If the dark mages are behind this invasion and their goal is Selana, I think you can see what I'm saying."

The King looked at his General. Gerak spoke, "I have no fear of facing the barbarians. I say let the baby live here and grow."

"So be it. Wizard, you have your wish. Welcome to Grecia."

Jeren turned to the General. "Sir, may I make a request of you?"

"What do you wish?"

"Arium and I have decided on a singular goal. Not only do we wish to become the greatest of wizards, we also want to become the greatest of warriors. There are no finer soldiers than here." The troops in the room shouted a deafening martial roar.

Gerak laughed. "I think you have no idea what you're proposing."

He came down the stairs, but straight up to Arium. Moving close, he stared into her eyes. It failed to intimidate her. Her wry smile tickled him.

"Arium, is it? You would be the first female ever to train in the Grecian Army. You do realize we grant no quarter, even in training. Are you willing to put your life at risk? I see you have a son."

She didn't hesitate. "Of course, I'm willing. If I was to fall, and I won't, I would trust you to take my son as your own that he can take my place as the greatest wizard and greatest warrior in history."

The soldiers shouted again, but this time they kept cheering. Gerak raised his fist and the cheering stopped.

"What a strange day this has become. These are directions and possibilities I could never have imagined. I'm moved to play this game to see where it leads. Sire, I ask that you also grant their wishes to train as Grecians."

"Granted."

Astounded, Grakar stared at Arium and Jeren liked they'd lost their minds. "What are you doing? This is suicide going against Grecian soldiers, even in training. They can injure or kill you."

"We realize that," Arium replied calmly.

"Do you? Your grand imaginings may not pan out in reality as you would like. Your fantasies are just that."

"Risk is a part of our lives now. It's unavoidable."

"You can avoid this foolish choice."

Gerak stood by with a wry smile of his own. Arium turned her face to him with a scowl. He shrugged.

"Perhaps you should heed the counsel of your friend. He's a man I respect. I cannot understate the danger with your newly chosen path."

Her eyes narrowed with challenge. "General, danger is a two-way street."

The surrounding soldiers cheered wildly and then Gerak laughed.

"Well said, Arium. You have genuine courage which I like very much. We will begin the work at sunup tomorrow. Obviously, you can't join the fray immediately. I will personally instruct you both, as well as instituting strengthening exercises to bring you at least up to minimum levels. Right now you'd get beaten down into the dirt."

Arium laughed. "Beaten down into the dirt, eh."

"I like you; you're brash and perhaps too cocky. Still, you may surprise me with what you can accomplish. It will be a first for me. I've never fought a beautiful woman."

She eyed him contemplatively. Like Brek, he was another heartthrob for women. Rugged, handsome, confident, and commanding in his approach, it was compelling to her on a deep level. His self-confidence came from success, not braggadocio.

Suddenly, she turned to look at Jeren gauging his reaction to the parade of handsome men seemingly vying for her attention. Jeren looked sour, which pleased Arium a great deal.

"General, we'll see you in the morning."

"You will, madam. I'll leave you to your final free night. Sleep well, you'll need it."

They were led to guest chambers where she surprised Jeren. Rather than separate rooms for them, Arium explained to the steward, "We must stay together due to the babies. Selana cannot be apart from Jeren, nor can she be away from me. I'm sorry if that offends your sensibilities, but those are the facts."

"As you wish, madam, the King has given you total latitude."

Following her into the bedroom, she turned to him. "This is no different than us lying side by side in the camp. This large bed can easily accommodate us and the babies. Do you have any objection?"

"I only worry about rolling over onto them. I can sleep on the floor."

She eyed him critically, but his point was a good one.

"If that's what you wish."

"This thick rug looks very comfortable." He smirked, trying to lighten her mood.

She shook her head in frustration, muttering to herself.

In the morning, she was feeding the babies when he awoke. Averting his eyes, she smiled. "Have you never seen a woman before? This is why we have these things, to provide sustenance for our young. It's normal and natural."

"I…eh, have not seen women in this way. I just feel I would disrespect you gaping like a schoolboy."

"Perhaps the fact I didn't try to hide this from you means something. Can you grasp the message?"

He continued to stare at the wall.

"I think I will soon be able to wean them off milk to start eating food. They're both growing rapidly. It seems each day, they're noticeably advanced over the prior day. Could there be a magical element at work here?"

"I don't know, perhaps. I will bathe quickly while you finish your childcare business."

"You do that." Her tone was abrupt, annoyed.

After a quick breakfast, the pair left the babies in the care of matrons and headed for the training pits to face their first day. Gerak had promised them hell, and they didn't doubt his words. As if a sign the day would be a misery, it rained steadily.

It was intimidating entering the huge training area where savage combat was already in progress. As they glanced about, it was like a real battle was happening. It wasn't rare to see red ribbons of seeping blood from the strikes of the combatants.

Gerak was sparring simultaneously with four opponents, all of whom seemed intent on killing him. His skill was amazing to watch, deftly holding off superb opponents, like it was no effort for him. Suddenly, they all desisted, turning to greet Arium.

Gerak spoke politely, but his smile was more a smirk. "Madam, welcome to the Grecian Army."

"Thank you, General. You're very good. I think you have a knack for fighting."

The five Grecians laughed heartily.

"Do I indeed? Thank you, madam. I believe you're right about that. Shall we begin?"

"That is why we're here."

He smirked. His four opponents left them alone together.

"First, I'd like for you to attack me so I can understand what skills you have, if any."

Arium smirked at him. "You're enjoying this, having us at your mercy."

"As I said, this is new ground. Perhaps I am…"

"Gloating?"

"*Touché.*"

Arium struck immediately. She surprised Gerak that she had any skills at all. Jeren joined the fray, but they were no threat at this early stage. Gerak deflected and parried every strike making no offensive moves to return the attack."

"That's right, don't hold back. We have a great deal of ground to cover, my friends, and not enough time to do it."

They battled for an hour before Gerak called a halt. Jeren was grateful as his arms were feeling leaden. Arium was huffing, but still had fire in her eyes.

"You have a better base than I anticipated. This is good. However, you need to strengthen and there is no rapid way to do that. We will suspend sparring for the time being while you do the necessary hard work. Do you agree?"

"Of course, master," Arium retorted, smirking. Her saucy manner affected Gerak which tickled her. "Should I refer to you as my liege?" Gerak pondered her taunts with amusement.

What followed was a first taste of the hell Gerak had promised. Lifting a heavy log, the two ran carrying it around the circumference of the training yards. It didn't take long before they were huffing and panting. Steeling his mind to the severe physical strain, Jeren concentrated on other things, a technique from his wizard training days. That Arium could endure such punishment amazed him, and to an extent inspired him to persevere and not let her down.

Gerak finally halted their circuits, but gave them no time to recover. Jeren was covered in sweat as he was led to a rack of objects used for weight training. Gerak gave heavy bars to Arium and Jeren to lift over their heads while they squatted up and down. It was a difficult exercise and soon had each straining with effort, grimacing at the growing fatigue.

Gerak seemed to sense when they were at their limits, halting the torture but quickly moving to the next series of tests, full wind sprints repeated over and over. Jeren had never faced such difficulty in his life. The thought of giving up nearly brought him to a halt, but watching Arium fight the same battle and endure forced him to keep fighting. His physical strength was ebbing rapidly, so in panic he sought answers. Without planning it, instinctively he accessed his power.

Suddenly, blue power and energy surged throughout his body. Seeing Arium start to glow also with a blue aura, whether he caused it in her, or she did it on her own, he didn't know.

The entire Grecian army stopped to watch the phenomenon as two wizards raced along seemingly impervious to physical stress and strain. Gerak signaled them to end the race. Pulling up to stop in front of him, he was at a loss for words.

Arium spoke, "What's next, Master?"

"What was that? Did you incorporate your magic into this combat training?"

Jeren answered, "As you said, we have too little time, so if magic can accelerate the learning process, it seems a prudent option to take."

"Amazing. As I watch this unfold, I think perhaps there is a chance for you to accomplish this impossible goal. What else can you do?"

Jeren thought for a moment. "If you're asking if we can suddenly jump ahead to skip all the steps of the martial training, that would be wrong. Supplementing our failing strength was what could be done in that situation. Learning fighting skills we must still do, as well as strengthening our muscles. There are no shortcuts because we have magical powers."

"That's good to know. It made me wonder if we would be easy marks for those other wizards, these dark mages you speak of."

"A dark mage is a serious threat, no doubt about that, but my order is a threat to them too."

"I'm glad to hear that. Grecia has never lost a war. We don't intend to lose now."

Arium asked again, "What should we do now, your eminence?" She batted her eyes.

Gerak eyed again at her continuing irreverence. He was not immune to her charms.

"We continue with strengthening work. Is that agreeable?"

"Don't bother asking," she replied. "In this, you're the expert and we want to receive maximum training and benefits."

"So be it."

The balance of the day was spent in more physical tests, most of which caused them to call on their powers. Neither realized what a boon it was, because when they ended the day and sat down together in the bedroom for

Jeren to continue Arium's lessons in magic, she made quantum leaps. Using her magic by instinct during the day granted her access and skill it had taken years for Jeren to achieve, and he'd been one of the fastest learners in academy history.

Arium took the whole thing in stride focused exclusively on her progress and caring nothing for his accolades.

Neither had any trouble falling asleep that night. Getting up early in the morning was a challenge feeling stiff and achy from the prior day exertions.

"I think it will take me some time to adjust to this schedule, Jeren."

"I wonder if I will ever fully adjust. I'm sore everywhere."

"I'm sore also. We share the pain, if that gives you any solace."

"It doesn't."

She smirked. "Do you crave your bed so greatly you would lie about all day?"

Her expression mildly irked him. "Do you crave the back of my hand to your rump?"

She laughed. "You may try it, but at your own peril, sir."

"Ah yes, Arium the daunting, terror of the realm."

"I like it. Perhaps such a reputation will help drive away those annoying suitors."

"Really? I only noticed your looks of awe in their presence."

She scowled and tossed a pillow at him. "I should have known better than to expect intelligent thoughts from any male. Why are you all such fools?"

"That is a part of our charm, madam."

"Charm? You call your idiocy charm?"

Now he laughed. "Come woman, it's time to begin our day of agony."

The attendants came to take the children for the day while Arium and Jeren plodded back to the training pits.

Gerak smiled as they came into his sight. "I'm surprised you returned. Seemingly, you don't learn the lessons those sore muscles have for you. So be it. There is no mercy here for you."

"We seek no quarter, General, nor do we give up short of our goals," Arium spouted angrily.

Jeren couldn't keep her from making these inflammatory remarks. She continued to glare at her teacher, the Commanding General of the Grecian Army.

"Let us resume where we left off, strengthening your muscles."

Jeren hated that heavy log. He muttered a soft complaint as they bent over to grasp it. Hoisting it to their shoulders, again he took the rear letting Arium lead and set the pace. It was a replay of the prior day struggling to cope with the physical stress and overtaxed muscles. Another entire day of misery accomplished one small achievement. They managed to refrain from accessing power for a longer time than the prior day before they reached the end of strength.

Gerak fought all day too, but kept a close eye on his students. If he noticed their small progress, he said nothing. When it was over, both felt equally as spent as the prior day. Going forward, it took a week of the hard work before they could notice strength increases and pain decreases.

After the miserable first week of aches and pains, progress came swiftly.

As encouraging as that was for them, the progress Arium made at night with her magic was gratifying for her and dazzling to Jeren. Always, it seemed Selana was quiet and attentive at those times. Daily, he tried to reassure himself she couldn't possibly have a hand in matters. With that, he failed.

Already, Arium could raise her power without fail, form some small magics, and grasp future steps she would be taking. She pushed him for more.

"Arium, we cannot go too fast. There are dangers with headlong speed without proper controls. You will accomplish our goals in due time."

"Who decides what is due time, you? I suspect I outpace your own training. Does that also intimidate you?"

"No, I'm happy you're gaining abilities so rapidly."

"Really, it doesn't seem that way to me."

"I'm sorry if you're unhappy with me as a mentor, but unfortunately, there are no others here to take my place."

"Which pleases you to no end, you're as bad as Gerak."

"No, it does not please me."

"I beg to differ."

"If you wish to paint me as vain, a small man in character; that is your choice. For my part, I will attempt to guide you in a safe manner. Remember, I was recently elevated, so I have little experience, and certainly none as a teacher."

She eyed him, unsatisfied with his answers. Finally, she spoke, "I will sleep now."

"Then I will also."

He picked up Selana to give her a hug.

Arium fussed with her son for a time.

Once she placed the babies into the bed, she climbed in, turning on her side facing away from Jeren.

He reluctantly rolled up in his rug, sad at how the night had ended with her. Rather than fall asleep instantly, and he was sleepy, he began soft chants from his own training days. They always calmed him from turmoil and he felt the need for calming.

Feeling his inner power simmer to life, he dwelled within the blue glow. It was purging and cleansing in a way. With eyes closed, he didn't see the blue aura emitting from his body which bathed the entire room in blue light. Arium was fast asleep, but Selana was not.

Her eyes were sharp as his power inadvertently enveloped her. When blue power touched her ruby amulet, there was a sudden spark in the clash between the blue aura and the encased red power. She let out a terrified cry, awakening Arium with a start and bringing Jeren up to his feet.

"What happened?" asked Arium. "Selana looks frightened."

"I don't know. I heard something, like a small spark of lightning. Now I smell the scent of lightning. Something magical has happened."

"Inside our room, how can that be?"

Jeren picked up Selana who was whimpering and shaking.

"It's all right, little one. We're here to protect you."

She continued to be restless and fussy, totally out of character for her.

Arium had a worried look. "Should we be worried about this, Jeren? I have no experience with magic and magical matters to make a judgment."

"And I have too little experience so I'm little better than you about this. I'm concerned too. Perhaps for one night, I'll set aside proper protocol and climb into the bed beside Selana. Hopefully, it will calm her so she can sleep."

"You could have been sleeping there all along, Jeren. I have no worries you would look to take liberties with me. You're being foolish about that."

"Regardless, at this point, I still believe I need to treat you with proper decorum."

"As I said before, I think you worry about what others think. I don't."

"I'd rather not have a debate. Tomorrow comes early and we both need to regain our strength."

Soon, four living beings were fast asleep in the bed. However, just before he went to sleep, Jeren placed a concealing magic. It just felt like the right thing to do.

Deep in the night, faint red power entered the palace wafting from room to room. Like a tracking dog, it sought a trace of the prey, but because it was evoked from so far away, it had only a fraction of its potency. Jeren's spell hid them in the bed from the hunt of dire beings and deterred them from their goal.

For the moment, all remained safe in the land of Grecia.

The morning came like any other. Rather than Jeren, it was Arium who looked about the room curiously.

"What is it?" asked Jeren.

"I don't know. There is oddness, whether the hint of a scent, a taste in the air, I can't explain it. Something doesn't seem right. Do you have any ideas?"

"I do not. I wouldn't have even noticed, but as you speak of it, if I extend my magical perceptions, I agree that something is different, and I don't believe in a good way."

"Should we do something?"

"Perhaps, but I have no idea what we should do. We can only continue our work to improve ourselves. Whatever progress we can make better prepares us if there is something coming for us."

Both felt disquieted and ill at ease for the entire day. Neither told Gerak about the disturbing night phenomenon.

Chapter 4

Gueldar

Time passed as Jeren and Arium both grew into their new bodies. Taut and sculpted to an extent neither had ever been before, or even dreamed of, they drew stares. In both cases, neither of them was comfortable with it.

Jeren could no longer exist on the periphery blending into the crowd seemingly as a man of little consequence, and where Arium had been annoyed by the pursuit of suitors, that developed into an onslaught of love-struck handsome men. Her response was to spend even more time in the physical and mental training of the two disciplines.

For his part, Gerak was awed by their astounding progress. Where he'd originally planned to pass them off to his underlings after bringing them up to a level where they could safely compete in the training exercises with the troops, that never happened as it didn't seem like the right choice for reasons he couldn't explain. She was physical perfection in female form and that was incredibly compelling.

Instead, they competed physically with him daily, fighting against the legendary man, the personification of the pinnacle of martial accomplishment. How rapidly they improved, and how daunting they became as opponents actually gave him pause. The possibility he could be exceeded as the mightiest of all warriors seemed a real chance in the not so distant future. If that was a good thing, he wasn't sure. Often during their matches, his troops would stop their own work to watch the three in action. It was a blur of motion and movement almost too fast for the eye to follow. Usually, Gerak was forced to use the maximum of his skills to survive the encounters and to avoid injuries. Already his two 'disciples' had no peers.

Eventually, it got to the point he could no longer battle both simultaneously but could only fight each of them separately.

Always, Arium wore that smirk on her face that evoked and provoked him. The combination of her perfected physical appearance, superb fighting skills, and aloofness of nature captivated him. No woman had ever reached such a place in his esteem and it was without her conscious design. He had no problem understanding she had no romantic interest in him. It seemed to Gerak that Jeren owned her secret desires, though Jeren was equally focused on his own goals of reaching for the utmost accomplishment, ignoring the obvious about Arium in the process.

At this point, years into the training, Darik and Selana were toddling about having passed the baby stage and moved into early childhood. Those children were as renowned in Grecia as Jeren and Arium. While the adults battled during the day, and chanted at night in magical practice, two little ones experienced their lives in the care of others each day.

Inevitably, that meant coming into contact with other children. One of those children they met was named Gueldar. Already in their twos and almost three years old, the children had full heads of hair. Selana's reddish tinge was only a hint now as her basic color was dark brown, though not quite black. It made for an unusual impression. People looked at her thinking her hair was redder than it really was. The tips were red, and there were red streaks interspersed, but most of the hair wasn't. Darik mirrored the dark hair of Arium, his birth mother.

Their new acquaintance, Gueldar, had jet black hair, full and thick, like the mane of a wild animal. His behaviors could be wild too, but in spite of that, people granted him plenty of leeway.

All three children spoke, advanced far beyond their tender ages. All three were compelling, though in different ways.

Gueldar seemed drawn to Selana, trying his utmost to dominate her time and attention. This irked Darik who competed with him for that attention. Meanwhile, Selana acted oblivious to the boys, other than seeing them as chums.

Her life was evolving so rapidly it foreshadowed a future of significance, or at least that was Jeren's reading of the situation.

When Jeren and Arium immersed in magic each evening, Selana was never far away, mouthing the chants silently in the background, learning and growing. Her innate power didn't require anybody to locate and release it. She was already magically awake and potent.

Darik watched her and mimicked each step in her quest to explore magic and power. In his case, however, the innate ability wasn't immediately accessible. Trying to duplicate what Selana could do so easily was like trying to capture smoke with his bare hands. It frustrated him.

She simply smiled at him and his struggles.

The fellow travelers in the flight out of Warmark, Arium's villager friends, and the Warmark troops under Captain Morstem, had blended into Grecian society. All of the men and older boys were training with the Grecian army, and the women had sought out jobs and homes. They took in any and all of the orphaned village children so none were left alone. Most women were married, or remarried, some with villager men, some with Warmark troops, or a few with Grecian citizens, those in the army. No woman wanted to be unprotected after the experience of the barbarian carnage. Therefore, picking capable fighters as new spouses was the only choice they allowed.

Lt. Brek Storig continued as one of those in the army of suitors pursuing Arium's hand for marriage. Remaining passive, she gave him attention as a friend and no more than that.

Third birthdays came and went for the children. Although Arium and Jeren were intent and focused on the magical challenges more so than the physical now, Arium finally took notice of Gueldar after seeing him in action one evening when she picked up the children. When she broke up their child game, he turned to her with a savage look in his eyes. Feeling genuinely in danger, from a child so young, it surprised her. Taking the children home, she pondered the development and began checking on this dark child.

Finding out after subtle inquiries he was living with a family, but was not their child, he'd been found on their doorstep in the past. They'd had no heart to ignore a helpless infant and took him in. Just like Selana, seemingly he was abandoned as a baby.

Again, she was confronted with a mystery, and again there was a 'special child' with a knack for magic.

Arium pondered, *Was it a gift for either orphaned baby?* It was a question without an answer at this point.

Arium pulled Jeren aside one evening. "Jeren, the children, Selana and Darik, they're observers to our evening exercises with the craft. I didn't think anything of it, but after I saw Gueldar that day, how the children interacted, and that strange hostile reaction from him, I wonder if we need to reassess things. If they're picking up skills, whether from us or some innate thing, is that something we should monitor? In the case of Gueldar, another mysterious refugee from whatever and wherever, do we start to include him in our actions? I sensed magical potential there, just like I sense in Selana."

"I'm sorry I've been so intent on my goals and inattentive to what's around me. You're right to have concerns. Obviously, I intended to evaluate Selana, but not for many years. It seems I was wrong to wait. I don't know about bringing Gueldar into our circle. Let me do my own visit to pick up the children tomorrow evening and I'll see what I feel about him."

"Good, thank you. I just don't think this is a matter to let lie. He's a disquieting child."

Glancing away, they pondered the matter for a moment before Jeren continued, "Are you ready to start with tonight's session?"

"I am. Are you ready for me?"

He chuckled. "I doubt it."

She smirked, like it was her nightly victory in a long line of victories. He looked at her with a wry smile.

"May I share an adage from the academy?"

Laughing, she answered, "Of course. I live to learn. This should be good."

"A haughty spirit cometh before a fall."

They both laughed heartily at that.

"We'll see who has the fall, sir."

"You're on, wench."

"Wench? You're very smug tonight. Why would that be?"

"Just a little banter with my…" he paused at what he was about to say.

"Your what?"

"Eh…"

"Very profound, Jeren. You almost did well, but then that stupid male brain kicked in."

She shook her head and closed her eyes. Instantly, he felt her mental magical contact with a jarring jolt and the sessions began in earnest. It took all of his abilities to handle it as she was provoked.

By the time they wrapped it up for the night, both were exhausted. Sleep came quickly. Neither was awake when a tendril of power, faint and nearly without any strength, wafted through the room. Gliding over Jeren curled up in his rug, and then over Darik, it swirled around Selana and started to coalesce, but instinctively, her innate abilities mustered a potent defense and the tendril was snuffed out. No one awoke and in the morning, they had no idea of the nocturnal event. However, Selana was uncharacteristically quiet and seemed preoccupied. That was totally out of character for a happy talkative child.

It caught Jeren and Arium's attention, her sudden reticence.

Returning to see Gerak, the combat training realistically had ended some time ago. What they did at this point was fine tune techniques and explore new strategies for fighting.

Arium never failed to impress with unconventional ideas that morphed into deadly methods. Sparring with her required the utmost care and concentration as she was more than capable of administering painful welts on any opponent, or lacing them with red ribbons if they irked her. In particular, those men with romantic aspirations learned quickly to avoid battling her as they were always painful lessons.

On this day, Gerak asked them what everybody wondered, "Have you incorporated magic into fighting with weapons?"

Arium gave a mercurial smile. "What do you think?"

Gerak smiled back. "I think you're well on the way to your goal, if not there already. I trust Grecia has adequately provided for all of your needs during your stay?"

"You already know that, General."

"I'd like to hear it, straight from your smug lips."

She smirked again.

"You smirk at me a great deal, more so with each passing day."

"I mean no disrespect. I think I'm guilty of basking too much in my current prowess. No longer being defenseless means so much to me. Do you think I'm ready to face the world?"

"That is a question which can't be answered. A person can prepare themselves to the ultimate, but if fate doesn't smile, a lucky arrow, an unexpected sword stroke, there are many things to go wrong. I have a reputation as the pinnacle as a warrior, yet every time I must fight, I feel fear. Without that fear, we can be foolish and not be properly attentive to the task. Do you understand?"

"Actually, I do. I feel that fear twice over, once with the physical fights, and the other with potential magical fights. I wouldn't say I'm ready to face down a dark mage."

"What does Jeren say?"

"Very little, only that he's never had a fight against a dark mage, so he has no answers for me."

"Where do you stand with the magical training?"

"I think at a similar state as with you. Jeren isn't sure there is much more to teach me. He's quick to point out it's only the limits of his knowledge and training we've reached. There is more out there beyond his exposure and experiences. That concerns me."

"I understand. When I prepare for a fight, I want answers for every contingency. The last thing anybody needs is a surprise on the battlefield."

"I agree with you. It's been a miracle we've been able to reside here for all of this time in safety and obscurity. We're far more prepared to face danger than when we crossed your border, but I wonder if it's enough. We may be easy meat for a dark mage."

"I don't think that's the case. My opinion is you're both daunting opponents against whatever challenge they try to pose. Working together, perhaps…well, I was going to say you have no peers."

"I hope you're right. I fear someday we'll find out. By the way, where is Jeren?"

She looked away for a time before answering.

"We have a concern regarding the children. Jeren was looking into a matter."

"What?" Gerak was instantly intent.

"Eh…Selana and Darik have a child friend, Gueldar. Lately, we've come to believe that the children have somehow accessed their innate power, all of them. It's a mystery how that could happen, however, our worry is about behaviors we've seen from Gueldar. He seems to have a singular focus on Selana that doesn't relent. As you know, he's like Selana in that they both have unknown origins. Whether those origins started in the same place, we have no way to know. We missed it totally. At age three, it isn't an issue we foresaw coming."

"When Gueldar showed up on a doorstep, there were many questions but no answers back then and still to this day. How somebody got across our border, past our patrols, and into the city without detection is a serious worry I have. We like to think we have covered every contingency."

"Understandable."

"What is Jeren doing?"

"He wanted to observe the children interact outside of their awareness. If there is magic in play, he will sense it."

"I see. Do you think Gueldar poses a problem?"

"Honestly, I can't answer that. Whatever is the case, we need a rapid clarification of the situation. It seems lately with too many things in our lives we're not fully prepared."

Gerak looked uncomfortable.

"What is it?"

"If the two of you are unprepared with magic at your disposal, how prepared can I be? Dark mages could be making preparations and plans that exceed what I can deal with. I and my men only have the strength of our arms to answer their challenge if they come for us. I don't know if it would be enough. I suspect not."

"I feel the same way. It's only the two of us, Jeren and me, to stand against them if they come in force. Where neither of us has fought against other wizards, I fear the worst."

"It's very troubling on both fronts, Arium. The Grecians have lived in what may be a false sense of security because our army has never lost. That may be because we've never faced this kind of foe. I must say, I have a bad feeling the near future is dangerous in ways we've never faced before."

Arium frowned, looking at the General sadly.

"However, I'd like to add, we're glad to have you with us."

That made her smile. "You're welcome."

Jeren wandered their way, lost in his thoughts. He nearly bumped into Arium.

"Hello," she barked at him impatiently.

"Oh, Arium, I'm sorry. I was—"

"Walking about in a trance?"

Both men chuckled.

"Perhaps I was," Jeren replied, smiling sheepishly.

"Try connecting your mind to your body. We don't need you mooning about."

"I'll do that."

"So what has you so detached and unawares? You could have wandered off a cliff."

"I watched the children at play and I share your concerns. When it's just Darik and Selana, they're different than when Gueldar joins them. He has this intense stare constantly looking at Selana, and yes, I sensed power brought into play. Although I didn't feel Selana was in danger or jeopardy, it made me feel ill-at-ease with the dynamics. At their young ages, I think with the three untrained about what they can do, maybe any potential threat is stymied to an extent.

"Selana appears far advanced, but in Gueldar, I sense great potency too. I doubt he exceeds her, but if he can affect her, that's what I worry. With time, maturation both physically and mentally, practice with magic, and especially if he was trained, I wonder if it's just a fatherly protectiveness awakening in me, or something in my magical essence being prodded. Does that make sense?"

"Perfect sense," Arium replied. "It sums up how I felt exactly. It may be my motherly instinct rising to a perceived threat." Both had worried expressions. Jeren blinked his eyes and continued.

"What were you talking about? Did I interrupt something important?" He glanced between Arium and Gerak.

Gerak answered, "It was much of what you're saying. I was worrying my army and I would be poor answers to an attack from dark mages. I've thought about that a great deal recently. Before now, I felt they had no reasons to come to Grecia."

"I doubt Arium and I are of any concern to them either. I have always believed Selana is the key figure. Whatever is her history apparently is important to them."

"I wonder also if Gueldar is tied into that same history," Arium added. "I talked to the mother in that family. She said he was an unusual baby right from the start."

"In what ways?"

"Initially, with his focus, older type facial expressions and actions, and then increasingly she suspected there was a secret side. She also suspected perhaps he was, well…taking some actions. They tried to dismiss the idea because of his age, but now they aren't so sure. Once Selana came onto the scene, he's blossomed, but it isn't matter of pride. The feeling something dire is close at hand worries them."

Jeren and Gerak stood in silence pondering the disquieting facts.

Arium continued, "Nowadays, she'll turn around to find Gueldar standing nearby watching, whether her or her husband. His intense stare is chilling. It gives her a creepy feeling."

Gerak asked, "Can children so young become wizards?"

Jeren looked at Arium. "Normally, I'd say no, but that's based on my own experiences. Because everybody I know started the same as I, persons with potential that was slowly developed, it's easy to assume it's that way for all people. Selana and Gueldar appear to be contradictions to my theory."

"If we tried to sever the relationships between our kids and Gueldar, I wonder what would happen?" asked Arium.

"I'd say we watch the situation far more closely. If Gueldar is capable of causing harm, I don't want to provoke him into action," Jeren answered.

"They're little more than babies," said Gerak.

"In age, that is true, but we need to be prepared for new realities. It's possible they're leading us all down a scary new path."

"Never in my life have I felt unsafe. I've trusted in my training and battle prowess. To feel vulnerable now is…"

"Distressing," said Arium. "Jeren and I can wield power, but we feel no safer than you. What he's told me about dark mages is blood chilling. I fear the day I must face one of them for the first time. If your armed forces have no peer in the military arena, it may be the dark mages are in that same category, magically speaking. That information came from his teachings at the wizard academy. Whether the truth of it is more or less, who knows? I wish I never had to find out."

"What have you shared with King Argost?" asked Jeren.

Gerak frowned. "Not enough to give him full understanding of the threat. Although he's a much better man than that dolt sitting on the Warmark throne, still, kings can be mercurial. I have all the potential trouble I need without adding him to the list. Also, he has his interests and priorities, and allowing him to dwell there, out of my hair, that's how I've been able to handle my job keeping the realm safe."

"You do a superb job," said Arium.

"What? Was that a compliment? I think the planet just wobbled in its orbit."

Arium chuckled, shaking her head. "Ah yes, the male brain again, it's my lifelong curse dealing with it."

Jeren and Gerak laughed.

****

Across the Warmark nation, although the direct assault and siege of Carngard had receded, the war throughout the realm had not. It wasn't a direct war strategy in play. Rather, the barbarian horde was loosed in the land to wreak havoc on the defenseless and the innocent. However, that was an undirected operation as the barbarian High Chief Kraga was strangely absent. Soon after the retreat from the attack against the Warmark capital city, Carngard, he was simply gone from camp one morning with no explanation.

Spreading word of his disappearance traveled rapidly and to an extent, cooled the battle fervor throughout the barbarian ranks. They were as frightened of the dark mages as anybody else. There was no other explanation for how their mightiest fighter and inspirational leader could be taken out of the middle of an invasion.

When Kraga had accepted the alliance with the dark mages, as a symbol to seal the pact, he was given the magical stave. The 'gift' was suddenly potent in a way any barbarian could sense, but none of them could wield it. Barbarians fought with bulging sinews, primitive weapons, and abundant endless hatred.

No citizen or soldier of Warmark had wronged them. It was the lust for slaughter that drove them. Other crimes they could commit were secondary. The dark mages stoked that underlying violence goading them to cross the Warmark border. No barbarian had any aspiration for conquest, patriotic compulsion, or redeeming goal. They were simple folk and thoughts were not their strong points.

Meanwhile, the Warmark army gradually took up doing raids, going increasingly farther afield from the city to fight the invaders. The people needed protection and only their army could provide it.

The 'war' had assumed a static phase with no new massive invader's moves threatening to topple the government. Royal forces managed to expand a bubble around the city, pushing Royal control outward backing away the barbarian warriors. The enemy tended to fight sporadically when confronted, but seldom made any stands to defend any particular territory.

Starving Warmark citizens tried to slink out of their hiding places to race into Royal Army held lands. Unfortunately with that, they were only partially successful.

The whereabouts of Kraga remained a mystery.

****

Arium sat down that evening with Jeren and the two children. Both agreed the time for assessing the situation had come.

Looking at Selana, it was like she could sense the moment with her enigmatic smile. It almost looked like a smirk, strange for a little girl's face.

Arium began, "Children, we'd like to ask that you allow us to investigate some things with you. Is that agreeable?"

"What, Mommy?" asked Darik.

At the same time, Selana also answered, but differently.

"Okay, Mommy."

Arium glanced at Jeren who took Selana onto his lap.

"Hello, Daddy," she whispered, wrapping her arms around him for a hug.

Arium took her son onto her lap.

"What are you going to do?" he asked. "Will it hurt?"

"Relax, son, I'm right here and I've got you."

Jeren shifted Selana around, cradling her in the crook of his arm. She smiled up at him.

"Darling, I love you."

"I know, Daddy."

"This might feel odd when I join my mind with you."

"I'm not afraid."

"That's my brave little girl. Close your eyes."

Closing his eyes too, he began the probe. Unlike his effort to open Arium to her magic, entering Selana's consciousness was supremely more difficult. He got no sense she was resisting him, but it was like jumping into the middle of the ocean surrounded by unimaginable depths. The feeling of being adrift and in danger of drowning frightened him. It required centering his power in a sphere of protection similar to the cloaking spells. Only after he could 'right his ship' could he continue the task.

No person he'd ever shared consciousness with was like Selana. She existed on a magical scale dwarfing anything in his experience and frankly beyond his conception. He could find no destination, her mind was structured differently. It was beyond daunting, it was terrifying.

This was a vast magical entity coexisting in a child body. He felt small and insignificant.

Suddenly, as he floundered, she was there in his mind. "Come, father," she whispered softly and gently. "Come to me."

Jeren was drawn forth by her power racing across the depths at incredible speed.

It wasn't that he could see where he was going, but rather he sensed it. In an instant, they met. For him, he felt like the most insignificant form of life possible, meeting a being from a higher plane. It was beyond disconcerting. It didn't feel right.

"You're welcome here, because for me, I see you as a father. Don't be daunted by your perceptions. Things will become clearer with time."

"You said you trusted me, and now I want to say I trust you also. I think both Arium and I were beyond naïve about the truth and had no sense of it. I apologize for our failings."

Do I really trust her? the thought came unbidden into his mind.

"There is no wrong here. You had no choice for your circumstances. Those were the choices of others. What I fear is you will no longer see me in the child stage. I rue that. No matter how you see me now, basking in the love and protection you both gave me was gratifying and also necessary. I needed time to adjust and gain my own bearings. I'm much developed from where I was. For that, I'm grateful."

"We always felt there was much more to you. I suspected Arium's incredible progress with her magic was somewhat due to your assistance."

"Perhaps I made her way easier, but she had the innate gift, and her possibilities are a marvel for me to behold."

"I have difficulty trying to find a description or category for you."

"Please continue to treat us the same way. The physical age of this little body serves so many purposes, part of which is keeping me concealed. There are difficult steps I must take and there are others who wish a different path for me."

"Are you referring to the dark mages?"

"They are one force, but one of numerous entities I must consider."

"We both worry about your little friend, Gueldar. I have the feeling he's a threat. Is he one of those others you refer to?"

"To an extent. He's also in a similar preliminary stage. Yes, he tries to extend influence over me, but that is a goal he could never accomplish. Essentially, we somewhat cancel each other."

"This level of contact, will I have this kind of access now? I like having an idea of where we stand and what's ahead for us."

"That is a difficult question with a complex answer. Yes, we can elevate our connection, but I'm not able to give answers to your satisfaction. The nature of the wheel of time is there are no absolutes, only possibilities. Occurrences can go in many different ways. Assuring triumph for your people is beyond any controlling. Victory can occur for dark forces as easily as for followers of the light. Do you understand?"

"Probably not."

He got the sense of her amusement with him.

"Jeren, you were properly chosen for this heavy task. I wish I could give you assurances, but they don't exist. What we must do and will do is follow the difficult path as it develops before us."

"Can I say, I'm worried?"

"My answer to your question is I feel confidence because of the man you are, your fine character, and high principles. I believe you can face any tests and prevail in the end, no matter how difficult."

"And Gueldar?"

"He's a true force in our little equation, no doubt. I'm able to meet any challenge he poses. And I'll endeavor to watch for consequential moves he might make."

"Like him alerting the dark mages?"

"Exactly."

"We've wondered about both of your origins."

"This is not the time for that story. We've made what progress we could for the moment. There are aspects you're not ready to handle."

"Is Arium sharing this same moment with her son, Darik?"

"Not really."

"What about his power, has it been released?"

"He is a true human child. Releasing power now in his life would be a very delicate matter. I've pondered that situation due to his presence in the dynamic of me and Gueldar. I've decided to unlock that nugget, but with my strict control. He'll be able to begin wielding his magic, but I will always be there to keep him safe."

"Will that provoke Gueldar? He's very driven about you."

"That's true, but he cannot harm Darik while I protect him. I can bring Darik along fairly rapidly to be able to protect himself. Does that suffice?"

"Of course it suffices. I—"

"Don't say it. See me as you formerly saw me, your precious daughter as I see you as my precious father."

"In spite of the fact I'm not a birth parent?"

"That is no factor. My birth family would have led me in different directions, but don't assume better directions. Biological parents grant no superior status in any sense for me."

"Amazing. This is such an awe-inspiring circumstance."

"That's true both ways."

"Can you tell us what to do next?"

"I cannot. As I said, the turns of the wheel of time bring endless possibilities and directions. All that one can do, including me and Gueldar, is cope. We do what we can."

"I know Arium will have many questions for me."

"I will touch her mind with all we have discussed. She will have your same knowledge."

"Should we take any steps?"

"That remains to be seen. Continue as usual. Don't treat Gueldar differently. I will deal with him."

"We will. He's out of our hands in any circumstance. Selana, I'm so grateful you allowed me to share this communion. I feel truly blessed."

"Don't deify me. That would be a mistake as I'm not a divine entity. I strive for purity as much as any other living being, perhaps more so. You don't understand the ramifications of what I'm telling you, but someday you will."

"I see. Thank you, Selana."

"This may be slightly uncomfortable."

Suddenly, he felt the sensation of dropping into a bottomless pit. The vertigo was so strong it gave him nausea. Suddenly opening his eyes in a panic, he was as he had been, holding little Selana in his arms. She smiled at him.

"Hi, Daddy."

"Hello, my darling."

Moments later, Arium jolted, opening her eyes startled and frightened. Rattled, she looked at Jeren.

He spoke rhetorically, "I know. Selana showed it all to me. She was going to awaken Darik's innate power."

Pausing, he waited for her to speak.

Arium got a sad look. "She did. He's no longer my innocent little baby boy. It's hard to digest his being a magical entity now."

"I wasn't ready for what Selana showed me. We were right all along. I feel like we could never have seen behind the curtain though. It took her revealing it, the truth."

"I agree. By the way, she shared with me about Gueldar. We will need to be incredibly careful not to betray what we now know to him."

"She will deal with him. I had so many questions she couldn't answer; it leaves me feeling totally incompetent and unprepared."

Glancing at Selana's face and serene expression, Jeren added, "I know that feeling. In her presence, I felt at peace, like things can work out. Sometimes I think we're mere spectators to something bigger going on we just don't see."

Arium eyed Selana also. "I hope that right things will work out. I have all the same fears about the dark mages, but now with the kids, now I have even more worries."

"Those fears can consume you, Arium. Try not to dwell on them."

"That's easy to say, Jeren, but not so easy to do. However, coming back to the issues at hand, do you think war is coming to Grecia? Now we can see why Selana was the object of their search. Perhaps they imagine controlling her to work their dark designs."

"That's very probable. Again I'll say they do no good in the world with their schemes. This we know as a certainty."

"I've never felt so close to my son. It was a wonderful experience establishing that magical link and that bond."

"With him suddenly possessing his magical power; it will certainly draw Gueldar's notice."

"We can only trust her to handle the matter. She's promised to deal with him, and I trust her to do so."

Selana said she would bring Darik up to a position to be able to defend himself."

"I was relieved when she shared that with me. I can say I will be there to protect him, but I can't be there at all times, plus, if Gueldar is like Selana where he exceeds both of us, what protections could I give?"

"It's out of our hands, so we should agree to stop worrying about what we can't control."

"As I just said, that's easy to say. I'm talking about the safety of my child here."

"I do understand, Arium. I'm just trying to be supportive."

"Well, in that you failed. I'll take my chances in trusting your little girl."

Again, Selana was smirking at him.

"Okay ladies, you win. I concede the point."

Chapter 5
Messenger

With the successful passage of two more years of practice, Darik had the opportunity to grow into his magic. By no means was he on a par with Selana or Gueldar, but he was competent, a tiny little wizard. Fifth birthdays had passed, Gueldar had been pacified seemingly as there were no dire developments or threatening acts taken against anybody, and Selana masked her inner *persona* completely. His danger was always present, but avoiding the worst counted as a success for the little magical group. As long as he remained near Selana, that seemed to suffice for him.

Increasingly, Jeren felt restlessness, a generalized feeling of discontent. At first he internalized the feelings, but soon those feelings refused to be contained. At last, he sat down with his pseudo-family. It was another miserable day in a week of miserable days as steady rain poured nonstop over the countryside soaking the ground and dampening spirits. Going outside into the drizzle meant slogging through muck and mire. Water pooled on the ground in frequent places, faster than the ground could absorb it.

Taking a deep breath to collect his thoughts, he began, "I know our lives are complicated already so I hate to add more turmoil. Lately, I've started to feel angst. It's unclear about what but it's stirring me nonetheless. I have no answer to where it comes from, or what it means, but it feels like I'm headed for an explosion."

None of them said a word, eyeing him with serious facial expressions.

"I tell you this because I feel we all need to be ready for anything. I hope I'm wrong, but with a feeling this strong, I don't think so. Does that make sense to you?"

"Father, none of us have experienced this angst of yours, but we don't disbelieve you," said Selana.

"Always it seems there are so many unknowns, I wonder if we can ever see the whole picture."

"We have each other," said Darik.

"We do, that's true." Jeren glanced at Arium who was eyeing her son lovingly.

As if on cue, they heard a commotion out in the courtyard. Hurrying out the door, a crowd was gathered around a spent horse. The rider had fallen off onto the ground and looked to be unconscious.

Hurrying over to the scene, Gerak was just arriving.

"Carry him into the palace to the doctors."

He looked at his magical friends questioningly, hoping for answers.

Jeren shrugged. He was curious too.

The horse was at the limit of its strength. Grooms led it away to the stables to water and feed it, and then nurse it back to full strength.

"That poor animal," said Arium.

Jeren ventured, "It had to be a bad situation that caused this. I feel badly too for the rider, but we need to find out what happened as quickly as possible."

Going into the palace following Gerak, they proceeded to the infirmary where doctors surrounded the stranger. He'd revived enough to gulp down considerable water. His complexion was flushed and his breathing was still accelerated.

Gerak moved to the side of the bed, eyeing the man. After his breathing calmed enough, he looked around at the sea of faces staring at him curiously. His attention fixed on Gerak.

"Are you General Kroll?"

"I am."

"I'm Gensten, a courier from Appia, a country far from here to the east."

"I've heard of Appia, though I think no Grecia has ever been to your country."

"I believe you're correct. It's a very long journey and incredibly perilous. I had no idea your Warmark neighbor had been invaded by the barbarians. I narrowly escaped capture on too many occasions. A single rider has advantages and disadvantages. I attribute my survival to nothing more than pure luck. Better men than me would have fallen."

"What brings you to our door, Gensten?"

"I was sent by our King with a dispatch intended for someone named Jeren?"

"You know Jeren?"

"I do not. In my country, we have an order of priests. How they know of a person in a land so distant with whom we have no treaties or political relations, I can't tell you. They're said to have magic."

"I see."

"Is there a Jeren residing here in Grecia?"

"Yes," said Jeren, stepping forward. "I am Jeren."

The courier stared at him.

"If you question my identity, I'm sorry, I have only my word to offer you. I'm a wizard and can show you magic, if that helps you decide."

He sat up slowly, still trying to regain strength. Lifting a pouch, he removed a large tome from it, handing it to Jeren.

Arium came over to join him and examine the heavy ornate volume.

"It looks to be ancient," she mentioned.

Opening the cover, a hush covered the room to the gasps of the onlookers. A strange scent tickled at their noses. It was neither pleasant nor unpleasant. Jeren blinked, Arium sneezed.

"Oh my, what was that?" she asked.

"Some spells protect inanimate objects as they can also protect living things."

"Can you read it?"

"As I look at the runes, it appears a very old language. I've seen such writing only a few times in the academy special library. I will try."

Gensten tried to get up, but was far too weak.

"What are you doing?" asked Arium.

"I must return to my own land."

"You barely made it to our door. At the very least, you need to rest and recuperate. We may have questions for you as we read this tome."

"I am no scholar to help you in such a way. My job is to be swift as a courier, nothing more."

Arium scowled at him.

"I'm sorry, madam, my duty is to my people."

"Did your people expect a reply from me?" asked Jeren. "Have you considered your task may not be done? I need time to study the book."

"That could take days, weeks, or months, perhaps years."

"We can't decide that standing here in this hospital." Jeren looked at Gerak.

Gerak eyed Gensten harshly. "I haven't given you my leave for you to depart. You will stay where you are until I say you may leave."

Gensten closed his eyes, secretly relieved. Showing a brave front wasn't the same as wanting to rush back into possible death all alone.

Arium knelt down at Gensten's bed. "You're among friends here. We'll nurse you back to full recovery, and then we'll see whatever steps come next. Racing back into that barbarian quagmire in Warmark because you miraculously passed through once is absolute foolishness, and it can still get you killed. I think your realm can survive without you for a time."

He eyed her, paying attention for the first time and seeing this stunning woman for the force of nature she was. She saw that transformation once again. A man awed and dumbstruck, losing his wits in an instant at her beauty and her commanding mien.

Before he could put his foot in his mouth, she stood up. "We'll leave you to the doctors. Rest well. You're a brave man who I respect a great deal."

Returning to their bedroom, the four sat down to deal with this ancient volume to ascertain what message was there waiting to be uncovered.

All of them stared at the first page like it was gibberish. Arium spoke first.

"I'm sorry I can provide nothing useful. I don't comprehend what was written here and I suspect as long as I might continue to stare, nothing will change. If you can interpret even a few of these writings, perhaps we can start to grasp why it was sent here through all of those hazards along the way, Jeren."

"At this point, nothing is meshing with me either. They seem very familiar, but I can't seem to remember any words or meanings."

"I'm hungry," Darik whispered.

"Darik," Selana complained.

"Well, I am hungry. I'm a growing boy."

"Yes, you are," said his mother. "Perhaps we should take our meal and resume this afterwards."

Later, trying again the book was no clearer, a tantalizing puzzle where they could see the pieces but couldn't put them together. Jeren felt answers were close, but that he was missing something like a key clue.

Late in the dark of evening, they finally gave up the effort and retired to sleep. On this night, the strange tendril of power returned wafting into the room, but stronger this time.

Rather than the prior method of gathering and condensing over Selana, it centered on the tome. It was an evoking discovery as suddenly, the phenomenon began to intensify into a whirling torrent of might, crackling with red power.

Selana's eyes opened and she sat up with a blaze of blue magic in her aura. Speaking ancient words of power, she attacked the threat in a battle of the two disparate magics, that of the light and of the darkness. This time, it was no longer a tendril easily dispatched.

The funnel of roiling red power responded to her attack with an attack aimed at her sleeping family. It required her focus to switch from offensive to defensive. Extending into the minds of Darik, Arium, and Jeren, she linked their magic into a single four-sided entity. The three sleepers awoke, sitting up and turning to fight the foe, but as anchors and vessels for Selana as she conducted the battle. Tapping their magic in addition to her own, she employed power beyond anything seen in this world since ancient times.

That meant in addition to battling the growing enemy menace, she had to employ an encasing bubble to contain the awesome force being employed so as not to destroy the palace and the city in the magical fight.

Speaking great words of old calling forth more than just the personal reserves of the four fighters for the light, she tapped into help from beyond, allies from an unending war between competing forces.

As the red power had tapped into a link to dark allies from knowledge in the book, so too did Selana in calling forth their antithesis.

A fight on this scale could have exceeded what she could contain, but her allies took action and in an instant of blazing blue power, suddenly the battle ended and the red tornado was gone.

The four sat gasping from the battle, their hearts thumping in terror.

Jeren stood up and went to the tome. Suddenly, he could read it, as could they all.

Two five-year-old children had become full wizards to match Jeren and Arium. None of them could manage to speak about the encounter. It was still raw, too vivid in their minds. None failed to understand how close to death and oblivion they'd come.

Lying back down, as impossible as it seemed they could sleep again, they were returned to slumber immediately. A new link existed and unseen allies stood guard over them for the night.

****

Not far away, Gueldar moaned in his bedroom, his headache was overpowering and the red aura still existed though nearly faded away at this point. He too had a new link, but with much different beings. It wasn't a comforting communion for him.

His body reacted physically as he felt nausea, liked he'd imbibed a foul substance and couldn't eliminate it.

Within himself, his living spirit recoiled and sought to hide from forces so powerful, dark and sinister; their very presence evoked the deepest of his fears down to his very core. Shuddering uncontrollably, there was no place to escape it. The link wasn't something he could control now. For them, it was a portal back into this world they would not relinquish.

Each living being has an essence and Gueldar's was under attack. Becoming the creature of these dark spirits, their avatar and instrument in the world, it was a battle he was doomed to lose.

Gueldar's mouth moved outside of his control. He too was speaking ancient words, but in this case, foul and noisome words. His spirit and essence was driven deep within his mind encased in a protection where he could only be a spectator as his body was manipulated like a puppet on the strings of vile masters.

Sleep for him was more like stasis lying on his bed with eyes wide open in a sightless stare at the ceiling.

The five-year-old child that arose out of bed in the morning walked out of the bedroom looking like an apparition with hair askew, disheveled clothing, and with eyes piercing in a stare that terrified. His parents huddled in a corner, fearful of what he could do, and would do to them.

The new Gueldar ate and drank prodigious amounts of food and drink before heading out the door. His destination was to meet the four other magicians, but he was too late.

Jeren knew what to do next and where to go. They'd arisen early and packed up their gear for the journey.

While Gueldar was searching their old room, the four had gone to the infirmary where Gensten was awake and alert.

"I'm ready," he said.

"Are you recovered enough?" asked Arium.

"In the night, I…eh…something happened to me. I'm better than I was in some strange way. I can't explain it."

"Come, we must make haste," said Jeren.

Gathering his gear, he followed them out of the hospital just as the suns fully emerged over the horizon. Being later fall, the air was chilled and in the distance they could see a weather front moving their way.

Heading to the stables, the Warmark troop who'd come with them so long ago were all gathered, packed up, and ready.

Jeren nodded to Grakar. Neither needed to speak, the plan was in all of their heads.

Moments later, Gerak appeared leading a hundred crack Grecian soldiers.

"I strongly desire to accompany you, but I'm forced to stay behind to lead the army here. I too have knowledge in my head about what's coming and that war is at our borders. I'm needed here. These men are the best I have. I've placed as their Captain, Drake Dorn. Although he is young, Drake is a born leader and inspires me. He will not fail you. You're precious to me, so be safe and make wise choices. This is a time to avoid battles if at all possible."

"We understand fully." Arium hugged Gerak. "What you've given to Jeren and me, it's a life debt we owe that I doubt we can ever repay. Know that you're precious to us too, and the same thing you advise us, you make prudent choices and don't seek out undue risk."

Gerak was moved. He returned her hug with a fierce embrace. Turning his head to Captain Dorn. "You know the heavy burden I'm putting upon you. You're going in my place to protect these people who I see as my family."

"I will not fail you, sir."

Gerak then looked at Gensten.

"You have perhaps the most critical role of all. You must choose wisely what paths you take. I suspect the enemy will be everywhere with a singular goal to capture and slay these soldiers until none remain alive and the quest is wiped out and ended in failure. That cannot be allowed to happen. I have faith in you all. For Grecian's, our lifetimes of training and dedication, our ultimate purpose has now become clear as we have a vital purpose protecting goodness from the advance of evil."

The troop gave a loud martial shout, none of them there were not moved by the gesture.

Mounting up, they galloped out the front gate and were gone. Gueldar arrived too late to stop the departure, but he took a horse of his own to give chase. The horse sensed the roiling evil inhabiting his body and tried to bolt, but the evil power merely captured the horse in the same stasis where Gueldar was exiled into a cocoon.

A five-year-old boy rode away, but this was no longer a little child. This was a living being possessed by evil, powerful and a true danger to anything he encountered.

The strange pursuit began. The magical four, Jeren, Arium, Darik, and Selana were well aware of Gueldar giving chase, just like Gueldar was well aware of them. He rode trying to close the distance, but that was not going to happen.

All of the four were transformed into new magical beings by what had happened in the night, but in Selana's case, she was virtually without peer now. With newly available unmatched powers within her, she was able to magically sustain the horses to ride like the wind without consequence and without cease. Although Gueldar could sustain his horse in the same way, he had no advantage over her and in fact was in a lesser position as she could link with Jeren, Arium, and Darik if need be to become invincible against Gueldar. Even fighting alone, it was doubtful Gueldar could ever prevail in single combat battling Selana.

Regardless, his new masters goaded him forward. Their deep hunger for evil had no bounds and their vile plans consumed them in the eternal war against the light. They were lost beings incapable of turning back to goodness. Imposing that horror onto Gueldar terrified him, but he was powerless to stop it from happening. He had no ability to reclaim his body and could only cower in fear waiting for the time they came for him in his hiding place.

Selana and Gueldar were able to tap into forces long absent from the world. Ultimately, whether that was a good or a bad thing was yet to be determined. The undeniable fact was turmoil was a guarantee in the world for the near future.

Meanwhile, ahead of him, the column of Grecian troops, Warmark troops, and the magicians rode determinedly heading eastward into the rising suns. The temperature rose very little and each wore heavy coats against the brisk wind. Crossing the border back into Warmark, the reinforced Grecian border forces cheered them as they rode by.

It wasn't long before they encountered their first elements of the approaching enemy army. Barbarians were re-energized with purpose as their dark master's reclaimed control of their weak minds, like goading herds of wild predatory animals into mayhem.

In the first battle the quest would face on this epic journey, barbarian war parties tried to block them, but that was a doomed strategy. Alone, the barbarians were a mere collection of physical fighters, and on foot. With magicians riding in the allied party, they had no chance in battle.

Although swords were drawn sweeping into the enemy with devastating effect, the blanket of power the four family members extended virtually safeguarded every allied soldier.

Predictably, it was a rapid battle that left a trail of dead barbarians in their wake.

Meanwhile, behind them, Gueldar approached the border at the full gallop. Grecia troops were uncertain what to do, as word of Gueldar's transformation hadn't reached them. There were no cheers as he raced by as they viewed his countenance with horror. There was no doubt this was evil riding through their midst.

The chase continued.

Gensten was a different man leading them through the dangerous ground. Where he'd existed day by day, fearful it would be his last on the trip to Grecia, this time he rode with total confidence. In the company of such a daunting force, he felt a part of something bigger than life. He was right in that feeling.

Behind them, the storm rolling in from the west overtook them and snows started to fall turning heavy quickly.

On another day, it would have been a pleasant sight over a scenic region, but they had no time for pleasantries. Their attention was focused on the mission, the long trek back to Gensten's home.

When they stopped for the evening each night, Jeren took out the book to read. It started out as a history telling the story of ancient times and the beginning of mankind on this world. Reading the saga was fascinating to him as well as the troop as he read to them to share the information:

"The original persons with power sought knowledge and purpose in a search for a better society, but one of their members, a flawed individual, took a different path looking into the opposite of the wholesome way. Darkness was too enticing and it warped the man into becoming dangerous. He sought out those with similar flaws of character and darkness gained entrance into the world. Henceforth two competing groups came into conflict and that battle never ended.

"The moral and ethical decay of the dark mages occurred rapidly and in every case, they irrevocably gave up their desire to seek goodness. The battle intensified and with the increase in magical powers on both sides, the war also took place in higher planes of existence.

"Countless eons passed in conflict, neither side willing or able to concede. There could be no truce, or surrender, ever.

"Death meant nothing to these beings, merely a move to a different higher plane to continue the fight. In spirit forms, the restraints of the body no longer applied and their capacity to access far more powerful and fearful abilities led to the opportunity to destroy all life.

"Only the intervention of the Creator, the Supreme Being canceled that threat as they were restricted from contact with their former world. However, there were links possible to individuals, and that is exactly what happened."

Weeks into the journey traversing Warmark, Jeren reached the end of the book. The last of the passages described a place, Evanshard Glade. Instantly, they knew the destination of this trek. It was a singular holdover from the creation of the world, holy ground. It wasn't a place a person could find to have a visit. It was a magical place hidden and protected by wards and defenses.

What they would find there was not explained, nor how to find their way. Even if they could gain entry was a definite question. That was a matter only the four magicians could tackle.

After he closed the book, it was like he'd completed a religious rite. No one said a word. There was nothing to say at that point. Such a view of their history boggled the mind. Expanding mental horizons to include beings of such vast power and presence was difficult and unsettling.

Finally, Grakar spoke, "This adventure into the unknown has shaken me, to say the least. If I've felt unimportant before, now I feel completely insignificant. The insects scurrying about beneath our feet have as much relevance."

"That's oversimplifying our lives, Grakar," Arium answered. "We have real purpose and because there are other great beings we've been exposed to, it doesn't diminish us. They don't live here any longer. We do and the fate of our future is in our hands."

"I can't argue with you, but that's how I feel."

"We all feel humbled," Jeren added. "Because the four of us have magic, don't think we're immune to those same doubts."

"I think I'd prefer to be in your shoes than ours," Grakar snickered and all of the soldiers laughed.

"Here, here," they voiced in unison.

Arium smiled. "I wish it was a simple matter of sharing our power into each of you. We could use more in our group wielding power. That's not an option."

"Do you think that child, Gueldar, is still approaching?"

"No," said Selana.

"Good, perhaps we can afford to rest a bit. Do I need to post sentries?"

"No," Selana said again. "I will keep watch over us. Nothing can approach here without alerting me. Neither can they escape my awareness, nor can they do us harm while I ward the camp."

She'd assumed Jeren's role, providing magical concealment and in her case also providing magical defenses.

Jeren and Arium had fully accepted these two children for the entities they'd become, and yet still, looking at those child bodies, it was still difficult to comprehend them in adult-type terms. The child behaviors seemed nearly permanently replaced after the event of transformation and enlightenment.

Nonetheless, they still craved affection and attention, the hugging, and parental attention and pride. Both children still asked what these parents thought about them.

It was a strange paradox. Seemingly for Selana, childhood was still alive in there somewhere in an otherwise adult mentality.

Each day, Gensten led them unerringly along some track only he seemed to see. Riding past Carngard brought plenty of emotions for those original refugees as they were technically still Warmark citizens. The King's standards still flapped from the battlements and the spires. A large Warmark patrol exited the main gate to start a patrol.

Grakar spoke, "I think we should let them pass before we continue. They would have questions for which I have no answers. We, as members of the Warmack army, are sworn to King and country. It would be easy to see us as deserters and traitors."

"Excellent point," Jeren answered. "We wait until they pass."

Selana turned her head to look behind.

"Is Gueldar getting too near?" asked Arium.

"No, there is something else trailing us."

"Do you have any idea what it might be?"

"I don't think an 'it', I think probably a 'they'."

Once the patrol was out of sight, the troop resumed the trek. However, Selana continued to glance behind them with a concerned expression.

"They draw near," she uttered.

Gensten spurred his mount and the command raced ahead until they reached the forest again. Riding into the trees, they were no longer in open ground. He led them for a short distance and suddenly made a sharp turn northward. That meant riding up an incline that grew steeper the farther they went. Reaching the summit of the hill, Gensten turned to go eastward again, but deep in the forest.

Arium looked at Selana.

"Are they still trailing us?"

"Yes, but Gensten's maneuvers have created space between us again. We should not stop at this time."

"Do you have a better feel for who is back there?"

"I think it may be some of those dark mages you speak of."

Now it was Jeren looking back with worry.

"They try to mask their approach, but that would never work with me."

Jeren slowed his mount to ride beside them.

"You act worried, Selana."

"I am. I don't fear their magic and I don't think they can hurt me, so what is so worrisome about them, I can't understand."

"You're not alone if it comes to a fight."

"I know. That gives me comfort and stress both at the same time. Having you here to stand with me is a great boon, but I worry about you being injured. Why you would have greater jeopardy than me, I don't know that either. It's something I feel."

The three rode in silence for a time before Selana commented, "Gensten is a good guide. We continue to gain separation from them. My angst is lessened."

"That's good, Daughter."

She looked at Jeren and beamed. "Thank you, Father."

Closing her eyes, Selana supplemented the strength and energy of the horses again. That influx of vitality spurred them to full gallops racing on through the heavy forest. Their animal perceptions seemed greatly increased too as they avoided all obstructions, and impediments seamlessly.

After a long period, she allowed the horses back to a normal gait.

"The threat is greatly reduced. At the heightened pace, they're unable to match us. I will know that if they draw close ever again."

"Avoiding any sort of fight is the first best choice," said Jeren. "In addition to avoiding casualties in our tiny army, we don't betray our position where they can start to amass forces to close in on us."

Grakar spoke, "May I ask if it's safe to stop for a rest period? We need to eat too."

"Yes," Selana replied. "We're safe for the moment."

Arium asked further, "Did Gueldar run into the dark mages?"

"I've lost contact with him at the moment. I don't think that means he's abandoned the pursuit. It's possible he's met those dark ones. If they've joined forces, it wouldn't surprise me."

"If he's with them, can he do for their horses what you do for ours?"

"That's a possibility."

"That's good news," said Grakar sourly.

Since a stream was nearby, first Arium took Selana with her for quick bathing, and then the men took turns. Being cleansed made everybody feel better. Guards stood nearby in both cases to avoid unpleasant surprises.

They accomplished it all, the stop, feeding the horses and themselves, and the cleansing of their bodies in about an hour. Gensten led them away starting the journey again.

Selana's sense of pursuit decreased, but that was worrisome too.

Jeren pondered, *If there is an enemy shift in tactics, what might be ahead waiting for us?*

The terrain became very difficult going through heavily overgrown stretches of underbrush, clinging vines, and briars. There was no path or animal trail to follow at this point. They had to depend on Gensten completely that he could find the way ahead.

It also made it difficult to get a sense of what was directly around them.

Suddenly, Selana sat up in her saddle. "Beware!" she shouted.

Bursting through the last of the undergrowth, they rode into a small copse and into a collection of barbarians in a makeshift camp.

The two sides took a moment to react before a serious fight began. In addition to the warriors in the opening, more emerged from the trees surrounding them. They were on the allied soldiers too fast for the magicians to unleash magic power. The troops fell back defensively to surround the magicians who stood back each facing in one of the four directions. Selana linked them in an instant so they fought as a four-sided single magical entity.

Getting clear shots was the difficulty. The barbarians were well aware of people with magical powers and stayed out of exposure as much as possible. Selana tried something new. What she'd done for the horses supplementing them, she attempted for the troops. It changed the battle from one in question into a mismatch. The allied troops gained not only the surge of energy and endurance, they also found their perceptions and fighting skills honed and sharpened. Suddenly, the barbarians were fighting the greatest battle force in existence.

There was no longer any question how this fight would go. The barbarians realized that quickly as their brethren were mowed down like a scythe in a field of grain. The enemy raced away, disappearing into the trees.

The allied command stood waiting, watching, and listening.

"Be cautious, boys," said Grakar. "This may not be over."

"They're gone," Selana announced. "We can move again. We should move. I sense Gueldar and those others are trailing us again. We need to be gone from here."

Mounting back onto the horses, they rode away eastward but speed wasn't possible in such terrain. Gensten decided to veer back toward open ground. Still it was some time before they could ride at a pace that satisfied Selana.

Her gauge of the danger stalking them had been uncanny. Everybody needed her advice with the uncertainties of this trek.

Jeren glanced at his daughter. The serious look on her face seemed to mirror a return of imminent danger. At least that was his opinion. Selana said nothing and remained focused on her task.

The sudden battle had been a wake-up call for the group. Their 'luck' at avoiding trouble was seemingly ended. For the balance of the ride that day, it was a somber group, tense and on edge.

When they stopped at night, they'd ridden farther than usual and waited much later to find a campsite. Being a large country, they were still in Warmark and had a sizeable journey remaining to reach the far border. After that, they'd be entering lands Grakar had never visited and they'd become even more dependent on Gensten guiding them safely.

Selana remained relatively quiet and still looked to be ill-at-ease.

Jeren spoke to her, "Are you okay?"

"I am, Father."

"If you need anything from us, just ask."

"Thank you, but I need nothing. There's nothing to be done other than continue with haste."

"Do you have any further insight on Gueldar, if he's somehow linked with the dark mages?"

"In a way, I think he was linked with them all along. To answer your question, I can't ascertain such things from afar. It's like a nebulous dark blob behind us for me. I sense the red power and the coalescing of the wrongness, but it's completely undifferentiated."

"Does it make you feel helpless? I know that is how I feel, and probably Arium and Darik too."

She displayed a rueful smile. "I know what you feel. It's regrettable we must endure this sad state, but there is no way around it. I'm sorry I cannot change it."

"Selana, this doesn't rest solely on your little shoulders. We're all in it together."

She got up to come over and hug him. "Thank you, Father."

Chapter 6

Hidden Hazards

Each day followed the same script, an early rising and a cold breakfast followed by long days in the saddle. That the two children could endure such a rigorous schedule was a tribute to Jeren and Arium, their training of the kids, attentive parental care, and of course, the ongoing magical communion supporting each other.

For Jeren, Selana—regardless of her birth parentage, inner nature with the exceptional being she contained—was his daughter. He could not have loved a birth daughter any more than he loved Selana. She gave his life the purpose he had previously lacked. Following the course of his training in the order had seemed the great path, but now he realized how empty he'd been as a person. The academy had been a mere step in his life journey and nothing more.

The idea of finally asking Arium 'the question' cropped in his mind much more so these days. Why he'd waited for all these years, he couldn't even answer. She was dear to him. They'd been a family, so why they hadn't formalized the reality, it was a senseless avoidance of his. A better word may have been foolish.

Glancing, he saw Selana staring at him intently. She wore that familiar enigmatic smile.

Can she read my mind? he wondered, and smiled back at her.

Returning to his question, taking action suddenly seemed incredibly daunting. His mind pondered, *Making an assumption about Arium's feelings for me, is that wise? She has endless options elsewhere, better options.*

It seemed any handsome man that came within her presence instantly fell in love and added his pursuit for her hand to the long line of other prior suitors.

Turning his head and eyeing her, she was a visual marvel, the pinnacle of womanhood in her prime. She could not fail to evoke men with her command presence in addition to her unmatched beauty. As much as he was moved to add his plea, his natural reserve and lack of practice wooing a woman made him hesitant. Taking a deep breath, he walked toward her, muttering the entire way, second-guessing the idea even before he made any attempt.

She was busy preparing Darik to mount his horse. She glanced up as Jeren approached her.

"What is it, Jeren? Has Selana sensed some new hazard?"

"Ah…no, it's not that."

Noting his sudden awkwardness with his eyes averted, she eyed him in puzzlement.

Clearing his throat, he tried not to stammer further. "I'd like to talk with you…" However, stammering with a woman was too easy; he'd had some practice with it.

"What, Jeren, we have no time to waste. What is this? The troop is waiting."

"Perhaps you're right that there's a better time to have this talk."

"About what?"

"Eh…I'll go to my horse now."

"Jeren, you can be annoying if you choose to. This is one of those times."

"I apologize."

Soon, the command was riding away eastward. The troops were aware of the awkward encounter. None of the men had any problem understanding what Jeren intended and most felt jealous.

However, the business at hand would not be denied. A sudden appearance of a barbarian patrol caused a slight detour to avoid a battle. It was like an omen for their day as not far away was another enemy trap, barbarians waiting in hiding.

This time, there was a fight, but more like a glancing blow as they fought off a vanguard and easily escaped from enemy warriors chasing them on foot.

"Something is different today," Jeren shouted, riding beside Arium.

"Yes, I agree. I wonder if this is a sign Gueldar and his friends are taking action directing these simpleton barbarians."

"That's a strong possibility."

They both glanced back at the two children riding side by side. Darik wore his usual determined glare, trying to cope with the discomforts of these endless daily rides. Selana had her eyes closed, concentrating on some matter of concern to her. When her eyes opened, she looked worried.

"Selana," he asked.

She merely shook her head and waved away his questions.

They took a break when the sun was at apex to rest and eat a quick meal. Jeren went to sit with his daughter.

She spoke preemptively, "Father, I'm fine. Don't worry. I don't wish to worry you but sometimes, what I must do, it can be taxing."

"Okay, but tell us enough so that we can be prepared. I don't want to have sudden surprises we have no answer for."

"I will."

At their next stop later, Arium came to sit down, along with Darik. Darik chatted silliness with Selana as they reverted back to childhood for a moment. Selana chuckled, visibly relaxing for a moment from her burdens.

"So, what's this talk you want, Jeren?" asked Arium. She stepped close, very close, eyeing him intently.

"Eh…"

"Enough with this dumb act please. It gets on my nerves, now talk to me."

"I'm sorry this is so difficult for me, and obviously it's the wrong place, but, I've been thinking about a number of matters. Honestly, why now, I don't have an answer to that."

"You keep sputtering, Jeren. That's not like you."

"In this area, actually, it is like me."

He eyed her sheepishly.

At last, it started to dawn on her.

"Arium, I have no doubts that you know how I feel…about you."

Her expression changed.

"So…what do you have to say to me?" Her confident smiled daunted him.

"I can't imagine being closer to a woman than I am with you."

"Well, we've been inside each other's heads. I can't disagree with you about that."

"Granted, but beyond that, I can't imagine a life without you in it."

"Oh…"

Now, for the first time, she acted shy.

"I know you have so many suitors, far better men than I. How an exceptional woman such as you could even consider a wretch of a choice like me—"

"Jeren, please stop that. Castigating yourself is a mistake. In my situation, thoughts of having a marriage again, dealing with a husband, I haven't considered it for a long time. Finding time to be together, in that way, I don't know how we could—"

"I wouldn't force myself upon you."

She smirked, shaking her head in amusement. "You don't understand. I'm not rejecting the marriage bed. Intimacy is a very consuming exercise, not a bad thing, but a blessing for the living. However, I need to refocus numerous things, if you're proposing that we…join in matrimony."

"That's exactly what I'm saying, if I can get my foot out of my mouth."

She smiled warmly. "I agree. I wish it hadn't taken so long for you to say this. Actually, you made me say it."

"I'm a coward." His sheepish grin was even more sheepish.

She laughed and kissed him deeply. "How do we do this? It isn't like we can conjure up a priest to perform a ceremony. For me, I don't require it to become your wife. About that, it's your choice."

Jeren flushed. Her statement was incredibly stimulating.

The troops stopped pretending they weren't eavesdropping. Standing, they made their way over to offer congratulations to the newly betrothed couple.

"This is a good thing, in spite of the circumstances," said Grakar. "Arium, you couldn't have picked a better man to be your new husband."

"Thank you, Captain."

"You know, you just broke a lot of hearts."

She smiled warmly and hugged Grakar.

Jeren spoke, "Grakar, would you be willing to speak words for us? I'd like some form of rite to seal our marriage. You're in the position of authority. I think your words and blessing would suffice to meet minimum requirements."

"I'd be happy to."

The impromptu wedding occurred in moments. Grakar did surprisingly well in officiating the ceremony in lending an air of solemnity and legitimacy.

When they stopped that evening, husband and wife took their bedding apart to find a secluded place, established magical protections for privacy and safety to consummate the marriage union. Jeren learned what Arium was saying about the power of intimacies. An entire new world opened for him as he discovered there was so much more to life. Two new people emerged in the morning agog in love's sweet bliss and acting love-struck and silly for a short time before resuming the heavy mantle of the trek.

For a day, the only thoughts in his mind were of this incredible stunning woman who was now his wife. It seemed impossible she'd said yes, and as far as him being her husband, it was so far beyond any expectation he could have ever had.

Glancing at her, riding flanked by both children, he couldn't help but wonder how she felt about him, if it was like how he felt about her.

Although they'd both changed, the trek had not, nor had the hazards lessened.

Toward dark, as they searched for a campsite, another enemy trap was sprung. This one was significant and imminently more dangerous. For the first time, the barbarian attackers were led by an actual dark mage.

Arium and Jeren were taken aback as it seemed a first magical fight had finally arrived. Darek stared at the dark mage curious, but Selana recoiled noticeably. Rather than launch a torrent of his red power at them, he started to chant. Selana suddenly put her hands over her ears. The assault seemed to be aimed at her. This spurred the remaining three into action.

While the soldiers in the troop fought against the barbarians who outnumbered them, Arium, Jeren, and Darik linked their minds into a single magical force. They were unable to include Selana who'd thrown up an impenetrable protective shield.

The three loosed a vast bolt of blue power at the dark mage. He'd already anticipated the attack and had surrounded himself in a bubble of red power. The two magic's crackled and snapped sizzling with raw power, opposites in all ways. The red dome held as they found alarmingly the dark mage could maintain his protection while continuing his verbal attack at Selana.

Being their first fight, the threesome of fledgling wizards of the light were unsure what to do other than increase the intensity their attack. As the soldiers battled the barbarians, some of the enemy warriors were forced backwards into the contesting beams of power. They were fried instantly zapped out of existence, whether by blue or red power. It helped with evening the odds in the conventional battle. Grakar knew this fight with standard arms was on them as their wizards couldn't help. He shouted, "Come on, boys, let's finish off these vermin."

The red dome thickened in deepening redness reflecting more power to match their attack. Seemingly, it didn't impact the dark mage's attack on Selana.

Jeren was at a loss for an answer. *If Selana is in imminent peril, this fight needs to end.* Closing his eyes, the thought of the tome came into his mind. With their communal first experience, the knowledge of that book had been imbedded in his mind. Suddenly, what had seemed a puzzle with no solutions crystallized and became a plan, without his conscious actions.

Without knowing how, calling forth power using ancient words from the beginning of time, they were no longer three fighting a dark mage. It felt like his mind and spirit expanded exponentially as he was filled with immense power through their sudden link to that higher plane. Mighty allies infused him with the awesome power. Being linked, Arium and Darik shared the experience and the benefits.

Striking immediately, the dark mage recoiled and lost the red cocoon and its protection in a loud pop, suddenly facing opponents he could not defeat. Rather than instantly strike him down, Arium surged to take charge of the meld to read this mage down to his core. Sifting through his life, memories, and actions, it was appalling. What he'd been asked to do, and what he'd done was sickening, but what was most disheartening was that moment of the key choice, his total surrender to evil, his free choice. The life he lived after that was predictably horrible.

Nearly equal to their outrage about him as a person, and the foulness of his order, was the nature of the attack against Selana. He wasn't trying to kill her at all. Instead, it was like he hoped to infect and pollute her. As impossible as that would have seemed, Selana seemed to have vulnerabilities he was able to access and exploit.

Whatever goodness and decency had ever been in this man were virtually extinguished, and by his own choices. There was nothing salvageable remaining. He couldn't be released from the evil yoke and reformed back to goodness. He didn't want that. They had no other choice at that point. Trying to take him captive would have exposed Selana to his continued mental attack. Taking a life is no small thing, and certainly something to consider carefully. Such actions have consequences.

In the end, the three did what they had to do. Instantly, the fighting around them ceased and the remaining barbarians ran away.

Selana was hollow-eyed, staring away into the forest. The three members of her blended family raced over to try to help her.

"Selana," said Jeren, with concern, wrapping her up in a fierce embrace.

She was unresponsive, remaining in a daze.

Grasping her in a three-person embrace, they tried to pierce her protective barrier, without success.

Jeren heard her muttering, whispering in that language of the ancients.

After a considerable time, they realized their efforts were not working. Whatever she needed, hugs were not going to accomplish it.

Having no other choice, they slept that night leaving her in stasis. Further, it was worrisome they couldn't get her to eat or drink.

Sitting watching his daughter, he spoke to Arium, "I didn't realize how dependent on her we were. Now we have no means to monitor Gueldar and his comrades. If they choose to ride all night to catch us, we'll never know it."

Arium shrugged. "I know, and I worry too. That poor child is carrying far too heavy a burden and too much responsibility. Fighting this aegis put on her by evil, all alone to face it is the last thing we want. We can be of no help to her at a time when she may desperately need us. That frustrates me."

"I also; perhaps I was naïve thinking a hug could remedy her distress. I need to stop thinking of her as a child."

"I believe she is still a child to some extent. The wondrous powers and abilities she has can mislead us into wrong conclusions about her."

He looked at Arium…as his wife. With his longing look at this wrong moment, she knew what was on his mind.

Shaking her head, she whispered, "I'm sorry, I would like to resume with our love, but I think we cannot afford to be away from her at these delicate times."

"Of course, you're correct, wife. I'm being selfish."

"No, you're not. We love each other and having these feelings is normal, natural, and a very good thing. I thought I'd experienced the greatest of love in my prior marriage, but Jeren, this new marriage dwarfs anything previous. Does that help you to know how I feel?"

"Yes, and I thank you. I worried if it was only I that felt such overpowering emotions."

"You're not alone with those feelings, my darling."

In the morning, they saw the first signs of progress for Selana. The malaise seemed diminished as she ate and drank for the first, and even said a few words.

Seeing her now, she did look her age. With the length of this journey, the children would reach their sixth birthdays, at the very least. However, it was another night and day, before she would converse normally, though only with family members.

Darik sat leaning against her holding her hand with a worried expression.

"Are you up to talking with us?" asked her father.

She looked up sadly, with a sullen expression seemingly permanently etched onto her face.

"It was awful," she whispered. "That person knew how to burrow into my mind, into the secret places we keep hidden. He was vile, and what he attempted was vile, trying to lure me to follow him into that life they live. It was like I was helpless to stop him. I've never felt that way before and it frightened me to my core."

"Did he threaten you with harm, or some such strategy?"

"It wasn't necessary. There is some part of me where darkness lives."

"I think that is true for all of us. However, my opinion is in their cases, they also have hidden places where the light still endures."

"That may true, as I hear you say it. Regardless, that lure was very strong to follow his path, too strong. Perhaps I am corrupt."

"Of course not, darling. If there was corruption present, it came from that dark mage."

"I'm not so certain of that, Father. You see me as this innocent little girl, and in most ways that is true. If there is a nugget of discord and discontent coexisting within me, it's a serious matter I have not yet come to terms with."

"Are you fit to continue our journey? Is Gueldar gaining ground?"

"They're not pressing the pace any longer. I think they've abandoned the strategy to race to overtake us. You're right that we must go. The quest must press ahead."

Shortly, resuming the ride, the unit tried to feel normal, but there was a pervasive dread affecting everyone that something dire was at hand.

Jeren rode up to the head of the column unexpectedly. "I'm going to ride ahead to join Gensten. Is that acceptable, Grakar?"

"That is your choice, but be careful. He treads dangerous ground as our singular vanguard and can't afford to be distracted. We trust him to ferret out traps and dangers in our path."

"I understand."

"Then ride swiftly; he doesn't hesitate."

Jeren could see Gensten ahead, but catching him proved to be a challenge. He was focused on his job and had no inkling anybody would try to join him.

At last, Jeren closed the gap.

"Gensten," he spoke. It startled the scout who looked back in surprise.

"Jeren? What are you doing here?"

"May I ride with you?"

"Okay, but this isn't the time or place for a leisurely ride exchanging pleasantries."

Jeren chuckled. "You're right about that."

"With the winter weather, I must devote all of my attention there."

Pulling up beside Gensten, he didn't slow the pace, nor did he engage Jeren with conversation.

Jeren rode in silence for a time as the terrain here was difficult. Ahead, they were about to climb into the foothills of the mountains which formed the border of Warmark.

Once they reached the top of the initial hillock, Gensten asked, "Whatever you came up here to say, you should say it. I must focus very intently to ferret out those hazards we must avoid, do you understand?"

"Gensten, the people in your land who gave you this difficult task, are they—"

"Magical? Perhaps yes or perhaps no, I don't know. If they're mere caretakers for the tome, or something more, I don't know that either. My occupation didn't include dealing with them. When they sent word for me to come, it was the first time I met them. To this day, I don't know why they picked me."

"Isn't it obvious? You were the best man for the job. Alone you made the perilous journey to deliver the book, and now you're taking it back to your country."

"Well, a great deal of it was luck."

"And most of it was not. However, the reason I ask is I wonder if those people, whether they're your priesthood, or some other thing, if they can discuss what I've seen. At this point, we seek a mysterious place and I have no idea where to even start to look."

"I can't answer that about them. I don't know. They're a secretive lot and share nothing of their ways."

Jeren pondered the dilemma as they continued to ride. They'd stopped for a moment to glance back at the troop making their way up the hillock. As always, Arium and the children tended to ride toward the back, just in front of the rear guard.

It warmed his heart to see her, his wife.

"Congratulations again," said Gensten. "You're the luckiest man alive."

"I can't disagree."

Once the unit arrived, they paused to eat.

"It's a beautiful view from here," said Arium.

Jeren was staring at her. Finally, she looked at him with a small smile.

"I'd forgotten what this is like, being the object of a husband's affection. It's nice to be cherished, but I'm the same person I was before, Jeren."

"I'm sorry to annoy you."

"It's not annoying, exactly, but just try to keep it relaxed between us so we can deal with this trek. Your focus must always be on the enemy, our children, and reaching that far distant destination. What did you talk about with Gensten?"

"About if there was help for us in his homeland. If we're meant to seek out this mysterious place, Evanshard Glade, we must find our way there. I have no idea where to start. For all we know, if there is such a place, it could be back where we came from."

She smiled. "I suppose that's true."

"Perhaps I create problems where there are none, but I'm a person who wants order in his life. The unknown rattles me."

"Being prepared is always a good thing, darling."

"Also, I'm of the opinion we're in the midst of matters of very great import, whether regarding us personally, or on a larger worldwide scale. It seems the dark mages have chosen this time in history to enact their plans. That isn't a good thing."

"I agree with that opinion. I feel the same way. Let me ask you, have you seen any sign of your brethren? You said they were all gone when you awoke."

"That's another concerning mystery. I find it hard to believe they were conquered in a single night by the dark mages. There were no dead lying about at the academy and no signs of battle. There has to be another explanation."

"We can only draw our conclusions from the facts at hand. They are gone without a trace. It seems all of our remaining available allies do not wield power."

"That worries me perhaps the most of all. If the enemy could wipe out the entire legion of wizards, what chance do we have with just the four of us?"

Arium had no answer. She frowned and glanced at the children.

"In the meantime, we continue the journey, stay vigilant, and survive. What else can we do?"

His rhetorical statement didn't require a response.

Ascending into the mountains slowed their progress as it was difficult travel. The animals were taxed and required more rest periods. Additionally, winter was at hand in the lowlands. In the upper altitudes, it was already an issue. Snow falls were frequent and snow accumulations posed an impediment as some areas were nearly impassable.

Making camp in a protected area between huge boulders, trying to sleep even with extra blankets was difficult. They could cast a protective spell to hide from magical searches, but a spell did nothing to impede the elements of nature. The little family huddled together under the blankets for warmth. The soldiers made due as best they could by sitting together or lying down shoulder to shoulder to share heat against the cold.

Waking in the morning with a large amount of snow on top of the blankets was an unpleasant surprise.

Grakar, Jeren, Brek, the Grecian captain, Drake Dorn, sat together while they ate a cold breakfast. They were talking to Gensten for his opinions.

Drake asked, "Do you have an idea how much farther before we reach better ground?"

"I wish I could say we're nearly there. This was one of the more difficult parts of the journey to Grecia."

Grakar added, "Our supplies are dwindling for a force of this size. We need to find a town or village to replenish them and sooner rather than later."

"We probably need to cut our rations in the meantime. Any potential source of the supplies we need is not close by."

Arium sat beside her husband embracing the two children to keep them warm as the wind had picked up. Blankets did a poor job insulating them under these difficult circumstances in the face of a frigid blast of winter.

Grakar shrugged. "I guess we limit the rations."

Gensten stood. "We need to move again. I suspect it will be another day of hard travel to reach the crest before we can start to descend. Prepare yourselves; this may be the worst day of all. The strong winds at the peak are nearly non-stop. I nearly froze to death coming here. The spirit to live in my horse allowed me to persevere and survive."

A somber collection of allied compatriots mounted the horses to start again. Gensten's prediction came true. The biting wind stung their faces, mixed with flecks of icy snow and hail. For the day, they decided to take the children onto horses with their parents. Arium placed her son in front of her on the saddle and Jeren did the same with Selana. Both wrapped a blanket around the children to try to temper the ferocity of the weather.

"In your arms, I feel safe," Selana muttered. "Thank you, Father."

"I like this too. I feel like I'm protecting you, even if it's just my feeling and nothing more."

"It's fine."

"By the way, your mother and I are sorry you guys had sixth birthdays and we could do nothing to celebrate."

"This isn't a place for such things. Peril is always too close. It requires constant attention."

The fierce weather did not relent and progress continued to be slow, too slow for Gensten's liking. They didn't reach his goal which was the highest point of the mountain pass. That meant camp that evening was in an unprotected place in full range of the wind. The entire unit huddled together *en masse* with the exception of the sentries. Sentry duty that night was half the normal time as being out alone posed a definite risk of freezing. Also, they paired up so no one could reach a serious physical state without help close at hand.

Again, a heavy snowfall that night buried them under the accumulation. The continuing gale combined with decreased rations led to near privation conditions. Each person was forced individually to seek out inner fortitude to endure the terrible hardships. Grim faced troops resumed the ride in the most difficult day of the journey. The horses had to fight through several feet of accumulated snow on the trail which required even more rest breaks for them. It was the afternoon before they finally got to the summit.

Gensten was right again, the wind was constant and the gale force of it nearly knocked them over, horses and all.

However, they could finally start the descent.

Just at a time they thought the worst was behind them, a pack of wolves struck, mostly going after the pack animals. It was difficult to fight them here on this treacherous terrain.

As a tribute to the Grecian training regimen where they were taught to cope with virtually anything, they did just that, pivoting their mounts for clean shots. Even bundled up, they soon brought their bows into play, expertly firing arrows to protect their essential livestock. Still, it took time to end the deadly threat. No other force could have handled the danger so well.

"Thank you, Drake," said Arium.

He smiled. "You're welcome, madam." She granted him a warm smile in return. Drake averted his eyes finally to mask his abiding longing for this incredible woman.

Resuming the trek, they made what time they could, but that wasn't far before they camped again. Fortunately, they found a place sheltered from the wind by a mountain crag.

Everybody was able to recoup some of the lost sleep from the prior night. Still, they woke to a skimpy meal.

Riding with hunger pangs was their new normal.

The following day farther down the slope, a different threat emerged. This time, armed attackers sprang the trap all around them.

It was a fight made serious by the place the enemy picked. This time, the troops were ready for a far quicker response. After the initial assault, the allies gained the advantage. These opponents weren't highly trained troops. Rather, they were locals, brigands looking for easy pickings.

The outcome of the battle was never in doubt, but still any threat was a serious matter in their weakened state.

When that fight was over, Gensten was able to ride back to join them. The brigands had let him pass by without revealing their positions until the main body arrived.

"Did you run into these kinds of issues before?" asked Grakar.

"No, as I said, it was remarkable I wasn't waylaid and slain. If I have any good news for you, our travel should get better quickly and we can descend to areas where travel is good. Finding a village should be soon afterwards, in maybe another day, or two."

"It's surprising to me how much shorter it takes to descend than it did to ascend the pass," said Arium.

Gensten explained, "The country we're entering is a much higher elevation. It's very hilly and the climate is frosty most of the time. Even their summers are cool. The people are a hearty breed, rugged and independent minded. Kings here are a different breed too. Unlike the lowland Kings, here they have no chance for lavish lifestyles. Individually, pursuing any poor moral choices and afflicting helpless servants, that wouldn't happen. Similarly, pursuing intrigues and plots either on their neighbors, or within the palace, the people here won't tolerate incompetence. Such a King would have a very short reign and an equally short life."

"It sounds like people I would like," said Grakar.

"They sound to me like people Grecians could appreciate. I like to think Grecians have such standards too."

"I'll let you make up your own minds about that when we get there."

Once they reached the end of the pass and entered the country of Nordca, the flora changes reflected the high altitude. Deciduous trees were replaced by conifers; the heavy undergrowth in the forests was missing here. That meant much faster travel, and a road to follow.

Presently, they approached a border post manned by a handful of guards. They were alert, smartly dressed, and all business. Their Captain eyed the approaching mini-army.

Putting up his hand, they halted. His dour expression changed when he recognized Gensten.

"It appears your mission went well in the lowlands. You brought friends for the return trip."

Gensten chuckled. "Yes, I did make new friends. For this return trip home, I realized traveling alone was too risky tempting fate again."

"That's a wise choice, my friend. I could ask all the usual questions, like what are your intentions entering our country, do you have proper papers, and so forth, but why waste our time."

"Thank you, Captain Svensic. We're in a hurry. By the way, let me warn you, we're something of a lightning rod as we have dire forces trailing us. If they approach your post, I'd suggest you ignore and avoid them. Dark mages aren't persons to confront with conventional arms. Basically, we're running to stay ahead of them."

"That is dire news. Thank you for the warning. I think it would be prudent to reinforce the border guard posts, and keep those reinforcements hidden. Do you suspect they would look to work their dark magic on the Nordcan people?"

"I don't think so, at least not those trailing us. Their focus is on us."

"Hmph."

"I'm sorry we've drawn you into their notice. By the way, where is the closest village, we're very low in our supplies and need to replenish soon."

"Your best choice isn't the first village you see, as they're too small and have no inn. Keep going as the larger town is near to them. You can meet all of your needs there."

Arium smiled. "It would be nice to sleep in a bed again, and have a tub to bathe in. I'd give anything for that." Immediately she scowled, noting the sudden smirks on all male faces.

"Not anything, you fools," she snapped, shaking her head in annoyance. "Males."

"You're free to pass," said the Captain. "Go in peace."

Riding ahead, it was half a day to pass through the little village and reach the town. The inn was surprisingly large for the remote location.

Architecture here was utilitarian meant to suit local needs of durability and function. Yet, there was a small attempt at stylish with the prominent lodging, in a town otherwise with no embellishments. They were actually met at the door as some workers came out along with the owner to greet them.

The allies weren't sure what reception to expect.

The large man smiled broadly. "Greetings, travelers, how can we be of help?"

Jeren spoke, "I'm sorry to come to you without notice or invitation. We need rooms for our sizeable group, food, and we need to replenish supplies in your town. Are we too large and daunting a force?"

"You are welcome here. I'll need to call in extra help, but new friends are always a good thing, don't you agree?"

"We do."

"Hello Gensten, I'm glad you survived your harrowing mission to the lowlands."

"Hello, Welstrom, I'm glad also to remain among the living."

"My people will take your horses to the stables. It looks like they could use rest and plenty of food. My girls will show you all to rooms."

The troop dismounted and carried there things into the inn. A group of young women waited there to guide them to rooms in the multi-level building.

"What is that pleasant scent?" asked Arium.

"It's a concoction we buy from a neighboring country. I think it includes scents of flowers and some other ingredients. I never inquired about the formula. It creates the right ambience for our needs. No one has ever complained."

Welstrom took a moment to eye Arium appraisingly. "My, my; what a sight you are, madam, I think perhaps the most beautiful woman to ever pass through these doors."

"I doubt that, but thank you for the nice words."

All of the servant girls were staring at her too, jealous of her beauty but equally of her command presence, dominating any male who came around her.

When they passed by the large dining room going to the staircase, it was about half full. Arium glanced in to notice four dark-clad men staring at the procession of allied troops. They stood out from the other patrons. Their sullen angry expressions gave Arium a bad feeling.

Chapter 7

Friends and Enemies

Getting into their room, there was one large bed, large enough for the four to sleep on comfortably. The servant girl happily showed them the few amenities, such as strawberries dipped in chocolate, like they were the height of luxury.

The two children made beelines for the treats, of which there were four. Two chocolate strawberries were gobbled and swallowed before Arium could stop them. The servant snickered.

Arium spoke to her, "Please, eat the remaining two, my dear. My husband and I don't need it and I suspect it's a treat you've never tried."

"I…we're not supposed to…"

"No one will know but us," Arium whispered conspiratorially, smirking.

The girl attacked the remaining treats savoring the taste like it was the best experience possible in the world.

"Thank you, madam, for your kindness. For us servant girls, you're a great example to try to emulate. Who and what you are, we all dream of such renown. To see the deference men show in your presence, it's like a miracle to behold."

Arium chuckled. "Believe me, dear, that male attention gets very old very fast. I would love to have my life to myself. Don't be misled to think my life is somehow superior to yours."

"I find that difficult to understand. What advice would you give us to improve our lots in life? I don't wish to live my whole life as a servant."

"There are far worse fates, child. Trust me about that. Evil stalks our world and ultimately what they can do remains to be seen. We endeavor to stand against them and in the process protect people such as yourself."

"In spite of what you say, I'm still envious of your life of great import. Your name will go down in the history books to stand forever. I know it."

"What's your name?"

"Millense, madam."

"Well, Millense, I appreciate your time and help. Don't waste time envying me. You're a pretty girl in your own right. Your beautiful long blonde hair makes me envious."

Millense blushed, fluffed her hair, and then beamed a warm smile. "You're too kind."

She stood for a moment.

"Oh, I'm sorry," said Arium. "It's been some time away from civilization so one forgets about amenities and proper protocol." She handed Millense a coin of gold, causing her to stare in awe.

"This is gold," she exclaimed in surprise.

"You've earned it."

Millense went to her knees, causing Arium to laugh.

"Stand up; I'm not a royal person. I grew from humble roots in a small village."

Millense stood, but then hugged Arium fiercely.

"My mother will be so surprised tonight."

Arium couldn't help but feel warmly at Millense's genuine reaction of unmitigated joy.

Arium pondered thoughtfully, *When Selana gets to a similar age, it will be such a joy to share that time as her mother.*

"I will leave you now, madam. It's been my honor to know and serve you. I am always your friend. Call if you have need of me, anything at all, just ask and it's yours without any questions."

"I will. Pass on to your parents how proud they should be of you. You're a dear person with a wonderful life ahead."

"Thank you, ma'am, you're too kind."

When the door closed, Arium pondered again, but this time sadly at her last well-intentioned words to the maiden. In truth, she couldn't guarantee what kind of life might be ahead for Millense, or any other person in the world. *I fear what is ahead for us all.*

After a brief time to freshen herself and the children, Arium took them downstairs. The entire command was gathered to have a meal. The kitchen had prepared a great vat of stew to feed the mob.

The scent of it wafting through the air as the containers were carried to the tables was overwhelming for near starving sojourners. Warm freshly baked bread lathered in butter, fresh fruits and nuts, assorted cheeses, vegetables, with ale or wine for the adults, and milk for the children, graced the tables and spirits lifted rapidly. A tasty variety of desserts ended the meal. Finally they could talk in safety. And the troops could banter. As idyllic as the scene started out, the instant the four ominous dark strangers came into the room, the four allied magicians of the quest turned their heads.

The strangers' 'auras' seemed muddied and unclear, but certainly weren't men they would ever trust. These men were bold, sauntering into the crowded dining room, eycing the allied soldiers contemptuously. Their attention focused on the eight at a particular table: Jeren, Arium, Selana, Darik, Grakar, Brek, Drake, and Gensten.

Displaying no fear of the moment, it seemed they looked to offend, first leering at Arium, and then moving too close to her muttering unseemly things within earshot of the table. They stopped short of laying hands on her. Jeren seethed, as well as the other men. Provoked, the room went silent as the soldiers readied to spring into action.

"We seem to have their attention," said the largest of the men. "Congratulations on making it this far, and frankly, I'm surprised. However, let me offer a warning. Don't bask in victory at this early point. There is still a long journey ahead, and dangers abound. You're aware that a determined search seeks for you and intends to close off all escape routes. Yes, we know about those few of you who wield power, four if I'm not wrong. That's not much of a force to face the entire might of the dark mages."

"Do you think your little book will save you then? I don't. When you're brought low, and you will be, we'll be there to see it. When you're stripped of all your power and defenses, we'll be there to share in the retribution and revel in your utter defeat and shaming. You intruded on matters out of your realm and far above you. There will be a terrible reckoning. Enjoy your evening and remember, we will never be far, as well as our friends."

Smirking, they turned and left the room.

Soldiers started to go after them.

"No," said Selana. "They're baiting you."

The troops sat back down.

The momentary euphoria of spirit was gone, stamped out by the cruel strangers. The fact they acted so dismissively implied they had a reason to feel confident.

"That was very distressing," said Jeren.

"Perhaps they were bluffing?" asked Brek.

"Or perhaps not," Arium replied. "I didn't get the impression of braggarts. I sensed genuine jeopardy with that group of men."

"Were they dark mages?" asked Drake.

"They very well could be," Jeren mused. His face was a mask of concern.

"Should we take preemptive action?" asked Arium. "I wouldn't mind knocking the smirks off their faces."

"Their taunt about having friends nearby, we can't ignore that. If they lured us into a fight against overwhelming odds, it could have tragic consequences. Plus, who else would know about the secret tome, other than dark mages?"

"After the meal, I believe we need to gather in your room to discuss measures to take, or even if there are any measures we could take," said Grakar.

Turning his head to Arium, "I'm sorry they disrespected you. As men we clamor to leap to your defense, but in truth you are greater than any of us and can defend yourself much better. You're right. I feel they could be evil wizards."

"This is a time for great caution about many things," Selana mentioned. "We should finish eating this food. We need to regain strength and vitality. That's our highest priority for the moment. The threat has passed for the time being."

The remainder of the meal was consumed relatively quietly. The staff of the inn had witnessed the bawdy men issue their brash slurs and threats. It dampened them too with worry.

The four dark clad strangers left the inn heading immediately out of the gates. The town let out a collective sigh of relief.

Grakar went to that gate moments later to speak to the guards' Captain. "Where did they go?"

"They headed east, Captain Morstem."

"I suspected as much."

"Use great care as they will be ahead of you. We'd be happy to assign one of our normal patrols to join you. They'll escort you to our eastern border."

"That's very generous, Captain. I'm inclined to accept the help. If we've drawn the barbarians to follow us this far, more troops would helpful. We may rest another day and eat a mountain of your delicious food before we resume the trek."

The gate guards all laughed with him.

Returning to the inn, he went to Jeren's room to join the strategy conference.

Everybody was assembled, staring at him when he walked in.

"It's what we expected; they went eastward along our future trail. I suspect they're planning a rude awakening somewhere out there. The Nordcans offered their patrol troops to accompany us to the border. I accepted."

"That's good," Jeren replied.

"Is there anything else we can do?"

"Not that I can suggest. If the threat is purely that of dark mages, it falls onto Arium and me and the children to wage that fight."

Arium asked, "What about the contemptuous things they said, discounting what we gained from the book?"

"I've considered that. Although it was alarming, as I think back of our prior few fights, the knowledge in the book is imbedded in us now and through it we have that link to…well whatever that other realm is, that higher plane of existence to those great beings. I think they have no fear of dark mages. As long as that portal can still be tapped, I believe we can face any threat from them. However, I want to explain, we don't control contacting that realm. They seem to act at critical times. Whether they monitor us is unknown. I can't initiate anything."

"At least that's something to feel optimistic about, added troops escorting us to the border," said Drake. "The Nordcan soldiers we've seen look to be decent. I'm happy for their help."

Grakar added, "I'd like to stay at least another day here. More food and rest can only help us."

"Yes," said both children in unison, smiling broadly. "I like a bed," Darik added. The group chuckled.

Arium pondered other aspects of the moment, including lighter topics. Remembering back to her simple life as a village wife compared to now, in the midst of this incredible epic quest, it was mindboggling the transformations she'd experienced. As a relatively young woman, to be seated here amongst incredibly handsome significant men nearby her, it was gratifying to her ego. Attentive to her, none of the men failed to stare at her at various times during the meeting. She noted, Jeren always handled it well, doing his best to ignore the romantic attention directed toward his stunning wife.

Selana uttered, "Darik is right. It's so nice to sleep in a bed again, and to have a real bath."

"Here, here," said the men.

"I guess there really isn't anything to plan," said Grakar. "Our strategies if we're attacked don't change, and our route forward is in Gensten's head. Once we cross the border, it will be just us again."

"The enemy was going to catch up to us sooner or later," Jeren replied. "You're right, essentially, nothing has changed."

"I don't know," Arium reflected. "That vile group of enemies gave me a very queasy feeling. I suspect we haven't seen the worst of our challenges."

"We'll deal with it, darling. There is no other choice."

She looked at the children. They were snickering, bumping each other in play. A stranger seeing them would conclude they were normal six-year-olds.

"We'll leave you now to enjoy your evening with the children," said Grakar.

"Goodnight, we'll see everybody at breakfast."

****

Meanwhile, beyond the town walls, the four riders didn't go far before they met a large group of their brethren.

In fact, they were dark mages and for so many of them to be gathered here in a country of no consequence to their plans and schemes, spoke to the importance of the allied travelers.

The speaker was Searik, a highly ranking dark mage and the leader of this pursuit group.

The brethren gathered around to hear him.

"She was there, I saw the child. I wasn't able to probe her, but simply being in her presence was enough to know she's all we were told she would be. Although I taunted her companions, I failed to provoke her to take action and reveal herself and her strengths. We must handle this very carefully."

"What of the others?"

"There is potency among them, but it was easy to see they're raw and untested to any great extent. I don't fear them individually. As a united group, they'll pose a threat, but not one I feel we cannot conquer. However in conjunction with Selana, the name they use for her, it's a different matter. With her included in a four part union, the difficulty ratchets up greatly. It will require we separate them to render them vulnerable."

"Selana? That name they've given to her? Do they not know what it means?"

"Obviously not, that helps demonstrate how clueless they are. It's incredible that they've come this far stumbling along in ignorance of the truth. However, it helps us because she is placed in a protected life, unawares as she grows and develops under their tutelage. This is why we didn't attack them immediately. We risk them growing into their full power with each passing day, but even reaching their maximum, it's still just them against our entire brotherhood."

"Is the woman the prize we've heard about?"

"She's an impressive physical specimen and her magic abilities are a nice addition, a tasty tidbit for us to consume at the proper time."

The brethren laughed, anxious at the prospect of the final conquest. As Searik spoke, he painted that idea as a certainty of victory. "You can see it, my friends, an unavoidable outcome for an ill-conceived quest by our hapless opponents."

He added, "Being misled and deluded adds to the impossibility they could ever prevail."

Searik looked about at the avid faces before he continued, "The glorious final day when the four are shattered, thrown down, and left at the mercy of the brotherhood is strong motivation on so many levels. Ages of secret rites, life in torment striving for the complete expulsion of any vestiges of goodness in favor of abject evil, this will be the ultimate reward by destroying goodness for all time. The world we intend to create will be a living hell, literally. We will be the benefactors."

The dark mages cheered at the thought reveling in the dark impulses it caused in them.

"We'll have an answer to this woman's arrogance, a stern answer teaching her proper role in the new world. At that point, with no force left to oppose us, we're free to unleash any horror we so choose, to indulge any impulse, and explore all conceivable excesses. This wizard of the light, Arium, will be our first victim. We'll show the world our great power, and the fact mercy is dead."

Searik skillfully stoked the pent up lusts of his followers with the idea to generate the level of blind commitment he required. However, masking his understating from them of the full truth was necessary. Those four wizards were far more a threat than he portrayed, and they were certainly no pushovers.

Without being able to probe any of them in that situation standing in the public inn, he was still able to pick up on possible reservoirs of great power within each, even the little boy. As far as Selana, she was beyond description, a simmering cauldron of power of immense proportions. Being near to her was disconcerting.

As a person, Searik had little concern for anyone other than himself. The contempt he showed toward the allies, he was no less contemptuous of his own flock. There were those individuals higher up in his order that he answered to, but it had never been a problem for him in the past and he didn't feel it would be a problem going forward.

"Yes, let this little story unfold, my friends," he muttered.

****

After the day of rest, the command mounted their revived horses and left the sanctuary of the town while the sun was still low on the horizon. It was a rare sunny day for this clime. Still, their breath and that of their horses billowed out in puffs, little clouds in the cold air as they plodded along.

Gensten rode at the front of the allies' column beside Grakar letting the Nordcan patrol take the lead. Where normally those patrols numbered around twenty, this time they were five times that size at a hundred. It was a daunting group in total also containing the hundred Grecian crack troops, the twenty skilled Warmark soldiers honed in Grecia, and now the best of the Nordcans.

Jeren, Arium, and the children rode right behind Grakar and Gensten. After them rode Brek leading the Warmark contingent, and then Drake leading the Grecians as the rear guard.

The Nordcans set a brisk pace and covered ground quickly.

Jeren glanced at his wife, riding along seemingly detached and impervious. She was all business with a determined look on her face. Her sword was always at her side and she was as deadly with it as any potential opponent she could ever meet.

Staring ahead, she was deep in thought.

I wonder what she thinks about? he mused. For him, it was a question without an answer.

As her expression became grim, he could only conclude it wasn't some pleasant memory she replayed. Concern for what awaited them was the probable culprit, but...

Imperviousness could work both ways as behind him he could hear the two children exchanging childish jibes and laughing, as if they were on a fun excursion rather than a deadly mission.

Moving past the site of the hidden dark mage camp, those mages fell in trailing after the allied troop far enough behind to avoid detection by their reckoning. They had no idea of what Selana could do.

At fifty brothers, their total numbers were far short of the allies totals. However, these were wielders of dark power and in that way posed at great threat to anyone they encountered.

A battle between the two forces would have been a serious encounter. For differing reasons, neither side sought that. For the allies, avoiding any fight with anyone to make best possible time was their directive. For the dark mages, herding the allies toward their 'destiny' of total defeat required no action on their part.

For Searik, restraining his own forces was the test. They were deprived beings for all of their lives, taught to nurture their vile inner hungers to the point they could barely be contained, making them potential explosions of wickedness waiting to happen. Sating their dark desires was counterproductive at this point of this quest, maintaining their focus was paramount. Their enemy had to be allowed to go unscathed to the designated place much farther ahead, both in time and place.

Ahead of them, the allied troop paused for brief rests when they took their meals and returned to travel rapidly. Selana continued to magically supplement the horses with vitality.

The grueling pace affected the dark mages who weren't trained for this outdoor life and rigorous strain. Though they experienced hardship on a daily basis, none were hardened into sufficient physical stamina. Even Searik was hard pressed to meet the demanding allied gait.

Far behind them all, an old foe pressed forward with a collection of ten dark mages. Gueldar always sensed Selana ahead in the distance as she sensed him too. They weren't looking to catch up to the quest any longer. That dubious plan had been abandoned long ago. Their new plan would have them arriving at the right time to join the final confrontation, an event about which he could barely contain his glee. Gueldar had his own fantasies about what he would do. In that imagined glorious moment of ultimate triumph when his dreams were fulfilled at last, his demons could be put to rest.

Gradually, the allies managed to expand the gap between them and the trailing enemy mages. At that point, they had no idea pursuit was near. Their superior physical stamina provided a perfect compensation, inadvertently decreasing their danger without their knowledge.

The only one of them to have any comprehension of this was Selana. The level of threat was always in her awareness. Jeren didn't understand what it meant, but he saw the changes in her countenance. When she was relaxed and relieved, so was he.

Riding into a Nordcan village just before dark, they stopped to spend the night there.

The villagers were happily surprised and tried to make it into an impromptu celebration.

They went to Arium with their offers.

"Thank you, friends, but we're hard pressed on this difficult journey. What we greatly need is sleep and food."

The head man spoke, "For us, this is the event of a lifetime. Please allow us some small event to mark the occasion."

Arium shook her head in defeat, smiling at him. It was unavoidable, these people wanted their moment.

"Fine, but we cannot be drawn into a lengthy—"

She never finished her sentence as the villagers cheered and suddenly food, drink, crude musical instruments and drums appeared and the impromptu 'fest' began. The Nordcan troops joined the merriment whole-heartedly and it infected the rest of the command. Relaxing into the party, putting aside their burdens for an evening, it swept over everyone.

Among the beverages provided was a brew of mead, some various other ales, berry wine, and another potent drink difficult to describe. With the exception of the children, everybody imbibed to greater or lesser extents.

Feeling the 'buzz' for the first time in a long time, Arium smiled and laughed as much as she had since before the attack on her village so long ago. She was the center of focus and for a night basked in it. Even the stoic Jeren let down his guard to savor the festivities, which for him was a radical departure.

The music and the rhythm of the drums were alluring and drew them to open their feelings to the lure.

The dancing started soon thereafter and Arium was in high demand as an endless line of partners took turns and that included village men and women. She felt like a teen girl again laughing and enjoying the fun. Her stress had been drawn away and it felt good to feel alive and safe again.

Equally, Jeren was surprised he was in high demand by village women for the dancing. It propped up his ego in an area he didn't see as his strength.

Selana danced as much as Arium, never lacking for partners either. So did Darik, pulled to his feet by village girls. His shyness with the opposite sex disappeared rapidly.

It was too late at night when they finally called a halt, the adults had imbibed too much bubbly, and nobody set up camp, they merely slept invited into the homes of various villagers.

It was their first real vulnerable time. Fortuitously, enemy forces couldn't take advantage as they were too far behind now, and too exhausted.

In the morning, with headaches, groggy from too little sleep, and ruing their dubious alcohol fueled choices, the command roused at different times. None of whom were particularly ready for another hard day in the saddle. This type of reverie had no place on a serious mission, but it was already done.

The villagers had their event of a lifetime, but the cost of it would be paid by the allies.

Leaving lasting memories had not been their intention in being solicitous of their host's wishes. However, it was done and behind them now. Eating ample breakfast and drinking plenty of coffee, they mounted up to resume the journey.

Jeren turned to Arium. "Are you okay?"

"Not really."

"It was some night, but I wish I'd drunk far less."

"I remember the start of it, but honestly not much of the end. Did we choose where we slept? I don't remember. All I know is waking up in a bed with some villagers, in their house."

"We all did, and no, I don't remember any choosing on our part. When I awoke, I didn't know what to think as it seems our own family slept in different homes."

"The children were together. No harm came to them. These villagers were not dangerous people, thankfully. Eh…did I change out of my riding clothes into a dress for the party?"

"I think I remember that later in the evening. As a matter of fact, you said dancing is easier in a dress, so yes, you did do that."

Arium frowned. "It's so vague. I just have no memory of, whatever else."

"This is a lesson. We can't make such mistakes in the future. If they were different sorts, well…"

She smiled at him. "I know, but we survived, and it was a great party. I do feel very relaxed and relieved. I will say I had very vivid dreams that seemed very real."

"I dreamt too, and they did seem like real."

"Maybe we're mixing up in our minds the end of the party with the sleep time afterwards? I'm not sure if I should be concerned."

"Perhaps."

"At any rate, it's over, so back to reality. We have a job to do."

Smirking, she snickered.

"What?" he asked.

"On the trip back, perhaps we could stop here again and have another party, even more grand than the first."

"You have a wild side, wife. I'm learning in stages about your other facets."

"Does it distress you? I do like to enjoy myself. Do you see this as bad?"

"No, I'm tickled by it, actually. You were the big hit at their party. I knew that would be the case. I'm fine with it."

"Good, you impress me. Most men would not be so understanding and tolerant. It was harmless fun, but men who can't control their jealousy make it seem otherwise. I always hated that aspect to dealing with men."

"You're welcome."

She grinned at him. "Don't get smug, sir. Remember your own adage, *A haughty spirit cometh before a fall.*"

"So true, ma'am, and I do realize you can knock me down into the dirt, and in an instant."

Arium looked at him like he was an idiot. "Always I have that male brain to deal with in my life. Are there no men who are not fools?"

He chuckled in return. It felt good, this rapport and connection with Arium. Truly, she was at the center of his life. It was hard to even remember life before her. "At least I'm your fool."

Arium didn't bother with a reply.

The swift travel went well with the Nordcan troops in the lead. The next evening in another village, a similar euphoria surfaced amongst the villagers, but the troop had agreed in advance, no more parties to dull their wits. This time they did set up camp to sleep as usual in their bedrolls. Wisely, they accepted no more alcohol to drink that evening.

The next morning was easier by far to get ready and depart without aches, pains, and throbbing heads.

When they stopped at high noon, sitting together for a brief meal, Arium addressed the men, Gensten, Grakar, Jeren, and Brek. Drake was busy meeting with his troops.

"I'm surprised the dark mages have set no traps after that scene in the inn. They were brazen and acted very confident we were helpless before them. Why wait?"

"I've thought about it," Jeren replied. "I think they were fostering feelings in us in response to the taunts. Whether they thought we'd make some ill-considered move, or something else, I don't know, but I didn't subscribe to what he said. It was either a half-truth, of a flat-out lie."

Arium shrugged. "I hesitate to discount them. Walking so boldly into our lair, they couldn't be helpless either. I think it's the timing about this whole thing. They have something serious waiting somewhere ahead. I'm confident of that opinion."

"I don't disagree. We all knew what we were getting into before we left Grecia."

Drake returned to join them.

"All is well," he mentioned in response to the stares of curiosity. "Just some minor Grecian matters to deal with."

It took another week before they approached the sentry post on the eastern border of Nordca. The Captain of the border guard post came out eyeing them in surprise.

"Are we invading our neighbors?"

The Nordcan patrol members laughed.

Jeren spoke to the Captain of the patrol troops. "We're so grateful for your help and companionship. It's a debt I intend to repay someday in some way."

"You owe us nothing. Riding in your company in this great quest exceeds anything we've done or will ever do in our lives."

Arium spoke, "When you return, be sure to give our profound thanks again at that village that opened their doors and their hearts to us. It was a memorable time living in safety with new friends. I will cherish it always."

"They will be gratified to hear it from a great lady like you, madam. Already, they deify you. Be safe with your journey and always be vigilant. The lands eastward are not as friendly as Nordca."

"We'll keep that in mind," Jeren replied.

Riding across the border reduced in their numbers brought back that nagging worry Arium had carried for so long. She looked back at Selana who also appeared to be discomfited.

Gensten resumed his place leading the column.

Although the vegetation didn't change substantially, the 'feel' in the new country did. It started with the border station where the guards were grim-faced, surly, and confrontational.

"Who are you, why are you bringing such an armed force into Stera?"

Grakar returned the grim stare. "Our business is to pass through your land on the way elsewhere."

"Elsewhere? What does that mean?"

"That's none of your concern."

The guards scowled, pondering a foolish move.

Arium smiled. "Test us, if you dare. This is as good a day to die as any other."

The guards glanced at the stern looks from the allied troop and quickly backed down.

Nodding, they admitted the quest into Stera.

Arium looked backed as they rode away from the border station at the sullen faces of the guards. Something didn't seem right and the farther they rode, the more that feeling escalated.

Gensten picked up the pace to a gallop for a time before slowing down to a normal pace. Even he looked behind them.

Jeren turned to Arium. "If Gensten is worried, I'm worried."

"This place has a bad aura. I wonder if the Sterans are in league with the dark mages."

"I feel it too."

Suddenly, for the first time, Gensten made a sharp turn to leave the main road riding into the cover of the nearby trees. However here, in coniferous forest, the trees didn't fully conceal them. Gensten kept riding leading them out of eyesight from the road. Going down into a gully of a dry stream bed, they followed that meandering path since generally it went eastward.

Searik came down the road, possibly an hour later. Gradually closing the gap between the two forces, he wanted to stay near enough to take advantage of any allied lapses. His lead scout had explained about the night of their revelry back in the Nordcan village. Such a lapse in the future would allow Searik to make them pay.

Searik's scout was forced to increase his pace when suddenly he couldn't spot them ahead any longer. Hours into racing along in a pointless chase, it finally dawned on him, they'd been duped.

Returning to the main body, Searik was not pleased.

"You fool, if you've allowed them to slip away from us, your torments will have no end."

Meanwhile, Gensten kept them in the gulch until it turned southward. By that time they were many miles away and farther along their journey.

Gensten led them to an alternate smaller road to continue the trek. It was fortuitous as it was far less well traveled with few eyes to notice their passing.

Returning to a gallop, he set another stiff pace to cover ground.

Reaching a good spot for a camp at dusk, they resumed usual protocols and set proper sentries as well as Jeren placing magical wards to conceal them.

Once he completed the spell, he sat down with his family.

"I didn't miss this," said Arium glumly.

Chapter 8

Antith

It was Selana who woke in the night with a fright.

"Father!" she cried.

The entire camp awoke in a panic, hearts thumping looking around for the danger. The sentries had seen nothing.

Quickly, Arium grasped Selana in a firm embrace; Jeren knelt down beside her, looking all around in the darkness.

"What is it, honey? We don't see anything."

"Something draws near, it's unclear to me. I feel anxiety."

"Could it be a bad dream?"

"I…I'm not sure. It's very strange. I'm sorry I startled everyone."

"Is it Gueldar, or the dark mages?"

"No, Father, it's not them. I sense them separately. This is a different threat."

"Does that mean a new magical threat?"

"I can't answer these questions. It's a nebulous darkness in our vicinity. For the moment, it has stopped coming toward us…now it is withdrawing."

"That's strange."

"Now we can sleep again." Her abrupt comment seemed odd.

Sleep was elusive in the camp after the incident, except for Selana.

In the morning, the entire command was groggy. Departing, they traveled for only an hour before they were interdicted by a patrol from the local Steran army. The surly expressions clued Jeren this was no warm welcome.

Grakar sat impassive as their Captain rode forward.

"You will accompany us to the city of King Crolar to explain your trespassing on royal lands."

Grakar eyed him grimly, deciding whether to fight.

"That would be foolish," said the Steran Captain. "What you see here is a fraction of the troops surrounding you."

"Lead the way, Captain."

It was several hours before they approached the gates of the seat of government for Stera, the capital city of Gondara.

As was the case in every other country they entered, the construction was geared toward defense. Inside, the city was sparsely populated with street traffic. Interior buildings were functional, but simple, some even crudely built.

What few citizens they saw were furtive, their faces fearful, glancing quickly at the quest members before scurrying into buildings.

The allied troops were edgy, ready for any form of attack. Jeren, Arium, and the children had silently formed their magical link in case of that kind of assault.

Tensions were high on both sides.

It was a short ride to reach the palace. The building looked to have lost its former grandeur as normal maintenance seemed to have ceased, and probably some time ago. The palace was no showplace for the realm. What the palace did have was considerable troops on guard with redundant reserves stationed nearby.

Their eyes were all focused on the approaching quest members, hands on their sword hilts.

"Get off your horses," the Steran captain commanded.

The command simply sat waiting for a response from Grakar. After a pause he dismounted. The troops followed his lead.

Servants raced out from the palace to take their horses, but none of the troops would allow it.

The Steran captain glowered. "You will relinquish the animals."

Grakar simply stared, leaving the Steran officer with the dilemma of a forceful response.

He pondered for a short time.

"My orders are those four are to enter the palace to meet the King." He pointed to Jeren, Arium, and the children. "The rest of you will stay out here."

Grakar smiled ruefully.

"Do you refuse the King's order?"

"Do you think we're fools?"

Again, the Steran officer was forced to make a difficult decision.

Grakar added, "We go together, all of us, or not at all."

"If I grant that, you must surrender all of your weapons."

"You may try to take them."

With a hand signal, the Warmark and Grecian soldiers deployed into battle formations with a martial shout, weapons drawn and ready.

The Sterans drew their weapons, but skilled Captains like Grakar and Drake could see they weren't anxious for a fight, nor was their Captain.

"I...eh..."

"Lead the way and stop wasting our time. We will meet this King of yours."

With another hand signal, the allied troops shouted again, seamlessly moving into marching ranks to enter the palace, the most formidable force ever to do so there.

The halls were lined with soldiers shoulder to shoulder, but uniformly, they had fear in their eyes.

The doors to the throne room were opened as they approached. Faded pennants and battalion standards hung limp adding to the impressions of shoddiness.

Marching in, they gave another great shout and deployed into fighting positions, weapons drawn at the ready. Archers aimed at the single figure sitting on the throne.

King Crolar was a middle-aged man who looked to have once been lively and fit. Currently, he was gaunt, hollow-eyed, and ashen-faced. It took a time before he snapped out of his stupor enough to stare at the skilled fighters arrayed before him.

"What is this? Who are you?"

"We are your guests," Grakar replied sarcastically. "Your troops waylaid us on the road and forced us here, supposedly at your command."

"My command, I don't remember..."

His attention wandered before his mind became lucid again.

"Captain?" he asked.

The Steran captain marched forward and bowed. "Your highness, we have standing orders to guard the realm against all foreigners."

"I gave such orders?"

"We were told that by the High Counselor."

At that moment, from behind a curtain behind the throne, a robed man emerged.

"You remember, your highness, we discussed this, about the army defending the realm from all threats."

The King lolled back into his stupor. The counselor turned to the allies, a sickly smile on his face. His eyes were hypnotizing with his piercing stare.

"Greetings our new friends, and welcome to Gondara, the splendor of Stera. My name is Antith, High Counselor to the throne."

His visual perusal of the allied troops stopped as he eyed Selana and Arium greedily.

"I'm sorry for any misunderstanding with your invitation to visit us here. I'm sure you can understand these are troubled times and we must be careful who enters our little realm. There are nefarious travelers roaming about who look to work mischief if left unchecked."

Grakar took a step forward. "Why are we here? We have pressing business elsewhere and have no time to waste."

"I understand and can appreciate your need for haste; however, taking a brief time to rest here and replenish your stores can only be a good thing, am I wrong?"

"Thank you for your invitation, however, we must respectfully decline."

"Captain, I cannot allow it. There is much about your quest you don't understand. I need to share this with your magicians to prepare them for what they will soon face. It will not take much of your time."

Grakar scowled but turned to look at Jeren and Arium.

Both of them were looking at Selana who was cowering, face averted from Antith.

Before they could reply, he made a slight movement with a twist of his hand. Arium and Jeren looked up. Their expressions were sudden curiosity.

Arium spoke, "Yes, Antith, we'd be happy to stay and hear your knowledge."

It struck Grakar badly, but he was at a loss at what to do.

"Excellent," said Antith. "Captain, you and your troops will be shown to comfortable rooms while I talk with these colleagues in the craft. Food and ale will be provided shortly. Please rest while you have the opportunity as you'll need all of your strength for what you will face."

Grakar looked at Arium. Her smile seemed very strange as did what she said. "It's fine, go take your rest. We'll hear from this scholar to further our knowledge and preparedness. There is no problem."

Reluctantly, Grakar led the troops out of the throne room following the servants to the guest rooms. Ample food and drink was brought soon afterwards, however, after the meals, all of the soldiers lapsed into a deep sleep. Steran troops removed all weapons and locked the doors imprisoning the allied soldiers in rooms with bars on the windows and reinforced doors impervious to escape.

Meanwhile, Antith led his four 'guests', his prey, like a pied piper into his private rooms. Separating them into different rooms because they were in a stupor of his making and unable to respond, he savored the moment.

Starting with Darik, he scanned his mind, assessed the level of his power and quickly dismissed him as inconsequential other than in union with the others. Moving to the next room to Jeren, again he assessed the man's abilities as only he could. Jeren was potent as a wizard and the fact that ancient knowledge was imbedded and indelible in his mind made him a significant factor not to be discounted. That tantalizing touch of the ancient power spurred Antith.

Moving with relish to Arium, she was similarly imbued with the ancient power. As he expected, in conjunction with the others, they became a formidable test. Her potential for Antith's purposes excited him, a perfect vessel for possibilities not only for the present but for the future.

At last, he came to Selana. Probing her was an incredible experience. She was unlike any creature he'd ever seen. The vast well of her potency was beyond description. The possibilities were endless to what she could do. She needed tutoring and development, but... He knew instantly the reason for the sudden emergence and widespread activities of the dark mages. This child was their goal and the pivot point of their schemes. From his perspective, they were limited, short-sighted, and weak proponents for their causes compared to him.

"At long last," he muttered in self-satisfaction. "I can take action. It's been far too long mired in this sty with these meaningless sots and fools." His contempt for the entire race of man inhabiting the world was colossal.

Starting first with the weakest link, he focused in Darik's mind. Affecting his real memories, planting false ones, redirecting imperatives, altering trust in his family, and adding memories of Antith as a lifelong acquaintance and trusted mentor, he smiled at the ease of it.

Moving to Jeren, his task escalated markedly reproducing the desired effects in a mature and a much stronger person. With time, he accomplished his task.

When he could finally address Arium, it had to be the next day.

For the four of them, mired in his imposed stasis, they had no awareness of the passage of time or what they were experiencing with his tampering.

Arium was a tantalizing puzzle requiring greater care and delicate approaches as with her, based on his findings there was so much more he planned to enact. She required an entire day and left him in need of rest. It required waiting to the following day to make his attempt with Selana.

All of these efforts were merely the preliminaries. So much more needed to be accomplished, but Antith didn't mind. At last he was taking steps toward his ultimate goals. Time was no factor as his control of them was for as long as he needed and they would have no idea of it.

Laying the groundwork of his plans into the remaining wielders of the power of the light, he smiled in satisfaction that after all of the eons, he could exact his revenge against his true enemies. Truth would be whatever he decided it would be on this pitiful world.

He sat by each day watching as his servants were admitted to cleanse and feed the captives. Still keeping them unconscious, he allowed their bodies to function normally, consuming food and drink, and so forth.

Gauging the proper time to wake them when they were sufficiently altered for him to take an active hand with them as conscious puppets, it was a choice. Getting his lies to stick, that was the first hurdle. If successful, thereafter everything else could fall into place.

Much later, waking them for the first time, they were prodded and revived one at a time.

Darik was numb-acting, disoriented, and somewhat unresponsive. Antith decided to wait another day before awakening Jeren. By that time, Darik had started to get some bearings. Still, he was confused and didn't readily recognize Antith.

Meanwhile, in the midst of his experiments, he ordered the allied soldiers transferred to the dungeons.

Watching Jeren's eyes open, Antith faced his first possible test. Just like Darik, Jeren was confused, unable to focus his mind, and suffering physical reactions, like nausea.

Trying to sit up, he was hit by vertigo and nearly slipped off the table.

"Careful, my friend," Antith whispered. "You need time to recover from your illness."

"Illness?" Jeren rasped, frowning while trying to get his bearings.

"Rest, you will feel better later. Go back to sleep."

With a wave of his hand, Jeren was rendered unconscious, but just into normal sleep.

Smiling, Antith moved on to Arium. Her reactions were the worst yet as she became violently ill when she tried to stand up and fell to the floor.

"Oh, oh...what's going on, what's wrong with me?" Her discomfort showed in her facial expression of pain.

"My darling, you're ill. Let me help you to your bed. You need to sleep."

Guards carried her out of the lab and into a bedroom. Again, with a wave of his hand, she was sent into normal sleep.

Servants appeared at his summons to receive his instructions. "Care for her as you've been doing. She'll sleep until tomorrow. I'll be back when she awakens to check on her progress. Answer none of her questions. Only I will speak to her."

They all nodded. None of them ever raised their eyes to look at his face. He was too frightening.

Finally attending to his last 'patient', he addressed Selana. She was the most intriguing, but also the one most probable to be a problem. Awakening just her consciousness without triggering her power was difficult, even for him. That anything of this paltry world could be a challenge was irksome. However the potential reward motivated him.

"Come child, rejoin this comedy and become another of my puppets."

Unlike the other three, Selana's eyes opened and she stared at him intently.

"Good morning," he wheedled, like a kindly grandfather. "Time to wake up, child."

"I..." she struggled, unable to find the right words. "Why do I feel this way?"

"You've been through a rough period of illness. I've been right here at your side to nurse you along. You're much better now. You should be able to get on your feet in a day or so."

"Illness?" She looked confused, which relieved his fears.

When she sat up, the strong reactions didn't cripple her as it had the others. Blinking her eyes, she looked out the window.

"It's daytime?" she spoke rhetorically.

"Yes, it is, little darling."

"Where am I?"

"I've attended to you here in this room during your convalescence. We can move you back to your room. I think you're well enough along in your recovery."

When she stood, she was momentarily wobbly, but gained her balance quickly.

"Come this way, child."

"Leading her down a hallway to a room beside Arium's, Antith placed them all separately in consecutive rooms. No longer boarding them together as a family, he'd tried to wipe away that memory in all of them, replaced by his lies.

"I'll let you collect your thoughts and rest. You've been through a lot. We'll try to gather later at dinner, if you're all able."

"We?"

"Yes, you have friends who suffered from the same malady. Their names are Jeren, Arium, and Darik."

Her expression changed to a scowl as his assertion troubled her jumbled mind. Something was amiss, but she knew not what.

Sitting down on the bed, she turned away waiting for him to leave.

Once the door closed, she got up to look out the bedroom window at the city below and beyond at the countryside. It was not at all familiar. There were memories in her head, but…it made her feel strange.

Blanking the troubling thoughts for the moment, Selana ate fruit from a platter on a small table and drank cold water. She kept on eating until all the fruit was gone.

Lying down on the bed, her brain continued to befuddle her. At last she dozed off to natural sleep.

The next morning was Antith's acid test as all four arose to leave their bedrooms and collect together. None had been able to attend dinner to prior night, so all four were famished.

"Good morning, it's so good to see all of you back on your feet." He peered at Arium.

She blinked. "I'm sorry, but would you mind explaining things. I can't seem to get my mind...straight."

"Of course, and please sit down all."

He walked over guiding her to a chair to his right. She looked at him, blinking her eyes again. "We are close?" She questioned. "I think maybe we are close?"

"We are, my darling. It's coming back to you." He kissed her cheek and hugged her.

"Thank you," she said demurely, as he pretended the gentleman with her chair as she sat down.

"For the others of you, please sit down. Let me explain, we're all friends, for a very long time actually. Jeren, you're an acquaintance of Arium's, as well as with the children. You children were orphans I took into my care. We've lived in my house for all these many years, since you were little tots."

Jeren looked confused, Darik even more confused, and Selana, she eyed him harshly for a moment before donning a placid expression.

"Yes, now I remember," she replied with a grin.

She was the one person he worried about going into the experiment and she was proving to be the challenge. Probing her, he could not verify if she was capable of a ruse. Nobody should be capable of a ruse in dealing with him. She merely smiled blithely.

"This food is delicious," she added, smiling brightly.

The others smiled and attacked their own plates.

Antith chatted pleasantly, mostly with Arium. Coaxing her along toward the planted memories, he acted the doting companion. Though she was still in flux struggling with the new reality he'd contrived, she didn't give any resistant behaviors.

Jeren gave him less of a problem than Antith had anticipated. Seemingly, he accepted Arium was not his wife and intimate partner. Nor was he a father for the children. Darik was acting very much a six-year-old, like his connection to his power and the link to the others was severed.

Selana remained the enigma, still impenetrable, even with her compliance. He wondered, *Could it be merely superficial?* With her, he would keep a close eye on. What she was capable of, he needed to know. When he looked at her, she plastered on that same blithe smile, and as days passed, he became less comfortable with it. The net result was, the time he wanted to spend working on Arium often had to be directed toward Selana to ascertain her state.

It delayed implementing his plans which annoyed him, but he couldn't afford to try to rush things. They were no threat to him, but a return of their faculties and true memories could not only complicate his agenda, it could force him to take action, possibly lethal actions. Losing his opportunities could not be tolerated, so he played the false part of pivotal member of the group.

Darik fell into a routine, once again, as a child, having no contact with his power. Antith felt he could now ignore the child.

Jeren too, seemed unable to recover any of his real life and also seemed to settle into the false life Antith created. He and Arium acted as mere acquaintances like they'd never been spouses.

Engendering affection from Arium, he took small steps to try to make her accept they were more than just friends. With that, she was slow to respond. She could be increasingly congenial, but going in such a direction with him, there seemed a line where she stopped and he dared not try to push past it…yet.

Selana increased the behaviors of her *persona* of total acceptance. Betraying no signs outwardly or inwardly she was deceiving him in any way; he still had trouble believing it. Continuing with draining away his time and effort, his plans were mired at a standstill.

"This can't be happening," he raged after several months of what was looking to be wasted effort. Each day was taking the same form, sessions with the females, and mostly with Selana, while the men idled their time away with nothing to do.

Arium couldn't be coaxed into any level of affections with Antith, still treating him as a friend and advisor. Pondering imposing his will on her flitted through his mind to push her ahead, but the risk was too great.

At last, he made a decision. He mused, *I will break this impasse. The time has come for more.* Calling them together, he explained his new plan.

"I've hesitated to tell you this after what you went through with the illnesses, but I feel the time has come to move ahead. We were entrusted with the onus of a great quest, the greatest of all time. During your time here recovering your faculties and your physical strength, I've waited patiently, but circumstances demand we resume the trek."

"What trek?" asked Darik. "What's a trek?"

"It's traveling to seek out a great secret, one we must discover to safeguard from those who wish to do harm in the world."

It was a dangerous ploy as he saw all of them struggle mentally. The quest was a strong enough memory that it could pop the bubble of his imposed ideas in their minds.

"Another thing I've decided to share is we had a troop of soldiers traveling with us that lost their minds in the epidemic of illness. They're recently returned to a state of health enough to share the journey. Of course, I'll bring along soldiers from our city too."

"When would we leave, sir?" asked Arium.

"There's no reason to delay. We leave at sunrise tomorrow. Tonight we retire early to be rested for what will be a difficult journey. Arium, with our relationship, remember you don't call me sir. We're so much more than that. I've given you time to remember it, but it seems you're stuck at a wall. I'd be happy to help you with your memories this evening, and I'll give you all the time you need in the session."

She eyed him, unable to remember any hint of what he intimated of their relationship and unsure what she should do. What he was proposing for that night was easy enough for her to understand. Something about it felt wrong. She frowned.

Antith cautiously tried to coax her mind and as he started to have success luring her along, suddenly she lurched mentally.

"I'm sorry, but there is something I cannot grasp about this. I think I must decline. Perhaps tomorrow I'll feel better and we can attempt it then?"

Concentrating on Arium, Antith didn't notice Selana's eyes had been closed, or her wry smile at his failure. Anyone evoking any power should have drawn his notice. It didn't.

Selana's ongoing evolutions were escaping him totally. Although recovery of her memories hadn't occurred yet, reemergence of her true nature and aversion of dark acts and schemes had occurred. Subtly countering Antith without his detection pleased her. Protecting Arium from his designs was her main mission at this point. Antith's efforts struck Selana as more than just misguided, but as unhealthy and inappropriate.

While Antith had sought to coax Arium toward his dubious goals, at the same time, Selana bolstered her against crumbling to the lures in her weakened state. Neither of them could recover what had been circumvented in their minds, but the wrongness of his aims gave them a point to focus on, like an anchor.

Late on the night before their departure, Antith was frustrated.

"This can't happen. How can a mere female resist me…I took away her power and…"

He paused pondering the implications.

"A mere woman couldn't. She should have fallen right at the start. There is something else in play here."

Extending his magical reach into her bedroom, he touched her sleeping mind. Delving deeply for any sign of the recovery of her powers, there was none. All he found was Arium in her REM dream state. There, he warped her dreams into what he wanted. Arium lurched and flailed about, trying to reject the jarring images suddenly appearing to interdict her dreams.

In the midst of concocting the dream, suddenly his access receded and then he was dismissed out of her head. She had not done it, and he could find no other outside source, it was another 'impossibility.' The only explanation was…

"It couldn't be them…" he whispered. That frightened him and he gave up the effort and went to bed.

In the morning, the reunion of the quest occurred, minus their memories. The soldiers were gaunt from the many months of privation not yet recovered to full strength. Their false planted memories were that of no companionship with the principals in charge. With Antith at the very head, the undisputed leader, they were mere vassals, serving at Antith's pleasure.

Jeren, Arium, and Darik looked on with virtually no recognition.

Columns of Steran troops rode ahead of and behind the allied force. Gensten was put on point as Antith had no idea where to go.

Though much of his memories had been interdicted, he retained his memory of the route of this journey.

The first night that they camped, he called Arium to place her bedding beside his.

"Tonight, we can attempt our communion again, darling. Does that suit you?"

"Of course, my darling, thank you for being patient with me."

Here was a difficult test for Selana with him so close. Also, she noted new vigilance on his part. Though he didn't seem to recognize her efforts, he acted as if there was some outside force at work.

Using new wards to keep his work protected, he plied Arium's mind to great effect, the most success he'd had with her. Convincing her she'd forgotten her former love for him, she felt helpless for the first time. Opening to him was near to happening.

Selana desperately sought a solution while there was still time. Deep within the fathomless well of her power, words came to her mind. Whispering softly, Selana tapped into that link, the mysterious access to the higher plane. Beings of awesome majesty and grandeur turned their countenance upon Selana and her plea.

Antith could create protections against any force on the planet, but now he was in the sight of far greater beings. What he wanted, they recognized instantly and reacted accordingly.

As he tried to ply her into acceptance and submission, they ended the communion and wiped his mind of the lusts. In one instant, all of his work was erased. The entire quest was purged, restored, and recovered as if his damage had never been done.

Arium awoke, stared at Antith, now helpless in his own right. In horror, she went over to her real husband.

"Jeren, I'm sorry."

"As am I, wife. I offered you and the children no protection."

Selana came over. "We must go, now."

While Antith and his Steran troops slept deep in an imposed stupor, the original command rode away into the darkness.

Gensten led them unerringly as they put ground between them and Antith.

Arium turned her head. "I remember now our real lives, but I also remember Antith and our time in his control. It could have been so much worse. He's so vile. Not the same as the dark mages threat, but a serious danger. I was helpless. I shudder to think how close he came to…"

"You have no fault. You did nothing. I was helpless and not even cognizant. If there is guilt, I'm as culpable as you. If we made errors of omission or commission, what purpose is served now wallowing in self-pity?" Rather than sounding conciliatory, Jeren's tone was harsh.

She did not fail to miss the ire in his tone.

"I know you're upset."

"How could I not be? None of that ire is directed at you, or any of our friends. Going forward, I wonder what else we could be vulnerable to. I still don't know how Antith took control of us all. If he catches us again, I have no defense to protect us from returning to that sorry state. I believe it was Selana who saved us somehow. I wasn't aware until after we were released from the mental shackles by those higher beings."

"Thankfully, she could do that. I realize she established some level of separation hidden from Antith's notice. From there, I believe she guarded me to thwart his evil designs. Without her, I was helpless just like you. Perhaps I was too taken with our ascension in the way of the light and too easily confident I could answer any danger. I will never feel that way again."

Jeren turned his head.

"I'm truly sorry for your ordeal, and I rejoice with you that nothing worse happened. I'm filled with hatred and a desire for revenge on Antith. At the same time, the captivity has taught me to ignore my emotions since I have no way to exact that revenge. I must seem a very weak husband."

"No, Jeren, of course not, don't castigate yourself. He could concoct any lie he chose and make us believe it."

"At all costs, we must avoid him, in addition to the dark mages already pursuing us."

"At least we can fight the dark mages. Whatever he is, it seems to be a higher level. I wonder if there are others like him waiting ahead in our path?"

"It's one of the many mysteries for us to solve, all of that while we try to stay alive."

Behind them, Darik and Selana were talking nonstop. She was trying to comfort and reassure him.

Both parents glanced back at them. Selana smiled. It failed to reassure either parent.

Meanwhile, the quest rode forward trying to escape their many foes.

Behind them, Antith drove his forces maniacally, but the horses had physical limits, in spite of his threats.

Farther behind, dark mages sensed the quest back on the road after a lengthy unexplained absence. They failed to sense Antith.

Much farther behind, Gueldar and his associates plodded along steadily. In their case, it was like he was a pied piper accumulating more and more dark mages as they went. The size of the pack now numbered in the hundreds and more arrived daily adding to the daunting total.

Similar to Darik and Selana, Gueldar developed faster than the normal child. He too had adult comprehension in many things, and in his case, he was developing a severe personality of arrogance toward others and a need to be in charge. Correcting or arguing with him was not a wise choice. Neither did he take the suggestions, nor did he treat the person decently. Rather, it meant a serious tirade and with him being a person of power, that could have serious and potentially deadly ramifications. Any empathy, moral persuasion, or even a sense of right and wrong was eroding away leaving an amoral sociopath.

There was a sense of urgency in all of the camps as in every case; they believed momentous events were approaching and close at hand.

The chase continued with the allies remaining the prey. None of the people on the quest, as forces of the light, were untouched or unchanged by their capture by Antith. In every case, total helplessness was a first. Antith could have taken every one of their lives if he chose to.

The memory of it was humiliating, frustrating, and it shattered their inner sense of security. Both Jeren and Arium had the same thought. *If we run into another Antith, we'll be helpless to stop it and there could be a far darker outcome.*

Of all of them, Arium struggled with it the most. No one said anything to her, but the fact she had been in Antith's total control, an evil man. Her mind mused on troubling questions. *Under his influence, would he act a gentleman in her helpless state? Did he?* That was not a question she could answer for sure, nor did she want to know at this point. With being judged, she was her own worst enemy, castigating herself internally.

Rather than share her angst with her husband, she tried to internalize it. He was lost in his own brand of misery and she didn't want to burden him further. *I'm sorry, Jeren*, she pondered often.

Reestablishing the familial bonds and rapport was the only thing she found therapeutic. Darik came around in time, but Selana seemed a different person.

That, she did talk about with Jeren.

"Has she outgrown us? I don't want to say she's standoffish or detached, but there is clearly a difference in her now. Maybe our failures as her protectors made her conclude she's better off without us?"

"I don't think that, Arium. I hope I'm right. She is different, but perhaps because she had the greatest tests of all of us."

"Perhaps."

Chapter 9

Tragedies

It was fortuitous for the allies, Antith had no way to send word in advance of them, so traveling across Stera they encountered only the usual glum looks from uninspired troops rather than aggressive resistance.

Though there was much distance to traverse, nothing slowed them and with Selana supplementing the energy of the horses, they were able to approach the far Steran border in weeks rather than months. The border guards didn't even bother challenging them.

Entering the next country, Gensten continued for a time before leading them off for a rest.

He waited patiently for the command to join him. Sitting down, he was pleasantly surprised when Arium opted to sit beside him.

Selana sat down beside her with Jeren and Darik on the other side. Grakar, Brek, and Drake completed their impromptu circle, all of the usual suspects.

Gensten mentioned to Arium, "Going through this trek, I realize now how lucky I was on the first journey. I had many frightening situations, but nothing on the scale of what we've faced this time going back across these lands."

"What country have we entered?"

"Roraika."

They stared at him, waiting for more.

"It's no place to relax. No country along the way is safe and that includes my home country. I thought we would get through Stera easily and we all saw what happened. With Roraika, who knows what hidden horrors they may have waiting for us."

"That's encouraging," said Brek.

"I could lie to you, but why? It's best we know the truth so we're ready."

"That's true," Drake added.

"I've seen as much of Stera as I ever care to," Arium commented.

"Here, here," they all agreed in unison.

"Good riddance," Grakar muttered.

Brek spoke, "It's good to see you happy again, Arium. You're too beautiful to be in a funk. It will cause frown lines in your face."

She eyed him wryly as the men chuckled. "Should I critique you also, Brek?"

"My shortcomings are clear enough," Brek replied. "Case in point, I could never garner your esteem, as much as I tried."

"There are many things I could say to that," she replied, smirking.

Jeren paid no attention to the attempt at banter in the group, and the fact his wife was constantly the center of attention failed to affect him, again. His concentration was elsewhere.

Selana looked at him. "What is it, Father?"

"I'm sorry, darling. I just keep going over what happened in my mind. I can't come to terms with…well…"

"Our failings," Selana added.

"I suppose that is true. In a person's thoughts, we imagined ourselves something more than we really are far too often. How to guard against that, I can find no solution and it irks me."

Arium spoke, "Husband, can we put all of that aside to enjoy this brief moment of companionship? Carrying weighty matters is a burden in itself. I, for one, need respite from that strain."

"Of course, Arium, I'm sorry, and I say that to all of you. I admit I wasn't paying attention. What are we talking about?"

Drake explained, "Brek was just saying how beautiful Arium is, and elusive."

"That's undeniable truth." Jeren responded blandly.

The others eyed him closely. Missing the point of the jibes seemed to happen to Jeren frequently these days. Grasping the nature of his perpetual distraction eluded them.

Brek spoke, "I meant no disrespect toward you or your wife. I assumed you know that."

"Of course, my friend; I'm just not a jealous person. If you're looking for such behavior from me, I'll always disappoint you. Our group banter is refreshing and a relief for me too. I don't worry about anybody going over any lines in my marriage if that's your concern. I trust my wife, and all of you. If we can't make light of our situation with some silly verbal play, we don't help ourselves in coping with the stress."

He glanced at Arium. She was eyeing him with a curious thoughtful expression. Understanding what she was feeling, and thinking, it wasn't his 'strength'. Being in the dark about her was the norm for him.

The wind picked up, rustling the trees, sounding like the rush of water in the distance.

"It does get cool in these alpine regions," Gensten muttered. "I never get accustomed to it."

"Is this country a large one?" asked Grakar.

"It's somewhat smaller than Stera, but a long journey nonetheless."

"If we're rested and fed, we should go," Grakar continued.

The command mounted up and rode back onto the main road. Rather the go out into the lead, Gensten stayed back to ride beside Jeren.

"In Roraika, I want to tell you, they're poorly administered by a weak government, so consequently, they have a significant problem with petty warlords and small armies of brigands roaming about and controlling much of the country. Royal forces no longer patrol and provide no protection for the people."

"How much of a threat to us do they pose?"

"Militarily, I'd say we're the measure of any challenge any of them could present, but being vigilant is prudent."

"More vigilant than we already are?"

"Not really, I just thought I'd give you an idea of what to expect."

Gensten spurred his horse to resume his place in advance of the column.

On this day, Arium had opted to ride beside Brek while Gensten was riding beside Jeren. Jeren paid virtually no attention, even when Arium looked at him directly.

Brek was chatting constantly at her. Frustrated with Jeren, she began to chat back with him, watching for her husband's reaction.

Jeren had slipped back lost into his detached state pondering issues again. That oblivious state of his seemed to irk her a great deal lately and it totally went past his notice.

Miles passed by riding the road with Jeren continuing in deep meditation and with Arium in ongoing conversation. This buoyed Brek who basked in any attention of hers that he could capture.

That evening when they stopped to make camp, Arium sat with Brek beside her, but invited handsome Drake to sit on her other side. Jeren merely walked past going over to talk with Grakar and Gensten, paying no attention. This further annoyed his wife.

Her sudden exaggerated fascination with the insanely handsome and dashing officers, Drake and Brek, failed to evoke any jealousy in her husband. Mimicking returning to her courtship phase with them to engender his attention, it made little practical sense other than a sign of developing new angst in her emotions.

Does he secretly hold some guilt against me, that I was culpable for being in the control of that heinous Antith? Her worries she tried to internalize, but…*will it lead to trouble later?*

Believing his stated words, she was increasingly having trouble with it. His actions were the gauge she used about uncovering his true feelings.

Guilt is a potent motivator. However, toying with the emotions of men not her husband was a dangerous game. Garnering their already strong interest was an easy step for her. What it could develop into was fraught with disaster on many levels.

Eyeing her husband sullenly in the middle of these two men any woman would die to claim; Jeren was scowling talking about whatever were the issues with Gensten and Grakar. Never once did he look over at her.

That night, she pondered radical steps to shock him into awareness. Moving her bedroll away to sleep by…them, it was a thought that gave her perverse satisfaction, like striking a blow against his apathy. It was a strange twist, a fit of such pettiness in the midst of this deadly quest.

When he came over as she was about to arise to walk away, he spoke.

"Arium, I've been thinking."

"Oh? What a surprise."

Her irritation came out in her tone. This time, he did not fail to notice.

"Eh…is something wrong, darling?"

That he wasn't aware and could ask that question nearly pushed her over the edge.

Shaking her head, she answered, "You could say that."

His face turned to concern, which pleased her.

"What is it? What can I do?"

She pondered how she wanted to approach this. Screaming at him, ranting and raving in the middle of the camp before the troops and the children, she restrained that explosion and took a deep breath.

"I'm…unhappy of late, but the fact you're unaware of it…well, it bothers me greatly."

"I'm sorry. Please tell me."

"We're husband and wife in the most desperate circumstances possible, so that is strain enough on a marriage. What I crave is what little we can salvage, your full love and attention. It's difficult to impossible to have the normal benefits of a couple, so making do without such pleasantries leads to pent up emotions with no outlet. Does that make sense to you?"

"It does. I feel it too. I haven't wanted to impose my burden on you. What burdens you carry already are difficult enough."

"You are such a dolt sometimes, Jeren. Some burdens, I want you to put on me."

He smiled. "You mean…?"

"Of course I do. I've been acting foolish, acting out with Drake and Brek, and you didn't bat an eye. It makes me want to smash you in the face."

He chuckled. "If I have an option, I'll pass on the violence."

"Well…?" she said.

Looking around, he eyed her sheepishly. "Perhaps we can slip away tonight?"

"Yes, and it's about time, sir."

"Should we bring along Drake and Brek since you've taken a shine to them?"

"You idiot." She smacked him on the arm while he chuckled again. "Stupid man, you're not funny."

"I'm sorry, I love you."

She continued to glower at him, but didn't resist his hug. Ultimately, in spite of her recent antics, it was his love she truly wanted.

In the morning, two spouses looked noticeably relaxed and revived. Seemingly, a budding serious problem had been successfully resolved, nipped in the bud in the nick of time.

Her return to usual left Brek and Drake disappointed. The thrill of the brief period of romantic connection with Arium resonated and wasn't easily dismissed. She was still tantalizing, a supreme prize, even as Jeren's wife.

They talked together that evening.

"I apologize, husband. My behaviors were not seemly for the wife of a great man. I wonder if the captivity changed me, weakened me to such lures?"

"Perhaps, I believe Antith devoted a great deal of his time and effort on you. Whatever he planned, I'm glad we escaped that noose. If there is some residual effect, I can't say, though I wouldn't be surprised. He was far more than a mage or a wizard."

"Thankfully, his reach doesn't seem to extend over distance, so staying ahead of him should keep us safe from being controlled."

"I agree. However, do you mind being controlled by me?"

She smirked. "Controlled by you...that will be the day."

They laughed, savoring the return of closeness and rapport in the marriage.

"You do realize, you broke two hearts with whatever this was you did."

"I'm not perfect. I make mistakes like any other person. I will apologize to both of them in private soon enough. It was so out of character for me."

"I know. Trying to garner male attention is a strange twist. You have all possible male attention already simply by doing nothing at all."

"Hopefully, you can put that matter to rest. I'm sorry. As long as you cherish me, that's all I need."

Selana suddenly got up and walked over looking worried.

"What is it?" asked Arium. "Is danger nearing us?"

"It's not that. Ahead, up ahead, I...we need to go there. Now."

They stood immediately. It caught the attention of the soldiers.

"Trouble?" asked Grakar.

"Selana sensed something ahead and feels we need to go there."

Presently, the command was mounted and riding forward. Selana rode beside Gensten, directing him to the new destination.

It was over an hour of riding before they saw smoke rising in the distance.

The soldiers drew their weapons.

Nearing what was a ruined village, they slowed to approach with caution. Entering the village, it was an appalling scene. Dead bodies were everywhere and that included women and children.

Selana was crying as they dismounted and walked about amongst the carnage. Darik was equally disturbed.

"What is this?" asked Arium. "These were not soldiers. They were peasants and their families. What could have been the reason for this senseless slaughter? These people were poor and I doubt they had anything of value. Doing such savagery accomplishes nothing."

The allied command seethed with rage at the atrocities. Selana suddenly looked at a hut. Two small faces ducked out of sight. She walked over.

"May I come in?"

The small faces appeared again. Their tear-stained cheeks and the terror in their eyes was heart-breaking to see.

"We aren't going to hurt you," Selana continued gently. "Please come out."

The children continued to pause, glancing at the soldiers before finally easing outside. They were dressed in simple clothes, little more than rags. Standing in front of these strangers, they shuddered visibly with fear.

Arium was heartbroken and knelt down to embrace them in a comforting hug.

"We're here now, children. You're safe with us."

The two looked to be in shock. Soldiers entered the hut to find their parents slain.

The children looked to be around age five, brother and sister.

The sister spoke first, softly, and only to Selana. She had a brief conversation. Turning to the troop, Arium explained.

"They're twins, and indeed it was their parents in the hut. The attack came after the 'bad men', to use her words, came with demands. The village paid this local band for protection but they came prematurely for another installment. The village had nothing to give, so they wiped them out as an example."

Arium stopped, taking a deep breath before continuing.

"These two survived because their mother hid them under a pile of blankets. What happened here is seared into their brains."

None of the allies were unmoved. All of them had murder and revenge in their eyes.

The trail of the marauders was clear enough to see, especially for an expert tracker like Gensten. They made no attempt to hide their path going away. There were none they feared. Peasants weren't ever a threat.

"What do we do?" asked Gensten.

"We take them with us," Selana replied.

"That puts them into our jeopardy," Jeren replied reflectively.

"I will safeguard them," Selana answered firmly.

No one argued with her. She took the brother, Amik, on her horse and Darik took the sister, Sari, on his horse.

Riding away at the gallop, there was no question where they would go. This heinous crime required a response.

The enemy camp was about an hour away far off the road in a clearing in the forest. The camp wasn't small, but they didn't bother posting sentries, plus they were drinking heavily celebrating their sins.

Over two hundred in that gang were no match for the sudden attack, or the righteous indignation of the quest forces. Neither Jeren nor Arium raised their power, other than what they normally did augmenting their physical fights. Scything through the rabble almost effortlessly, at the end only the leader and his few lieutenants remained.

"Who are you?" he wheezed in fear.

"We're retribution for your lifetime of killing, leaving innocent victims in your wake. Today is your day of reckoning."

"Please spare us. We will follow a new way, I promise."

"Your promise is as worthless as you. There can be no forgiveness in this world for you with what you've done. Perhaps you can find pardon in the next world, but I suspect you'll be welcomed to hell."

Puncturing the remaining enemies with a barrage of arrows ended their miserable lives.

However, killing off this gang hadn't given the allies any feeling of closure and had done nothing for the little twins.

Tragedy had already entered their lives and irrevocably so. There was no winding back the clock to restore their lives with their family.

"No," said Selana to the unspoken questions. "They're a part of us now. They're brother and sister to Darik and me, any questions?"

The group was shocked at her challenging tone.

"Nope," Jeren answered.

They rode away to return to the road. Selana began a process as they rode, probing his little mind as Darik did the same with his sister. Seeking out any sign of that tiny nugget, the kernel of innate magic; in both cases, they were blessed to have it.

"You will begin a new life path," she muttered in his ear.

"Yes," both Amik and Sari answered simultaneously.

"Good."

Even on the road, the two new disciples for the light were taught preliminary lessons and given small mental exercises. It became an ongoing education during the rides each day and at each stop.

Jeren and Arium joined the communion after some time to add their teaching and their assessment.

The twins had clear abilities and expanding the small circle of four magicians had no downside, other than greatly increasing the hazards in the lives of the twins.

If Jeren's entire order, the wizards of the light, had been incapacitated or wiped out altogether, beginning to rebuild the ranks was a must. The dark mages could not be left unchallenged.

Far away, Gueldar was aware of the two new entities of magic, even in such a fledgling state. Antith also knew of the awakenings. For him, it was insignificant and inconsequential. Only one thing mattered, recapturing and subjugating them, the members in the quest, to resume his vile schemes. Two tiny additions were nothing.

Back with Selana, calming the twins, giving them both feelings of security and new purpose, it was gratifying. For the twins, it was like a vast door had opened and they stepped into a new world of wonder. All of their terror was packed away deep in some hidden corner of their minds while they learned the lessons Selana had to teach them.

The bond they experienced between the six gave them communion in a way they would never have known. Viewing Jeren as Father, and Arium as Mother, it came easily. Their love for their birth parents wasn't replaced or diminished, but the new familial bond filled the void of their traumatic loss.

The knowledge contained in the tome was passed on gradually as the twins were able to comprehend and digest it. Consequently, their progress was beyond remarkable and far beyond what they would have accomplished in the academy.

By the time they approached the far Roraikan border, months later, they had a level of command and skill fully trained students of the academy would have envied. Using complex magic's, they could act if faced by adverse enemies now with some real chance at success and survival. In conjunction with the entire group, that formidable array of wizardry was far stronger and more daunting.

Along their trail, various bands of miscreants attempted to waylay them to overpower and capture the group. It was a foolish plan and the allies showed no mercy excising their ire about the slaughter of the twin's village on any criminals in their path.

There were noticeably fewer criminals left alive as they prepared to exit the land. Grecian troops didn't lose battles to anybody.

The border guards and their Captain stepped out to meet the approaching small army, took a good look at approaching death and quickly went back out of the way.

The quest entered the next country.

Bandar was a change in numerous ways as they descended out of mountain countries quickly returning to the lowlands. It meant even in winter, temperatures were warmer, though not warm.

Bandarian patrols were frequent after the relative free travel in Roraika. With colorful pennants flapping in the breeze, they rode toward the quest looking like a parade display. Their multicolor uniforms were as colorful as their pennants. With their comical appearance, none of them looked to be combat veterans.

Drake looked at Grakar.

"Peacocks," he muttered.

The troops heard him and chuckled.

"Be ready anyway," Grakar replied.

Though the size of the two forces was approximately equal, their relative strength was not.

The Bandarian commander waved them to halt.

Grakar merely slowed the approach until they were very close.

"What is your business traveling on Bandarian roads?"

"Our business is traveling through Bandar."

His contempt at the patrol transmitted through his tone and his rude response.

The patrol commander bristled. Grakar smirked.

"Who are you and from where do you come?"

"We come from the west and who we are is none of your business."

"I'll have you know, I'm Blanak, divine commander and high exemplar of her majesty's auspicious host. You will show proper respect, or face the consequences."

"What consequences would that be?"

Arium rode forward as the encounter spiraled out of control.

"Excuse me, your imminence," she said smoothly. "Blanak, is it? I think we're both a bit on edge. We've had a difficult journey so perhaps our manners are a little lacking. Can you forgive us?"

She gave him her sweetest smile.

He was awed, as are all men meeting Arium.

"Well…in this one instance, as a kindness to you, my lady, I will make an exception."

He smiled, full of self-importance. Turning to his men a made a loud pronouncement, mostly for Arium's benefit.

"Forces of her majesty, you will deter from your terrible and righteous wrath and refrain from punishing these intruders as they so justly deserve."

"Thank you so much for your generous forgiveness and forbearance." Her manner was so insipid and silly, it was a shock Blanak didn't recognize it. He was so lost in her allure.

It was supremely difficult for the allied troops to keep from laughing outright at the absurdity of the exchange.

"As a gesture of friendship, we will forgo our normal patrolling and accompany you to the Capital City of Glorium to meet her august majesty the Queen, the divine ruler of rulers, Sobrina, *deus rex,* the divine goddess come down into this world."

"Thank you for such an honor. We look forward to meeting her."

"We will protect and keep you safe from all peril, My Lady. I will grant you may ride here by my side. Please ride to my right in high honor as my companion."

"What?" Jeren muttered.

"Quiet," she whispered, giving them a hand signal to let it rest.

"Thank you so much, Blanak. I feel very safe."

His reaction, beaming like a child, entertained everybody in the quest, except Jeren.

She rode ahead to join him while the quest fell in behind the Bandarian troop.

"What a fool," Drake whispered to Grakar. "He's a clown with a toy weapon."

Gensten said nothing, staring ahead in deep contemplation, choosing not to share his musings or any concerns at that point in time.

Jeren was further annoyed watching the exchanges ahead of them as the Bandarian officer attempted to romance Arium. She acted coy, playing the part of a timid blushing maiden dazzled by a uniform. Seeing him wheedle his pleas for her companionship for later that evening, his putting a hand to her shoulder and rubbing her back, it irked Jeren, even with the understanding that Arium was in control. She used subtle magic to manipulate the moment, and the fool wooing her, and was never in any danger of an inappropriate dilemma. For whatever the reason, this display evoked his jealousy for the first time and it took great effort to refrain from zapping the man out of his saddle with a bolt of blue power.

Selana sensed his struggle and rode up to his side.

"Father, I'm here," she said. "There is no danger. Calm your storm; this is not the time for a foolish fight. They are no threat to us."

He would have ignored her request, dwelling instead in his childish snit, but as she could do, and had done before, she drained away the troublesome emotions and suddenly the rage was gone.

Jeren was left feeling empty momentarily before his emotions returned, minus the discord.

Selana rode along sublimely, as if her intervention never happened. Darik knew though, and now the twins knew it too. Amik and Sari rode their own horses, having quickly left the vulnerable stage. They had potency and that gave them confidence and a restored sense of security.

Meanwhile, the absurd parade continued. The multicolored soldiers followed Blanak and Arium into the front city gates past a line of massive statues of former rulers. Blanak beamed at the sudden crowds of citizens gaping and exclaiming over the visitors, and in particular, Arium riding with a Bandarian officer. Capturing the heart of the most beautiful woman ever to enter Glorium was a feat of romantic prowess unheard of in the realm. Instantly, Blanak ascended in the esteem of the populace to near legendary status. Tales and speculation on how it could have happened were as diverse

146

as the numerous minds could conceive. Those theories were tame, or lurid, depending on the person speaking.

Arium was oblivious of the commotion and ado. Her attention was concentrated on scanning the area and the palace for any signs of magicians, or magic. Meeting another Antith was her worry. Probing ahead with her magic, she found nothing worrisome.

The procession, which had developed into a victory parade, stopped at the palace stairway. Troops were stationed on each step all the way up the entire lengthy structure. Again, they looked to be ceremonial fixtures, not combat troops.

Those palace guards were dressed in different uniforms of a basic royal blue, but also with needless embellishment taking away from any chance they could look fearsome.

"Your friends shall remain outside the palace," said Blanak. He saw Arium scowl.

"I'm sorry, my dear, but those are the rules. Only the queen can issue an invitation for them to make an appearance. Don't fear, you'll always be safe under my protection."

Looking back at the command, she gave another hand signal. Selana was right beside Jeren, just in case. He sat impassive.

To walk up the staircase, Blanak offered his arm, staring at her. Refusing his gesture in front of the throng would have caused an incident. Arium linked arms with him to the raucous cheers of the crowd. Jeren was not cheering. A faint aura of blue power came to life, but Selana grabbed his arm to shake him out of it.

"No," she whispered.

The halls of the palace were choked with courtesans gawking at the spectacle, the biggest event in virtually all time for this backwater country.

Arium nodded with a sublime smile, like she was a ruler come for an official visit.

Blanak was agog with his moment, the notoriety and acclaim, and with this vision of perfection walking at his side. His dreams and aspirations were running rampant in his mind.

At the doors into the throne room, for the first time, Arium saw some real soldiers, large men who could handle themselves with weapons. Dressed in plain dark brown uniforms, they eyed the procession balefully.

147

"Are these guards Bandarians?" she asked in a whisper.

"No, they're on loan to us from our neighbors to the east in Cronda. They are a serious lot, stay to themselves much of the time, except for…well, you understand men."

"I understand men very well," she replied softly.

"Their burly gruff ways appeal to some of our women. I don't understand it, but there it is."

"I see."

"It's confusing for you, I'm sure. A refined, cultured, and educated woman such as you could never find merit in such beastly men."

"I try to keep an open mind in all things," she replied, smirking inwardly.

The remark caught Blanak by surprise and he wasn't sure what to make of it.

"Eh…" he stammered, but then the throne room doors were flung open and they marched in.

Arium looked around. This room was the first time she'd seen any level of taste in the *décor* and the first time any wealth was on display. There were no silly displays like in the hallway with huge tapestries celebrating phantom battles and false victories which had never occurred.

In the throne room, she saw some people who looked competent and possibly even intelligent. Also, standing by the throne were more brown-clad Crondan soldiers, and they were huge, man-mountains of muscle.

Sitting on the throne was Arium's biggest surprise. The queen was a young woman, little more than a girl actually. Her crown was too big for her head, so she sat it on one of the throne supports.

Eyeing Arium closely as she was led right to her feet, Arium smiled to her. Blanak knelt down, so Arium followed his lead, they bowed their heads in deference.

"Your majesty, we've returned with travelers to our land. I've had the pleasure of making the acquaintance of the esteemed Lady Arium. I'm pleased to present her to the crown."

When the queen replied, her tiny voice made her seem even younger than she looked.

"Thank you, Blanak. You may rise."

Arium stood looking first at the two guards. Their eyes were fixed on her, but like predators about to consume prey. Fierce expressions seemed to be the norm for these soldiers.

Although they were imposing physical beings, with her powers they were not a threat to Arium.

The queen stared at Arium, who waited in silence under her appraising scrutiny.

Blanak turned his head. "You may speak to her highness."

"I'm sorry, your majesty. I'm unaware of your protocols. May I say I and my companions are happy to visit your land, and to see your wonderful palace? I hope you don't see us as trespassers as we had no such intention. We have pressing business elsewhere and are making all haste to complete our journey."

It caught her attention. "What is this business?" She asked in true curiosity.

"I'm afraid that to an extent, we're not sure. We have a general sense that this is a momentous quest, but the details remain unclear at this point."

"That sounds very dangerous."

"There is certainly danger involved. We've come through a number of harrowing experiences thus far and I suspect we have more to come."

"I don't experience danger, or adventure. I spend my days here in the palace like a bird in a gilded cage."

"Your majesty," Blanak interrupted. "You are the jewel of our land and our people. We realize we ask a great deal, but it's a price you must pay so the people have your divine leadership and inspiration."

"Inspiration? I suspect this woman, Lady Arium, knows about real inspiration."

Arium smiled ruefully. "Your majesty, not every test we face in life grants inspiring outcomes. There is too much evil in the world to hope for gentle and blessed lives."

She looked at the Crondars. "I suspect your personal guards could give you a different explanation of what resides beyond your borders."

They grinned at her.

Chapter 10

Difficulties

What else was in their eyes made her blush, and for Arium, blushing was nearly unheard of. At this point in time, that she was being affected or even paying attention to any male notice surprised her. These men were a different breed of male and had little concern for polite niceties or gentlemanly decorum.

Blinking her eyes, she looked back at the young queen. "Is it permissible to admit the other members of our quest into the palace? They would appreciate the opportunity to meet with you and see the splendors of your home."

"Of course, Lady Arium. Banak, why didn't you tell me there were others waiting here?"

"I'm sorry, your highness. I thought…"

He glanced at Arium. Suddenly, his dreams, those warm fantasies of bliss, had developed a tinny hollow ring. Seducing her seemed beyond a ridiculous thought. He felt shamed and embarrassed. Of course, she'd helped him along with that realization.

"I'll see that they're brought forth immediately."

Bowing, he hurried out of the room.

Arium glanced again at the guards for a moment. They were locked onto her with piercing stares.

"May I ask how many of you are stationed here?" she asked.

The guard on the right answered. "Enough."

She couldn't help but smile. Even the guards relaxed their hostile looks.

She could hear them coming, the allied troops, marching, singing and shouting as they entered the throne room. Arium smiled with pride.

The Crondarians jumped to attention, weapons at the ready. Captain Grakar ignored them completely, simply continuing to march into the ceremonial room. The clop of boots on the granite floors resounded loudly.

Once they were all inside, he gave a shout and they executed a dazzling deployment and display of sword mastery.

The guards looked on, fascinated. At long last in this spineless country, they were around comrades in arms, men they could respect.

With a final loud stamp of their boots, the allies ended the performance. Within moments, a contingent of Crondar troops rushed into the room, weapons drawn. The man leading them was another giant of a figure. Dashing in appearance, another man's man, ruggedly handsome, he accomplished a rare thing—Arium noticed him. Evoking her almost on a primal level, his aura wasn't one of magic. Rather, it was one that set female hearts a flutter. The strong flush in her reddened cheeks embarrassed her. Glancing down with worry to see if Jeren noticed, he didn't. He was clinically watching the man and his troops to assess any potential threat.

Initially confused by the scene, this officer made his way to the throne when the allies offered no attack.

"Your majesty, are you harmed?"

"No, of course not. Meet our new friends, Brogan. These are travelers through our lands. Meet the Lady Arium and her retainers."

"My Lady," he said with a bow, and then he kissed her hand.

"Thank you, Brogan. May I tell you, your troops are very impressive? Actually, they're among the finest I've ever seen."

"Thank you, My Lady, and as I see your troops, they're similarly impressive. May I know where you're coming from?"

"We're from countries far to the west, to answer your question. Our journey takes us eastward. I don't know if you've heard of the countries, Warmark and Grecia."

"Truly? Are these the famed Grecians?"

"We are," Drake answered.

"Your army is legendary, even here in these obscure reaches."

"I'm sorry word of the Cronda hasn't reached us. It should. Your troops are the envy of any commander."

The Crondar troops gave a martial shout of their own.

"I hope we can have an opportunity to talk and spend time together," said Arium. "It seems we'll be traveling through your homeland next."

"Then we definitely need to talk. Our country is not like Bandar."

The queen arose, standing up from her throne. Smiling, she announced,

"I declare we will stage a great ball for this evening to celebrate your historic visit and form new bonds of friendship. Lady Arium, your compatriots will be taken into suitable rooms to rest, have food, and cleanse for the event tonight. I invite you to stay in my royal suites. I wish to know you, if that's agreeable."

"Certainly, your majesty, I would be honored."

"Would you consent to wearing a ballroom gown this evening?"

"I…it's been a while, but yes, I can do that."

"Riding clothes are for out on the trail. Here, they're not necessary."

She was taken behind the throne past curtains to the hidden entrance into her majesty's suites. The rooms were surprisingly lavish, and to Arium's surprise, Brogan had a room there too.

"Perhaps we can talk much sooner than you expected," he said.

"So it would seem," Arium answered.

"Does this offend you that I have the Commander living so close at hand?"

"I take offense to very little in my life, and I certainly have no need or desire to judge anybody else. Whatever relationships you have are your own business."

"I think if I wanted to have that kind of relationship, Brogan would refuse me, and I think he would drive away any other person I wanted."

He frowned. "Your majesty, you need to grow and mature in many ways. Rushing such an important matter as a romantic companionship; now is not the time for you."

"Do you see what I mean, Lady Arium?"

"Queen Sobrina, don't rue meeting men with principles. Regretfully, there are far too few in the world. Men looking to take advantage, they seem to be infinite in number."

Brogan laughed. He commented, "Men are simple creatures; we have just a few basic needs."

"Basic needs," Arium smirked, shaking her head. "I can think of truer names for it."

Again, Brogan laughed. This time he eyed her. Arium had been 'perused' so many times in her life she was surprised it took him so long. Why it caused her to fight from smiling at him, she couldn't understand, though he was a very appealing man in a number of areas.

"This, what you two have here, this playful banter, why must I be denied that privilege?"

Arium and Brogan stared at each other a moment. Arium spoke.

"Queen Sobrina, matters of the heart can be a slippery slope. Taking time to gain maturity is the only choice you should consider."

"Just call me by my name, Sobrina. That's not a satisfying answer, Lady Arium."

"Your satisfaction must wait, I'm sorry. And just call me by my name, Arium."

At that moment scowling, she looked a girl rather than the monarch of monarchs.

Brogan looked at her. "These troops, Lady Arium, are they your vassals? They're from different countries?"

"Brogan, will you just call me Arium too? And no, it's not like that among us. We act as equals in all things."

"Do they need your counsel or instruction?"

"Hardly, and I doubt they would take it anyway."

"Your lands are much different than ours."

"May I ask in what way?"

"Strife is not unknown in Cronda. There is intrigue, plots and schemes. The King and his brother compete constantly. The reason we're here rather than at home is we support the brother, so the King looked to weaken his position sending his supporters away. I suspect that civil war could break out soon. Already there have been skirmishes all over the land."

"I'm sorry to hear that."

"The army is split, just like the citizenry. I see no chance those competing brothers could ever reconcile. My opinion is the King is the lesser of the choices. He's far too impulsive, demanding, and indulgent. Without the tempering influence of his brother, things would have been much worse. That could be our future."

"Will we be in danger trying to cross the land?"

"I can't say you would be safe on that journey."

She frowned.

"Arium, I can only be honest with you. I never lie and am honest in all things."

"Interesting," she replied.

"In what way is it interesting?"

"That's a bold allegation that you never lie. I wonder if it's possible for any person never to lie?"

"It is the choice I make."

"Do you have a wife back home?"

"No, it wouldn't have worked out."

"Does that say you have no desire for a wife?"

His eyes narrowed. "What game do we play, My Lady? I have the thought of a wife, of course."

"My question was do you lack a desire to have a wife?"

The queen chuckled. "She will make you say it, Brogan. You pretend you're above desire and even lust. I never believed that. I haven't seen you slip away with your men when they seek nights with women, but what lurks in your heart? Will you answer that question?"

"This is unseemly for your ears, your majesty."

"I'll decide that for myself."

"I'm sorry," Arium interrupted. "I didn't mean to go off onto the topic of men pursuing...well."

"Coming back to your question, I haven't dismissed the possibility of having a wife. I would answer it must be a particular person, a woman I can respect, has a brain, and evokes me."

"Have you ever met such a woman?"

He paused. Arium smirked and the queen laughed.

The queen said, "Arium, I doubt he will answer because meeting you has fulfilled all of his requirements."

Arium eyed him thoughtfully. The embarrassment on his face lent credence to Sobrina's theory. It was gratifying that this mighty man apparently longed for her and honestly, he had a strong masculine appeal that resonated in her, perhaps too strongly. He looked away.

"Ladies, I won't hold you from your bath and rest before the ball. I need to check on a small matter but will be back a little later."

He bowed and left.

Sobrina was tickled. "That was so much fun, the most I've had as a queen. Thank you, Arium. Can we continue to talk? My bath is actually a large pool. We can converse while we soak in hot water and float around. We have plenty of time to savor the experience."

"I don't want to intrude."

"Of course not. I'm alone so much it's a pleasure to have someone to spend time with."

"As you wish, Sobrina."

"Leave your clothes here so the laundry maids can wash them. As I said, we'll get an appropriate ballroom gown for you."

Arium peeled off the clothes that were definitely in need of cleaning. Servants appeared from the background to take them away. Arium followed the queen into the bathing area, a huge in-ground pool of heated water. Climbing in, she experienced luxury far beyond her wildest imaginations.

"Did I not tell you it is luxurious?" Sobrina chuckled. "Woo-hoo!" Diving under the water, she broke the surface with another whoop.

"It is wonderful, Sobrina. I haven't…"

Sobrina grabbed her arm to pull down fully immersed in the luxurious heat. Arium laughed. It was exhilarating.

It was impossible not to enjoy this sumptuous time of luxury. Relaxing enough to trust Sobrina was an easy step.

Sobrina took advantage of the moment to ask pointed questions about virtually every topic imaginable.

Arium fielded the inquiries answering as tactfully as she could. The thought crossed her mind, *this could be Selana in the future when she grows out of childhood into womanhood.*

Losing track of time, Brogan returned while they were still basking in the water. Unsure where to find them, he checked the pool, only to find them unclothed still immersed in the water.

"Oh, I'm sorry, ladies, I didn't realize you were in here. Please forgive my error."

He'd averted his eyes, but not instantly, only after a time. Sobrina was pleased, Arium was conflicted. She'd done nothing with Brogan, yet strangely she felt guilty. Neither woman had voiced outrage at the compromising view he got, or demanded he hurry away.

Arium pondered, *Is that leading him on? Why didn't I chastise him?*

He went into his room while the women dried and went to don their party dresses.

The dress they brought was incredible and fit Arium perfectly. She wouldn't have chosen a bare shoulder red satin gown, but it made a dazzling impression. It highlighted her superb physique.

Sobrina's gown was white satin and also bare shoulder.

Brogan had bathed quickly and produced a dress uniform of Cronda. It was jet black with gold epaulets, piping, shiny black boots, and surprisingly modern looking. It displayed his considerable medals and badges of honors. Just like with the Grecians, these were not false awards. They were genuine achievements, the marks of a battle survivor, many times over.

"Oh my," said Arium. "You clean up well." She couldn't manage to mask her appreciative smile.

In return, his stare at her, openly in awe, ignited a tingle in her body. "I can think of no words for you, My Lady. Your aura is unmatched. No person could resist you."

"You're too kind, Commander."

Later after some wine, far more relaxed together as they let their collective guards down with him, he took two beautiful women to the ball, one on each arm.

Entering the already filled enclosure, a herald announced their arrival.

"Brogan, High Commander of the Crondar military contingent, the Lady Arium, esteemed leader of the holy quest and friend to our sovereign, and her supreme majesty Sobrina, Queen of Bandar, High Sovereign of the World."

The assembled cheered wildly.

Jeren stood to the side with the children. He made no attempt to claim his bride as she entered to drums and trumpets with great fanfare. Mobbed by the curious and the fascinated, she was nearly permanently totally surrounded.

Selana said nothing, merely watching the spectacle. Drake came over looking for him.

"Jeren, why are you standing back here? Arium has come to join us."

"I didn't want to become embroiled in that whirlwind of bodies. I'm content to stand out of the way. Parties are not my preference. I'll let her enjoy the adoration of the masses and the company of local leaders."

"What?"

"Dinner is served," announced the rotund head chef.

At that point, Jeren had no choice but to weave through the mass of bodies toward the banquet tables to join the festivities.

Arium was laughing and talking happily as numerous admirers guided her along beside her majesty, the Queen.

Jeren wasn't surprised when his seat wasn't with his wife, or anywhere near the main table. That fact only dawned on her when her name card was placed on the table to the right of the queen. Brogan sat beside her. Various courtesans were seated relatively close or far depending on their status in the realm. The allied contingent was seated somewhat toward the front but away from the main characters, placed on both sides of the room.

Arium had to stand up and crane her neck to see them. When Jeren saw her looking and turned his head away, she pondered going over to her people.

"Is there a problem, my dear?" asked the queen.

"I didn't realize I wouldn't be sitting with my people."

"They have you the rest of the time. For tonight, you're mine. They'll be fine. I don't want to lose a precious moment of your attention."

Arium sat down.

The feast was sumptuous and involved seemingly endless courses. At last after many delicious desserts had been served, musicians began to play and soon afterwards, the large dance floor was packed.

Arium was in the highest demand along with the queen. In spite of the seating snub, the allied troops had no problem getting into the spirit, grabbing any female that could stand to twirl around the room with them.

Selana joined the dancing and dragged Jeren out to the edge of the dancers. Grabbing his hand to keep him from slipping away, soon he was partnered dancing with a small person. After the first dance, his next partner was Sari, an even smaller partner. Women noticed and took him to be a kind man. Thereafter, he never escaped the dances as stranger after stranger swirled into his arms and tried to make an impression. No one knew he was the husband of Arium, the star of the ball. He didn't share that news, or anything else. Merely acting polite, he finally relaxed into the event. It was mildly therapeutic. Neither did he ever see Arium out on the floor, nor did he look for her.

What he did notice mirthfully were the two boys, Darik and Amik, trying their hands at dancing. It was very entertaining as they struggled initially to duplicate the actions of the grown men around them. Their partners were very patient teaching the boys to the point they actually gained some skill. Selana and Sari danced continuously also. They were competent right from the start.

Jeren tried to keep his dancing within sight of all the children, not that he feared for their safety in this tame city, but it seemed the appropriate thing to do. With all four children armed with magic, none here that could have ever threatened them in any meaningful way.

Mixed with the merriment, ample delicious wine flowed the entire time. It was a local vintage and it went down very smooth. Hours passed by in dancing, and then more hours of the fun for Arium entrenched in the middle of the royal party. Similar to her festival experience in the Nordcan village, she lost track of time, imbibed far too much, and let down her guard.

And just like then, she was the center of focus dancing with endless strangers including ladies. After the kitchen closed, the portly 'head chef' corralled her first his turn at a dance. Considering his girth, he was surprisingly agile and whirled her around as skillfully as any other.

The person who claimed the most dances with Arium was Brogan. He was charming, solicitous of her, dashing, ruggedly handsome, and again he evoked her on a deep level. The fact he could stir her so strongly was something she tried to temper, but it was too much fun being with him, so she dismissed the niggling worry with too much wine.

The Queen paid close attention to Arium's considerable dance skills, honing her own to match the sassy nature and later the sensuousness. It was her majesty's first major venture into too much wine.

With senses and sensibilities dulled with drink, Arium no longer bothered rationalizing the 'exhilarating evening' like, *it's just harmless fun.*

The celebration swept her away and she loved it. Just like with that Nordcan party, she didn't remember the end of the night. An entire room full of partiers experienced the same dulled senses and foggy departures. Not everyone ended up in their own beds.

Jeren had also drunk too much to drown his sorrows, but he had the children along to safeguard him from any dubious situations. Some women were getting insistent with him.

On the other hand, Arium did not have any buffers against such contingencies. Jeren was already gone when Arium's night at the party ended. Wobbly from drink, she lolled into Brogan's strong arms when he escorted her to the royal suite, a task he repeated carrying the queen also. Neither woman remembered the particulars of afterwards.

Her night in bed again featured dreams even more vivid and life-like than in Nordca.

Breakfast never happened as with the late hour the celebration ended, everyone slept in, including the head chef.

Arium awoke in the late morning with a throbbing headache and moaned. Rubbing her eyes trying to get her bearings, her mouth had an aftertaste, whether the alcohol, or something she ate. Glancing over, her dress and other clothes were on the floor. Sleeping nude wasn't her norm.

"Oh my," she whispered. Stretching her arms, yawning, and sinking back on the ultra-soft bed, she smiled at the luxury after the hardships of the trail. "I could get accustomed to this very easily."

The queen awoke, answering Arium's comment. "I'd love for you to get accustomed to living here."

Arium sat back up with a start. "What? I'm sorry…am I in your bed? I apologize profusely, Sobrina. I don't remember, eh…you should have pointed me toward my own bed."

"It's not a problem. We were both loopy. Was that not the best party ever?"

"It was a grand bash, Sobrina. I'll pay a price for it today though."

"I have a headache too, but it's worth it."

"How did we get…like this?"

"The servants are always nearby and I'm sure they helped us with undressing for bed when we were unable. Let's jump into the pool to refresh. I'm in need of a bath."

Swimming and soaking again, it did help, along with ample cups of coffee that waited when they came out. Brogan was sipping a cup at the small table dressed in a robe.

"Good morning, esteemed ladies." He smiled warmly at Arium. Both women were in robes too.

"Morning," she whispered softly. As with that prior feeling from Nordca, relaxed and relieved, this time she couldn't dismiss niggling doubt. *What if?* The concern was in her mind.

"I trust you slept well?"

"I, we, don't remember the end of last night."

"I helped you both back here. Fortunately, it's a short walk from the throne room to these suites."

"Did you enjoy yourself?" asked Sobrina with a smirk.

"You know I did," he replied with a broad warm smile.

"I've never seen you so congenial and pleasant. I must say I like this new Brogan. You cut a dashing figure at the ball. There were no women who didn't notice you."

"You're too kind, your majesty. None could match your shinning stars gracing our presence."

"I did feel beautiful last night, however none could match Arium. I felt the best about myself on so many levels and being her friend is the biggest reason. Arium, I learn so much from you. Would you be willing to stay here? At the very least, spend time teaching me, and for your superb fighting force, if they could train my hapless soldiers, this country might be able to develop a real defense force rather than the farce army there are now."

"I...think that could be arranged, however, the Grecians train in a way which could injure your troops. Their poor skill level jumped out at us when we first met them on the road. They may want to start by ditching those silly uniforms."

She turned to Brogan. "Do your people train others?"

"For you, my dear Arium, there is nothing I wouldn't do."

Drawing up against her, taking her hand and then kissing her cheek, the familiarity stoked her worries back to life. Honestly, she had no memories and it was concerning. Fighting off the thumping of her heart was a further test.

Later, after eating a noon meal, she went with the queen to the rooms of her quest cohorts. The first person she met was Selana.

"Good morning, My Lady," she said with a pleasant smile and a curtsy.

"Good morning, Selana."

"Good morning, Your Majesty."

"Good morning, did you enjoy the party, little one?"

"I did, very much so. It was a first for me."

"Are the others of your party awake?"

"Not all of them have returned yet, but most are here."

"Oh," said Sobrina, as it dawned on her. "At any rate, I'd like to speak to your officers."

"I'll fetch them. Please give me a moment to see if they're all here and up for the day."

Arium waited with the queen, like she wasn't a member of the quest any longer. *Did Jeren...no, don't be silly.* It was an unusual thought for her, she having jealous worries for a change.

Drake, Brek, Grakar, Gensten, and finally Jeren came out.

She stared at her husband and his passive expression. He only watched the queen and it annoyed Arium.

"Good morning, esteemed ladies," he spoke in a deferential tone, lowering his head. "What can we do for you?"

"The queen has asked for our assistance, and that we delay our departure for a time. She knows her soldiers are a joke and has asked that we join the Crondars in training them up to a decent level. Her country is not properly protected at this point."

"Did you tell her about Grecian training methods?"

"I did. Can you all scale back enough to keep from wiping out her entire army?"

The men laughed, even Jeren.

Arium continued, "Also, I need to get out there and battle with you. This luxury of life in the palace can make me weak. I need to keep my edge."

"You can fight?" asked Sobrina. "Will you teach me?"

She turned her head. "Perhaps on a small scale, I can show you some fundamentals."

"Thank you so much, Arium, and all of you. Is now too soon?"

Grakar answered, "We can work today, but once all of our comrades return. Is that acceptable?"

"It is. Come Arium, let's go into the city to the shops. It will be so much fun."

Arium looked at amused faces of the men, all but Jeren.

"You should go shop," said Drake, smirking. "It will be fun."

She scowled at him, but turned her head to smile at the young Queen.

Uninterested, Jeren was the first to turn and walk away. Selana had been standing nearby watching Arium closely. She turned and followed Jeren back into the rooms.

Arium felt out of sorts emotionally. This wasn't how she wanted this visit to go. The initial ruse entering the city had long ago outlived its usefulness. Now Arium was stuck with this fiction instead of reality and pieces of the puzzle were moving independently of her control. Not the least of which was living with Brogan. His aspirations for her, a blind woman couldn't miss.

What troubled her now, those aspirations she saw so frequently from men and easily dismissed; smothering them, this time seemed so very difficult. The possible answers were a very troubling matter.

She mused regretfully, *I'm culpable for not telling anybody about being married, and for allowing him to think me available. In his mind, the choice for a wife seemingly has been made. How could I allow this to happen? Am I truly weak to this temptation?*

After the kinds of serious issues they'd fought through on this trek, this kind of self-inflicted wound was the last thing she could have anticipated.

Going with the queen into the city on this lark amongst the shop owners to see their wares, it would have been impossible to the Arium that rode into the city. Wasting time was not allowed in her world, and yet here she was doing just that very thing.

"What are you doing," she muttered

"Did you say something?" asked Sobrina.

"I was just thinking about something."

"Oh, please tell me. I want to know everything about you."

"It's…nothing. This is a lovely fabric."

"Would you like it? It can be my gift to you."

"No, no, what would I do with fine fabrics with my journey back on the road? Thank you for the offer though."

Several hours later, with Arium back in her usual garb and the Sobrina dressed in pants, they went with Brogan to the training yard.

It was jammed with Bandarian troops. Arium saw Blanak for the first since his awakening in the throne room. He was reserved and embarrassed to see her. He averted his eyes quickly.

His forces had replaced the flamboyant uniforms with functional dark green ones.

Beginning the training, the Grecians put on a dazzling display that terrified the Bandarians. Afterwards, the Grecians, the Warmarks, and the Crondars all gathered groups of Bandarians to start their quest for competence.

It gave the quest members a task rather than sitting idly by. Even the four children joined training as each was in no danger. The twins had progressed with their magic to be able to incorporate magic into physical fighting so they could be as daunting as a fully grown soldier.

Days, weeks and then months passed by in the work as the Bandarian army rapidly improved. However, Jeren could never relax and wondered how they were free of Antith or the dark mages for this long time span.

Arium saw her family each day in training, but she'd never managed to set Brogan straight. His pursuit, which the queen relished as a matchmaker, was persistent, and in any other circumstances, his chances to win her heart would have been excellent. There was no fault on Sobrina or Brogan. They didn't know the truth.

He was intriguing and more so each day she lived with him. Watching how Jeren reacted, he'd buried the jealousy, reverting back to that impassive detached phase she so hated.

The weather got better as winter had passed and spring was nearly over. Time was moving and very soon would be seventh birthdays for Selana and Darik. Darik was another dilemma for Arium. Her son played the same part as the others of the quest, like she was a separate independent entity only attached to them in some peripheral way and not the heart of the group, or his mother. Hugs, exchanges of affection, they were gone from her life as a palace resident and she missed it terribly.

The stimulus that finally convinced Arium she had to do something was Sobrina had recently started intimating Brogan and Arium should wed. Those hints developed into statements and when word started to spread throughout the court a major wedding could be on the horizon, Arium shook out of her doldrums.

I must end this.

That day in the training yards, she walked over to Jeren. He turned his head. "Yes, My Lady, what is it we can do for you today?"

"You can drop the act. Things are spiraling out of control. I realize I've been a fool to allow the ruse to go on for this length of time."

The others were listening and stepped close—Grakar, Drake, Brek, Gensten, and the children.

"I apologize to you all. Jeren, I know I've hurt you with my poor choices."

Jeren shrugged his shoulders. "So what did you have in mind?"

"We've done what we could for her army. I think we need to leave promptly because I'm standing in quicksand."

"I hear that will break Brogan's heart. He looked to marry you in the not too distant future." Jeren failed to keep the ire from his voice.

Arium stared straight ahead with a pained expression. "I know that. I will explain the truth to him." Her reply was terse and frosty.

"I don't know if that's wise. Telling him you've deceived him all of this time letting him think you were his sweetheart, his reaction may be a violent one. I'll admit, you would have made a stunning couple." He was irked and struggled to rein in his own ire.

She looked at her husband carefully. Anger was rising in her in response to his. "I won't rise to the bait, Jeren. You have every right to be angry with me. I was foolish and in that way, I put our quest in jeopardy."

"Perhaps you shouldn't have this talk with Brogan and the queen alone." Grakar suggested. It headed off the developing explosion.

"That makes sense," Drake added. "Antagonizing a fighter of his rank and abilities can be a dangerous task. Being deceived to this scale before the masses is a great humiliation and an affront."

Arium glowered, looking around the group. "I know that you all have strong opinions and feel the need to punish me with these stiff rebukes. You think I don't know it, or that I'm just as hard on myself? I have the fault for this mess, but castigating me now, how does that help us?"

Grakar spoke, "I think you worried us all with your ongoing antics. We need to be able to trust each other and this radical departure from your normal behaviors is alarming. You get wooed on a daily basis and dismiss it without incident. Why this time you seemed to struggle, we questioned. Is there more to this companionship you wish to explain?"

Arium's face hardened. She glared at Grakar. "Did we do unseemly things? Is that what you ask me? I tell you I'm married to Jeren. I set out to do nothing to shame him or our marriage."

He faced the challenge on her face and in her tone coolly. After a moment, he replied. "That feels like a cautious answer, ma'am. Not setting out to err doesn't say if you erred nonetheless."

Arium got a serious expression. Looking at the faces of the children, she was embarrassed. "In front of you all, I'll say, I had no indiscretions I'm aware of. However, after that royal ball, I had too much wine and lost track of...it was like after that Nordcan party. I was vulnerable for that night. I awoke with no memories of...anything. If advantage was taken of me, I honestly can't say.

I don't think so, but that's the truth as I see it. I believe Brogan is an honorable man. You must make up your own minds. I can only leave it at that. Whatever happened or didn't happen, it's over, so I've moved on."

The men looked at Jeren. He put up his hand. "As Arium says, it's over. There's nothing to be done about the past. When we married, I felt incredulous I could have her for my wife. That awe has never left me. At the same time, I acknowledge she's unique and a lightning rod to people coming around her. Standing up daily to the tremendous temptations put on her, I admire she does so well. If there was an incident of an intimate nature, it does not make me love her less. I have no need to rail against her."

With tears streaming from her eyes, Arium grabbed him in a fierce embrace.

"Thank you, I'm so sorry for my weakness."

"Arium, this isn't necessary."

"Yes, it is. Your putting up with this game of mine for all of this time here, and with such dignity, Jeren, it was so needless of me, stupid really. Letting my ego loose to bask in Brogan's attention, I'm so ashamed of myself. I will make this right."

Provoked, the entire group, including Selana, went immediately to meet with the queen and with Brogan. When Arium entered the royal suites, Sobrina was laughing sitting at the table talking with Brogan.

They looked up in question at the approaching group.

"Hello, Arium. What is it? I see many glum faces."

"I must say some difficult things to you both. I want to apologize in advance. I meant no harm for I love you both. I'll explain how this happened, but I fear it will sound like an excuse. I don't attempt to sound blameless because I'm not. Will you listen to me?"

"Of course," Sobrina replied.

"When we came to your country and met Blanak on the road, there was some posturing and confusion. I'm ashamed to say we saw your patrol in comical terms."

"You were right in that," said Brogan.

"Blanak thought to seduce me, so I pretended to go along to gain entrance to the city to assess the level of threat. I allowed him to believe the ruse all the way into your presence, Your Majesty. At that point, I should have explained the truth, but I allowed the ruse to go on. Treating me as a royal lady, I should have said, I'm not royalty, I was a villager wife of a slain farmer, widowed with my son, Darik."

"You have a son?"

"I'm remarried to Jeren, who is a far greater person than you mistakenly think I am. We share together along with Darik and Selana as a family, and now also orphaned Amik and Sari as purveyors of the power of the light."

"You're wizards?"

"I have no real defense for continuing the lie with you both, letting you make wrong assumptions, the worst of which was the fallacy of me being available as a possible wife. Brogan, I'm so sorry. I…eh…this is difficult to say in front of my family and friends. I was lured and moved, deeply moved. You're a wonderful man and a great prize for any woman. However, it's unseemly for a wife to be in such a state, especially one of her own doing."

Sobrina got up to hug Arium. "If you're asking for my forgiveness, you have it. You're closer to me than any other living person. I never knew my mother who died in childbirth. I fear you're about to leave us."

"We must."

Chapter 11
Civil War

The enraged response they feared from Brogan never came. He merely looked sad and regretful.

Standing, instead of Arium, he walked straight to Jeren. "Sir, I sincerely beg your pardon for my behavior."

"There is no need. You knew nothing of my marriage and from what I saw, conducted yourself with dignity and proper decorum."

"I…eh, I'm not perfect, and for that, I apologize."

Jeren didn't ask what that meant. None of the possibilities were particularly palatable.

"Just as the queen gave her forgiveness, I do the same following her noble example. Whatever you mean with your statement, I don't wish to know. The past is over. We in this quest have too much uncertainty still ahead of us. Dwelling on such issues as this, we can't allow. As long as Arium wishes to remain my wife, I'm content with that."

Brogan looked stunned at Jeren's reply. "Amazing, I'm awed by your character for it's far beyond what I could manage to do in your situation. I'll admit, I'm in love with your wife. That is no reflection on you."

"Let us agree the matter is over."

"I want to discuss one other thing. I and my men are here, as you know, at the behest of our King. It's clear we'll never be recalled home. The latest I've heard is actual civil war has broken out. We cannot sit here idle while our countrymen carry on the fight for our future. I ask you to allow us to ride with you across the border into Cronda. You'll be in jeopardy riding into a war and having us along to guide you will be fortuitous. We know the landscape and the people."

Jeren looked at Grakar.

"I have no objection, Jeren."

"Anybody else?" asked Jeren. No one voiced a complaint. Arium had a pinched look, like she was conflicted.

Sobrina spoke, "I so envy you all. I wish I could join you with acts of such significance in my life."

"Don't belittle yourself or your circumstances. Being the leader for your people is no small thing," Arium answered. She lifted Sobrina's chin noting her downcast and sad expression.

Speaking gently, she continued, "What you said about our closeness, it's the same for me. I'll never forget my time here and yes, I learned many things from you also."

Sobrina smiled warmly. "That makes me happy. Can we milk a few more days or maybe a week, or possibly a month? Would a year be too much to ask?"

Arium laughed. "You know we must go. We've delayed far too long already."

Turning to Brogan, Arium asked, "How long do you need to prepare your forces for departure?"

"We can be ready immediately. Duty here has been monotonous without real danger. Going back home to lend our support to the cause of freedom for Crondar; that motivates us greatly."

She looked at Grakar. "There you have it, Captain. I'll pack my things and join you presently."

For the last time in Bandar, Jeren watched his wife walk away with Sobrina and Brogan, but this time, he didn't have that nagging worry of something seriously amiss. Seemingly, she'd reawakened from her temptations and was again the trustworthy Arium of old. *That's my hope*, he mused as his deep angst remained.

An hour later, bolstered by the added Crondar forces, the ranks of the quest assembled in the courtyard, formed up their columns and left the queen standing on her palace staircase waving at them. She cried out loudly. "Goodbye, my dear friends. Safe travels."

Brogan and his Crondar troops took the lead. Gensten rode at the front beside Brogan talking constantly to get information on what was ahead.

Arium took her place riding beside Jeren. There was a great deal she wanted to say, but this wasn't the time or place. That was a conversation meant to be private as she felt the need to be brutally honest and that went beyond what had already been said.

Selana was in her usual place, riding right behind Jeren. Her face was serious as she searched for threats nearby or far away. Her saying nothing to them, Jeren assumed for the moment they were in no danger. He most feared Antith catching them.

Returning to his usual contemplative state, he ran all manner of hazards through his mind trying to develop ready responses and solutions. That thinking always met an impasse with the matter of Antith. There were no answers to his threat.

For Arium, seeing that face of his again, it irked her. She mused, *If he plans on dismissing me from his thoughts again, it is…mistaken on so many levels. He fails to comprehend the extent of Brogan's allure, and now Brogan is riding with us.*

She'd pondered her current feelings a great deal, and her time living apart in the royal suite, as many elements were adding up to conclusions which were problematic at the very least. Brogan's *mea culpa* had shocked her. What he meant, it may have been much more than she thought it could be, and her finding any outrage at the prospect, it was appallingly far too elusive for her. *Why? Might I actually be in love with Brogan?* That thought should not have been tantalizing, but it was.

Two spouses rode along locked within their own minds wrestling with completely different problems, equally consuming in both cases.

Looking ahead, she stared at Brogan's broad shoulders and back. *Of all men, why him and why now?* Forbidden feelings simmered to life for her too often these days, just below the surface. It was strangely difficult to dismiss those stubborn urges.

Suddenly, she felt a light brush of magic. Looking back, Selana was staring at her. Arium smiled and nodded. Selana smiled back.

Suddenly, the temptations and troubling thoughts were absent.

Arium sat up from slouching in her saddle, her mood greatly improved. Jeren turned his head, curious. "Is there something troubling you, Arium?"

"No, I'm fine."

She smiled at him and he finally responded to her, smiling back. She touched his shoulder gently.

Behind her, she heard Selana whispering. Looking back, her eyes were closed and Arium sensed powerful magic she was creating.

"I think Selana has made a protection over us."

Jeren looked back. "She is so much more now than ever before. She's growing and evolving so much and so fast. Already I believe she far surpasses us, and we know of no other wizards in existence. I'm afraid we're poor vessels as her mentors and teachers."

"I can't disagree. Tonight, perhaps we should resume our nightly communions, the six of us."

"Yes, we should."

"Selana has been teaching the twins far beyond what we could have done."

"That's true also."

"They seem to exhibit that accelerated physical maturation too. Selana and Darik at seven look older than that."

"Her magic is a wonder."

The trek across Bandar to the border was uneventful. The only issue, which Arium kept to herself, was vivid dreams every night, and Brogan was always at the center of them. Each morning, she awoke feeling unsettled and evoked.

One evening, she sat up in the wee hours to see Brogan sitting up too. The overpowering urge to go to each other pushed them into motion, but Selana sat up chanting her magic. For a difficult time caught in a struggle, Selana did battle while Arium and Brogan were suspended in the throes of imposed lust. At last, Selana prevailed and the urges disappeared.

Arium couldn't keep her eyes open and fell back to sleep in an instant. However, in the morning, she remembered it all, as did Brogan.

He came over to sit with Selana and Jeren in talking with Arium about the nocturnal occurrence.

Selana explained, "I know you've been troubled, Mother, and questioned your seeming weakness about Brogan, and Brogan, you're driven wild with unseemly urges for Arium. Last night I picked up a thread of magic directed into the camp at you both. This lure to…you know, it's coming from outside the camp. We wondered why our enemies have seemed to be passive for so long a time. My suspicion is they haven't. Focusing on you, coaxing you into mistakes to break apart our communion, I see it now. Whether it is Antith, which I doubt, or the dark mages, I can't say.

"If there is another enemy we have yet to meet, that's possible too. I think this whole time, keeping you apart from us living together in the royal suite; it was part of their plan. Gradually eroding your faith in your inner defenses and even your morals, it gathered momentum toward their goals. Apart, we're vulnerable in ways we are not when together. Do you see? Neither of you are flawed or of low character."

"Thank you," said Arium. Brogan smiled.

He spoke, "I've never battled against temptations of the flesh. It's not that I've never…well, but here it was so constant, I was always too near to failure."

"It was true for me too, the desire to succumb. There was never relief or release from the stress."

She hugged Jeren.

Selana continued, "Tonight, I think we will set a magical trap for the perpetrator. Brogan, you will need to sleep beside my mother to provide a seemingly tempting lure for them, like our guard is down and their success at hand."

Brogan asked, "Will there be a danger to Arium?"

"No, we'll all be here with a magical link established. Arium won't really be asleep."

When they camped, the Crondar border was near that night they set the trap.

As always, deep in the night, sinister magic wafted toward their targets. Arium sensed it instantly, but this time she was awake and ready. As the foulness flowed over and into her and Brogan, when the usual inflaming emotions ignited, the six with power in the camp acted as a unit grasping the flow of dire magic with a recoiling response of immense blue power. It sizzled and crackled as it zapped back along the red path to the origin. Far away, they witnessed a massive concussion so strong it shook the ground and lit up the night sky with a rainbow of colors, much of it blue and red.

Whom they attacked and to what extent, they had no way to know, other than knowing they'd struck a serious blow.

The falsely enhanced lusts were gone completely and they both had the feeling a dire link had been severed and they were set free.

"I think we have a great success," said Selana rhetorically. "That avenue for attack has been silenced."

She stared at the looks on Arium and Brogan's faces.

"Can you understand now, you're not flawed. The feelings were normal and natural, which they exploited. Brogan, any of these other men here could have been the victim. That you shared real love for each other; don't see it as a bad thing. Sharing such bonds is always a blessing."

"I hope I'm no longer a scourge to plague you, Arium."

She laughed. "Don't talk silly. I was equally affected mooning over you like a schoolgirl." They spoke the right words, but their stares lingered.

Mounting up in the morning, the allies crossed the border heading for the Crondar border station. It gave them a taste of what to expect. The guards were followers of the King. Their Captain challenged Brogan.

"Why have you come? Your directive was to remain in that feeble land as lackeys for their girl queen."

"Well, Captain, as a Commander, I'm not subject to your authority. We're traveling on a quest going through Crondar. It has nothing to do with politics here."

"What? Who released you from the authority of the King? Are you saying you're no longer subjects of Crondar?"

"I'm not saying any such thing. It seems you're looking for a fight."

The Captain glowered. His hand rested on his sword hilt.

Grakar, Drake, and Arium rode up beside Brogan. Jeren assembled the children nearby in case of hostilities. Everybody eyed the border guard Captain grimly.

Drake spoke this time, "I'm Drake Dorn, Captain in the Grecian army. I'm happy to make your acquaintance. If you're offering us a chance to spar, we always relish that. As a matter of fact, I'd be happy to fight you alone, you and your guards. Of course, that would leave your border unguarded afterwards."

"You're Grecians?" he asked weakly.

"I see you've heard of us. Would you like to find out if the stories about our battle prowess are true? It's been a while since we've had the pleasure of open battle."

"Eh…no, that won't be necessary."

"Are you sure, I don't mind."

"Please continue your journey. Make haste in crossing our country."

His guards had pulled back out of range of Grecian swords as they rode by.

"Not much of a threat," Drake muttered to Grakar.

Arium turned her head to Jeren a little later.

172

"I think the evil aegis has passed. I feel normal again. That is such a relief at last. I wonder how I could have missed what Selana detected. All of that time thinking me a terrible person, feeling those wrong needs…"

"Arium, it's fine. Perhaps we can talk at a later time. I fear we have new dangers close at hand and we need to return to vigilance."

"Of course, you're right. It's just such a relief at last."

"I rejoice with you."

Those dangers were not far away as they heard the sounds of battle ahead. Brogan spurred his horse to a gallop. The allies came upon a village embroiled in a battle. How Brogan could recognize friend from foe, Jeren couldn't understand, but he never slowed down, riding into the teeth of the fight with devastating effect. Those loyal to the King had been pushing back those who favored his brother. In a moment, a serious defeat evaporated as not only were the rebels augmented by like-minded Crondar brethren, the Warmark and Grecian soldiers scythed through the royal soldiers leaving none to carry the tale back to the capital.

Those rebels spared from defeat and death looked at their benefactors with great relief. Their leader spoke.

"Brogan, you've returned from exile?"

"In a way, we're no longer residing in Bandar, that's true."

"Have you come to lend your sword to the cause? This is an incredible victory which will inspire our side. Who are these brave allies of yours? They're incredible fighters."

"Before you are living breathing Grecians, and also Warmark soldiers, as well as wizards. It's been my honor to know and respect them all. Stories about the Grecians military prowess are all true, as you just saw."

"They're daunting to watch. The precision and skill is unlike anything I've ever seen. Are you joining us?"

"Sadly, we cannot. We're now a part of a great quest traveling east to face whatever fate intends for us all."

"But…our country is in crisis."

"I know, and I don't mean to imply it's unimportant, but this imperative outweighs all other matters. The prince will not prevail or fall because of us. Brave souls like you carry that banner. Your courage and tenacity can turn the tide."

"I'm sorry to hear that. Having you with us would be a great boon."

"I'm sorry also, but we must go. Good fortune to you and be brave. Your cause is just."

Later when they stopped, the officers gathered around Brogan. Arium spoke, "We had no idea you intended to join us to complete this quest. Though you're welcome, do you not regret leaving the battle for Crondar to others?"

"Of course, but I've come to understand what you're about. Our mission has consequence for all people everywhere. This is the greatest task we could ever do."

"So be it," said Jeren. "Welcome to the brethren of the quest."

"We must go, quickly," said Selana.

The troop mounted up and galloped away.

"What is it?" asked Arium, as they rode along.

"I think we stirred up a great deal of frenzy in our enemies with our ploy. They attempt to close on us."

"Dark mages or Antith?"

"I'm not certain, As I said, we could have other opponents out there also."

Jeren glanced at Arium. "There's really nothing else to do but keep going, in my opinion." He then asked Selana, "Are they closing the gap?"

"No, but we should continue making haste."

The farther they went into the countryside, the more skirmishes they came upon. Some were villagers at odds with each other, some involved small units of army troops from each side. Then they located a full scale battle between rival military armies in serious struggle.

Brogan led them up a hill to survey the fight below. "This is a terrible thing, brothers fighting against each other. It sickens me. This war can not only disintegrate the country, but fuel a war with no end but one. Neither royal brother will relent at this point, which means annihilating the foe until none remains alive, I shudder to think. What has become of our decency and compassion? Can foolish sibling rivalry surpass good sense and genuine care for the welfare of the citizens?"

Arium rode to his side, eyeing him sympathetically. "I'm so sorry, Brogan. I wish we had an answer."

"Emotionally, I'm drawn to join this fight against a King so petty and apathetic to the suffering of the people he could command such things. He's no better than these neighboring monarchs we mock."

"If you choose to leave the quest, no one will think less of you."

"I could never leave." He looked at her directly. "You know that."

She blushed. Although stoked artificially from afar, the emotions created were real enough in both of them and had taken root deeply.

"I should apologize, Arium, but…I'm not sorry. I doubt I could ever stop loving you, even if I wanted to."

"I must…go," she whispered, and then rode back to Jeren. He was talking with Drake and Grakar. Brek smiled at Arium. She nodded.

Brek spoke, "Your friend is conflicted?"

"Of course, this is his home and his people are dying down there. He chooses to stay with us of the quest, a very difficult choice."

"Yes, of course, he would stay with the quest."

She scowled at his smirk, and his implication.

The battle raged on with neither side able to gain an advantage. Finally, Brogan turned and led them away at the gallop, Gensten returned to his side.

Brogan tried to skirt the conflict, but there were too many patrols and moving columns of troops to totally escape notice.

Meeting approaching reinforcements for the King, the quest was suddenly confronted with a fight or flight decision. Jeren looked at Selana. For the first time in the communion of the six wizards, Selana grasped control to lead the group.

When the Commander of the opposing force recognized and challenged Brogan, hostilities broke out quickly, but before the King's soldiers could charge into the midst of the allied troops, Selana acted unleashing a blue wave of power sweeping them out of their saddles, though leaving them still alive. Thereby a huge column of enemy troops far outnumbering the allies was dismounted and disoriented sitting on the ground. Neither the enemy Commander, nor his troops could manage to regain their faculties as the allies rode away, unscathed.

It wasn't the last threat they faced, but it was the most serious. Skirmishes thereafter, Selana left to the soldiers to handle as they had no peer in battle.

After a long day riding evasively, they stopped much later than normal. Brogan knew where to go for a safe camp site. Double guards were stationed all around to protect them. The remainder of the troops bedded much closer together on this night, virtually shoulder to shoulder. They all listened to the magician's conversation.

"Selana, we're curious about that guarded and controlled attack. Where did you learn it because it's beyond what Arium or I know, or can do?"

"As I've continued my studies, I seem to have benefit of a deep pool of knowledge. I think absorbing the knowledge of that tome is the trigger."

"It's strange that neither Arium, nor I, have experienced a similar phenomenon. I'm not saying it's bad, just curious."

"You're right to be on guard about everything, Father. I haven't sensed anything sinister or dangerous thus far. I stay constantly on guard."

"That's good to hear."

"Another observation I've made, and it seems to be true for Darik, once we aged to seven, it seems a significant development."

"Seven is a number of significance for growing children in any realm."

"My mind is expanded, my powers further unlocked, and my ability to think, as adults think, has blossomed. I know I'm not an adult, but that is this body. I suspect in virtually any other way, I'm on par with you."

She saw looks of worry with Arium and Jeren.

"Does this displease you?"

"Displease is not the right word. We're daunted by the challenge of trying to be your parents. You're unique."

"I'm still your daughter. I love you the same as before."

Arium hugged her. "And I'm your Mother."

"Does my continued awakening and expansion frighten you?"

"Again, that's a wrong word. Ascending to a higher level isn't bad," Jeren explained. "It just happens in your case it's on an unprecedented scale. When you say awakening, what do you mean?"

"In light of your reactions, I think I'll refrain from explaining that for the moment. If I experience an issue in any area, I'll certainly tell you. I will say, as you experienced vivid dreams, mother, I have them some nights too now."

"Could that strange outside force be affecting you also?"

"I don't believe so, which doesn't mean that there couldn't be other attacks coming from other sources."

"Have you ever picked up any sense of my brethren being out there somewhere?"

"No, Father, I'm sorry I haven't. Only the six of us here carry the flame of blue power, at least that I'm aware of."

Arium commented, "Brogan has done well steering around trouble for the most part. That's a good thing."

"That's a very good thing. I'm glad Gensten is riding with him to learn from such a great soldier and a great man. That can only help us." Jeren noticed she didn't look at him when bringing up the subject of Brogan.

Arium stared straight ahead, in Brogan's direction.

"Feelings," he muttered reflectively. Though much different, his own were no less a problem than hers.

In spite of Brogan's skillful guidance, this was still a country in conflict and not every snare could be avoided. An ambush provoked sudden conflict as troops loyal to the King sprang out from forest concealment to engage the allies. Instantly the two forces mixed together, so the wave of power to knock them down harmlessly wasn't available. They were not a small force, so a serious battle developed.

Jeren's first concern was keeping the children safe. All had been taught combat with weapons, but they were still small in size versus grown men. Only Selana, by augmenting her skills with her magic, could have been able to prevail. The other children were not at her stage.

"Stay with me," he shouted to the children. Arium looked conflicted. "Go, I can defend them."

She spurred her horse to ride ahead to where Brogan was locked in a dangerous fight against three enemy troops.

Seeing her flash past racing into the teeth of the danger, Drake shouted and the Grecian troops executed a precision movement attacking behind her ferociously. They were madmen in an instant and enemy troops started to fall in droves.

Arium arrived at her target enraged and glowing blue with her power as she jumped into Brogan's fight. Felling the enemy to her right and her left, she also freed Gensten. She was magically protected and extended small protections to Brogan and then Gensten making the three invincible. They fought in tandem allowing no opening or weakness for the enemy to exploit. In moments, the fierce Grecian attack swept through enemy ranks decimating them in startling swiftness.

What could have been a precarious situation teetered for just a short time before the allies gained the upper hand. The ambush failed and the remaining King's soldiers were driven away in defeat.

Jeren had been forced to kill also as the enemy intended no mercy toward the children. Selana linked the five of them to make Jeren a glowing avatar of doom. He too was invincible, but at the opposite end of the battle from Arium.

She would not relent in her battle until the enemy was gone from sight back into the forest.

Brogan looked at her in awe. "That was amazing, darling."

"I…just reacted when you were imperiled. They made me angry."

Brogan laughed. "Remind me never to make you angry."

She smiled, and then chuckled. "Are you injured?"

"No, I'm fine, thanks to you."

"Gensten?"

"I'm fine also, ma'am. I agree with Brogan, you were awe-inspiring."

Drake and Grakar joined them. Drake spoke, "We seem to have only minor injuries. Having wizards amongst us is a very good idea."

They all laughed while Arium beamed. These were the dear people in her life and feeling their love showered unto her was gratifying.

"I'm glad I could help, gentlemen."

"Let's get out of here," said Brogan.

Brogan spurred his horse and they galloped away. He was pleased on a number of levels. Their victory had struck another serious blow for the rebels against the King. Arium had displayed deep a connection with him and residual strong feelings. Whether she should have shown such a public display racing to him, he didn't care. She would always be the woman he loved.

Without conscious thought, she rode on at his right side with Gensten riding on his left.

Brogan glanced at her, his face aglow. Her actual magical glow, her aura, had been released, but her face was happy.

It was only after several hours riding to clear out of the area that they slowed to a normal riding pace.

"There's a place ahead we can pull off the road, rest and feed the horses, and have some food."

"That's good. We can't tire them out in case something else pops up unexpectedly."

Riding into the forest, they traveled to a small clearing and set up camp.

"It's afternoon, but I say let's stop for the night. There's no better spot nearby and we've just come through a battle."

"Certainly."

The troops knew what to do in the field and set about the chores of caring for their animals and then themselves.

Rather than immediately search out Jeren and the children, Arium lingered talking softly with Brogan. No one said anything to them, but everyone noticed. Not the least of which was her husband.

When she finally parted from the man that occupied her attention, and perhaps a place in her heart, she wondered what to expect back with her family. Jeren was busy doing mundane things, talking with the kids.

Her mixed feelings made her act a little defensive. When Jeren pretended he didn't see her coming, and only turned when Selana called out to her, "Mother", Arium's resentment simmered. It was totally unfair of her, but it was there.

"All is well up front?" he asked, his stoic look and bland response annoyed her immensely.

"Thankfully, it is."

"I saw no major injuries amongst our troops. We're blessed to have the finest soldiers on the globe."

"That is true. They're remarkable."

She eyed him very intently, expecting retribution which never came. What also did not come was a hug or a kiss. That irked her into a retort.

"I'm fine too, by the way."

Rather than the argument she would have relished at that moment, he looked bewildered.

"We can see you're uninjured, Arium. What are you upset about?"

"Nothing," she snapped.

"Hello, Mother," said Selana, interrupting and stepping near to give her that hug. It spurred Darik, Amik, and Sari to join in hugging their 'mother'. Only then did Jeren join the group embrace, but by putting arms around the children.

She so wanted him to rail at him. Her mind was active. *Why does he not understand the simplest things about a woman!*

She kissed the top of the head of each child. Finally, Jeren kissed her cheek. That didn't suit her mood, or her needs. Silly thoughts of childish retribution flitted through her mind, like going to sleep beside Brogan.

Jeren went back to his work. That included laying out her bedroll beside his. It was something of a tonic for her spirit; that he still cared in spite of her actions.

Selana stuck to her like glue drawing her attention off her issues and back to the children. Amik and Sari in particular still needed a great deal of mothering affection on this night.

They had a group magical communion that evening after eating. For Arium, she could purge her troubling feelings for a time, or at least sublimate them.

Selana took control of the meld and took them along with her as she cast her surveillance abroad searching for enemies. They were able to see what she saw of Antith and his group, as well as a number of dark masses that could only be dark mages, or similar beings of power. None were in a position to close the gap and none were moving.

She released the communion, returning to them to alertness.

"All is well," she announced.

Jeren spoke, "Thank you, Selana. We always wondered about your view of things. That was enlightening. However, I'm curious why all of our foes are content to merely trail after us?"

Arium interjected, "Perhaps it isn't us they're after. Perhaps it's where they think we will lead them?"

"Arium, you might be right. I never thought of that."

"Jeren, there is much that seems to pass you by these days." Immediately, she regretted the barb, but her annoyance wasn't easily dismissed.

He thought for a moment before speaking. "There is less passing me by than you think."

He wasn't argumentative, his tone was gentle. That irked her too.

Turning his face to stare, he asked, "Do you require—"

She cut him off sharply, "No."

Jeren shrugged in mock surrender. Marriage to the most beautiful woman in existence was proving to be a test in many ways, too many for his liking. The fact she was not happy with him was obvious. He pondered thoughtfully, *Which one of my many potential shortcomings is she focusing on this time?*

It was dusk, but regardless, Arium announced to him, "I will sleep now."

Whether to merely taunt him, or for another reason, she looked longingly toward Brogan. Brogan spotted her stare and turning directly toward her, they locked eyes for an uncomfortable amount of time.

Jeren turned his back and went about seeing to the children getting them situated before crawling into his own bedding. By that time, she was lying under her cover on her side, facing away.

Two spouses were emotionally percolating, but for different reasons.

Unawares by both of her parents, Selana was awake and alert, closely monitoring their emotional powder keg, searching for outside tampering. If the attack had taken more subtle means, she meant to root it out ruthlessly and destroy the perpetrators just as forcefully. Her comprehension of the world, including adults and their issues, was remarkable.

Unable to detect any thread of red power, at last she closed her eyes, but hours later. The camp was safe.

Guards moved about in the stillness of the night. There were no weak links in this superior assemblage of military might. None of the sentries ever fell asleep on the job, failed to note anything of significance, or failed be ready to react instantly to threats. In spite of the nightly magical shield, any manner of intruder could wander into the unseen barrier, including animal predators.

As they watched, prey sprang from a hiding place under a bramble bush as a predator slunk close. A frantic chase ensued as a life hung in the balance. That animal had none of the protections of the quest, only native speed and elusiveness.

This was the cycle of life played out in its most brutal form. Being too close to the terrified prey, the cat pounced onto the creature, which squealed in terror for a moment as its life was taken away in the jaws and teeth of its killer. Now, it was just food.

Nonetheless, it bothered the guards to witness it.

Chapter 12
Lair of Mobokta

Finding villages to replenish food and water became a problem as the war caused a great deal of destruction, death and displacement of the populace. Villages were often completely destroyed and damaged to the point they couldn't spare the few precious supplies they had.

It got to the point the quest had to risk going into a town and on this side of the country, those towns tended toward the King over his brother. As they rode down a street, they were met by suspicious stares from the locals.

Stopping at a store, Arium went in with Selana and Sari to present the most innocent look to the proprietor. Even so, he scowled at them.

"Sir, I need to order supplies for my travel companions."

"Who are you? That looks like an army out there. We've already lost huge amounts of profits to government troops conscripting supplies without paying. Are you mercenaries?"

"We're just passing through. I have gold to pay."

His expression changed radically. "Well, well, why didn't you say so, madam? Your daughters are lovely, by the way." This was moments after he'd glowered at them for touching several items on the shelves as children will do.

Arium looked at the girls and smirked. They were displaying their sweetest smiles batting their eyes at the portly man.

"I'll call my servants from the back storage room to carry your order out to your caravan."

"Thank you."

While those broad-backed men grunted with the strain of moving the heavy grain sacks, crates of various foods, and kegs of drink, the greedy owner's eyes sparkled as she opened her purse to pay him the gold. It was a considerable order and a considerable payment she made.

"Excellent," he said. "This puts my accounts back in order for the year. If you come back this way returning from your journey, be sure to stop here again. I'm happy to serve legitimate customers. My only purpose is to serve your needs in whatever manner I can."

She turned her head to hide her skeptical look. *Your purpose is to line your pockets. I wonder how much your workers will get out of this large payment.* She mused further, *it's obvious you've never lifted a hand in hard labor, or have ever missed a meal.*

His frank perusal of her form was followed by, "I must say, my lady, we've never had such an angel of beauty cross our threshold. I pray you will return. I'd love to offer an invitation for you to share dinner with me."

His seamy smile disgusted her. However, she continued the game, "I'll consider your generous offer for another time. I'm sure it would be memorable, a divine event."

"Indeed it would be."

Turning her back, the two daughters were smirking at her ruse.

When they left the store, Selana muttered, "Divine in his dreams, perhaps."

Arium and Selana laughed, as did Sari, although Sari didn't fully understand the joke.

Jeren watched them as they approached. "What is funny?"

"It doesn't matter," Arium answered.

Selana explained, "That addled shopkeeper invited Mother to dinner. What a comedy. To expect a woman such as mother to grace a pig like him with her time, what a lunatic he is. I'm learning how many needy men there are in the world. It's appalling."

"I see, daughter." Jeren turned and walked away to help with loading the supplies. It annoyed Arium, his seeming indifference.

Brogan made his way back, supposedly going to oversee the supplies, but he stopped near the females.

"Excellent work, ladies. We could have picked no better representatives for this task. These much needed supplies will carry us out of Cronda. I'd say you made quite the impression judging by the look on his face."

"She did," said Selana, chuckling.

Arium smiled warmly at Brogan.

"I'm happy to serve in whatever manner I can. That is what he said, and then he invited me to a private dinner."

Brogan laughed, shaking his head. "Arium, your effect on people is always amazing. Nobody is immune to your charm."

"You're welcome."

They both laughed and then stared deeply into each other's eyes.

"Ah, yes…well, I must see to the children." It took strong force of will for her to break the visual connection and turn her face away.

"And I must see to the supplies. It's always lovely talking with you, Arium."

"And with you as well, Brogan."

The warm tingle she felt should have alarmed her, but she merely smiled. It was too easy to rationalize this dangerous dance. *This is harmless, it's fun, and gives me good feelings to buoy my spirits through the difficulties. I haven't crossed any lines.*

She didn't add the word 'yet' to her train of thought. Nor did she choose to further consider if lines had already been crossed. That too shouldn't have been a possibility that evoked her; however, it did. What Brogan had said to Jeren…she mused dismissively, *it could mean so many different things."*

Turning to the children, she was somewhat more lively and animated than usual.

Selana had a contemplative look, like she could read everybody's thoughts, and she was looking at Arium.

In her case, who knows what she's capable of? Arium wondered at the perusal.

In her seven-year-old child body, it was still hard to equate the vast consciousness residing within her. Certainly, Darik was a much different child than he would have been otherwise without the advent of magic within him and in his life.

The allied command opted to remain in the relative safety of the town to dine at an eatery before they resumed the journey.

Ahead, Cronda flattened out into lowlands as they put distance between them and the mountains. The original forest had been cut back to provide arable land for farmers. Travel was swifter here and the effects of the war far less pronounced. Being a larger country than Bandar, much more time elapsed on this leg of the trek. Weeks became months of monotony in the saddle and camping at night.

Arium joined the magical evening of communions as usual, but they'd taken something of a routine there too. She didn't seem engaged like in the past.

Brogan abandoned any pretense of keeping his distance and was a frequent visitor whether sharing in a mealtime, talking with the children, and of course, carving out time with Arium.

Arium did nothing to discourage the advances and even stopped eyeing Jeren to gauge his reaction.

Outside Jeren was placid, cementing his unflappable facade; but inside, not so much. As galling as it felt for him as his wife was publicly wooed for all the camp to see, he'd decided his impartial gauge would be Selana. If there was genuine trouble brewing, even if just two grown adults traveling a mutual path of impulsiveness, he trusted she would identify it and if any action was required, she was probably better suited to reasonableness in response as Jeren's probable responses would have been problematic at the very least.

Brogan tried banter with Jeren, but it never got far. Jeren had no interest. Brogan didn't really seem to care what effect it had on Jeren. He claimed more of her time and attention each day. With the exception her bedding was always beside him, the rest of the time she placed no limit on the 'friendship' of a man not her husband.

Nobody could fail to notice and of course, whispers and opinions abounded; however, there was never any open discussion with any of the involved parties. Jeren was the aggrieved husband and if he chose to tolerate the seeming affront, so be it.

Jeren was no fool and sensed the judgment around him in the minds of his compatriots. That was an additional log on the blazing fire of his turmoil.

Though Arium continued to ride beside Jeren on the road, she tended to be lost in her thoughts and conversed little with her husband. Jeren took it as both a sign and a symptom, and not in a good way.

Selana started up a conversation one day talking with Jeren.

Arium didn't pay attention initially. Her daydream consumed her.

"Father, I sense something ahead."

"Another magical threat?"

"No, it's…unclear."

"Do you think it's a threat of another kind?"

"I don't know. It's unlike anything I've sensed before."

"Are you worried?"

"It's difficult to explain. There's no aura or magical signature I can discern, but it's a considerable presence. I'm not inclined to dismiss this, whatever it is."

Jeren dropped back to ride beside Selana. Arium rode alone for a short time before spurring her horse ahead to join Brogan and Gensten in the lead.

He was aware of Arium's action, but chose to focus on Selana and the needs of the quest.

"Are there any preparations we need to make?"

"I wish I could say…and also, regarding Mother, I know you look to me to guide you. That is not a role I can fully accept. Where I was able to sever that evil magic that created the first problem, the residual affect is real feelings were fostered in them. You see the result every day. Although I'm greater in many ways, in other areas, I'm not. I'm still a little girl about those things. For me to try to school my mother about her feelings and her choices, that is beyond me. Do you understand?"

"That's fair, Selana. You're right; I should have made my own choices."

They looked ahead at Arium happily talking and laughing with Brogan. Gensten had dropped back to exit out of the awkward meeting.

"It may be that the time for my deciding anything has already passed." Jeren muttered.

More than one of the soldiers glanced back at Jeren. That included Brogan's own men.

She rode with him the balance of the day. Both of them walked over as Jeren and the children ate food and talked.

Arium spoke, "You and Selana seemed to have some heavy matters to discuss. Should we be worried?"

"I don't know," Selana answered.

"We talked a great deal but I suspect there were no answers to be found. All that we can do is proceed with great caution." Jeren added.

"We already do that," said Brogan. His voice came out a little terse, eyeing Jeren severely.

Jeren replied evenly, "I realize that, and you do an excellent job guiding the troop, Brogan. I was not criticizing. I'm merely passing on to you Selana's information. I leave it to you and the other leaders to make military decisions. I've explained that before."

Brogan scowled, like he had hoped for an argument, and more.

Jeren continued, "Whatever she sensed is unlike anything we've faced before. It's not making any threatening moves yet, but that could change, and with each passing day, we draw closer."

Brogan's surly expression finally started to change as he reassumed the role of leader for the Crondar contingent.

"I'll think on this. Perhaps we can send a small fast riding group of troops ahead to determine the nature of this presence."

"Use great care," said Selana. "I have no proof, but I get a bad feeling."

"We will." It was a rare time for Jeren seeing Brogan not totally focused on Arium. At the same time, Arium still looked at him instead of Jeren. She talked to him, touched his hand, and counseled him with her opinions.

Why Jeren did it, he didn't understand, but in a rare impulsive childish reaction, he concocted a misleading statement.

"Arium, if you two need to seek a meeting with the others about plans, the children and I have already decided a nightly communion isn't necessary any longer. If anything develops requiring the use of power, we'll deal with it at that time. I don't want to stand in the way of the proper defense of this quest. Please, do whatever you must. I'll watch over the children…here."

In spite of her ongoing slide and loss of perspective about what she was doing, this was a total shock. She stared at Jeren with her mouth agape. Even Brogan looked daunted at the possibilities and the implications.

"What?" she whispered. The hurt on her face was the last thing Jeren expected to see. Assuming she was nearly out the door of kicking him to the curb, causing her pain was the last thing he intended, or wanted.

"I…don't know what to say, Jeren. Do you no longer…"

For him, the dam burst. He couldn't continue the façade. His pain matched hers.

"Arium, I'm so sorry. I had no intention of hurting you."

"It sounded like you're driving me away," she uttered with an unsteady voice.

Selana was sobbing. She whimpered, "I couldn't stop this. I'm sorry."

Arium got up when Selana ran over to her.

Brogan stood too. Surprising Jeren, he said, "Much of the error is mine. I chose to chase after your wife, again. You know my feelings for her, but that doesn't excuse my behavior. I will leave now to allow your family important time together. I would like to say, I wished no harm on anybody either. It was purely selfishness and therefore, inexcusable."

He departed. Arium would not look at Jeren, so Jeren got up to go join Selana's hug. The other children quickly ran over too.

There was a visible sense of relaxing in the camp, like the ship had been righted.

Jeren whispered into his wife's ear, "I think in this marriage you got the worst of the deal."

She hugged him fiercely and sobbed on his shoulder. It was a cathartic act for both of them. The second time down this road of doubts about the marriage, neither of them could believe the sad state they'd allowed to happen.

"Your father and I are going to talk," said Arium.

"Yes, we'll leave you," said Selana, leading the other children away.

Jeren and Arium sat down talking softly while the troops gave them what privacy they could under the crowded circumstances.

"I take the blame," said Jeren. "Why I couldn't see how you saw me, I don't know, and I have no excuse. We both realize you could have done so much better than me in a husband. My pitiful actions are a perfect object lesson."

"That's generous of you to take that approach, but you know I was the one out there acting poorly. I was and I am a married woman, and I've never regretted marrying you. What was going on inside me, granted it had a beginning from that foul magic, but once Selana shattered that link, I have no excuse for what we did next. I admit that the residual feelings still simmered and I did too little to check my behaviors. I rationalized I wasn't cheating, but was I, in a way? Not consummating the lust we both nurtured didn't absolve me, and barely avoiding disastrous choices, I shudder to think where this was going.

"Brogan is a wonderful man and on certain levels he's very appealing, but I've faced very appealing men all of my life, so why this was different, I honestly don't know. I can point to your dismissive actions as reasons, but that's not right. I think I formed this image that suited my flawed needs. Painting you as a husband indifferent and uncaring, oblivious and unwilling to fight for his wife, it worked for fueling the fires of discontent. I was unreasonable and then stupidly I acted worse.

"I'm going to try to explain something you may not get. I know my body is a huge lure for men. What I'm saying is, you weren't one of the army of men trying to simply bed me. You loved me, my soul, and the person I am. I knew this because we've been in each other's heads."

"Before you make me seem blameless, I want to say, I was flawed in my own way. I acted childish and yes it could be seen as indifferent. I think it was as much a defense as conscious choice. From the beginning I could never believe you could pick a slug like me, so in a way, I felt sooner or later you'd realize what a mistake you made and wake up to reality, a husband filled with flaws and weakness, and a man who doesn't make his wife happy.

"Kicking me to the curb was the only path that made sense. Whether it was with any of these handsome men riding with us, it didn't matter which one. Trying to pretend you weren't hurting me when my insides were being ripped to shreds, I don't know what I thought."

"I pray we can finally put this away, once and for all."

"Do you think Brogan will be a problem? I know how hard it will be for him. I know what it's like to love you, to live, breathe, and dream about you, Arium."

"That's always been a heavy burden, all these things other people put on me. I just wanted to have a normal life."

"There's no chance of normal for either of us."

"I'm sorry to say, you're right."

"Maybe we can—"

"Yes," she whispered quickly, cutting him off and chuckling. "I'll make the separate cloaking spell for you and me while you make your usual one for hiding the camp."

"Yes ma'am."

In the morning, husband and wife once again tried to implement renaissance, a rebirth and renewal of their marriage union. When she started to give her promises about Brogan going forward, he stopped her.

"Those feelings are real and for me to expect to no longer care for him is unrealistic. He is a good man, and he will love you until the day he dies. Let's agree to accept the truth and move forward understanding it. Your feelings don't just dissipate overnight. If you are close and a dear friend with him, I need to handle that as a man who needs to act worthy of such an incredible wife."

189

"Enough with the compliments, it gets on my nerves." She brandished her fist. He snickered.

As a week passed and they approached the far Crondar border, Selana became quiet, concentrating on what was ahead. The night before leaving Crondar, the leaders sat talking.

"Gensten, what can you tell us about new country ahead?" asked Grakar.

"It was early in my journey and probably it was a place I had the most luck. I was terrified so I took every chance to avoid main roads, stay away from people and especially their troops. They're the least civilized of any land I entered. Those barbarians that attacked Warmark are probably a good way to think of our new hosts. I wouldn't be surprised if they're related. This dark threat Selana has detected, I have no recollection of any such thing in my travels. Obviously it doesn't mean it wasn't there. Again, I think fate smiled upon me for the whole journey westward."

Selana had come to share in the meeting along with Jeren and Arium.

They looked at her. "I regret I have no more information than before. It's still an amorphous mass of something. I can't even pinpoint a particular place. Whether that is for magical reasons, I can't say. I don't sense that, but…in this I could be wrong. There could be powerful magic at work beyond what we've faced before."

"That's not reassuring," said Brogan. "I think I speak for all of the soldiers here saying there is no natural danger in this world we fear to face, but when we face magic, it's angering to be rendered helpless."

Jeren added, "I wish there were more than just the six of us, but those are the facts and we must find a way to cope."

"Should we return to the practice of me riding ahead as our scout?" asked Gensten. "Brogan could lead us through his lands, but we're about to leave his country. Alone, I can do my job better, no offense to anybody else."

The group chuckled.

"None taken," said Brogan, smirking.

Jeren spoke, "I'd say tomorrow, entering this next country, that we continue making haste. My goal has always been getting to Gensten's home to visit with the people who sent the tome to us. Whether that will ultimately help us find our destination we don't know, but I have nothing else at this point. Selana?"

190

"I cannot guide you either. The extent of my usefulness is in gauging the level of threats around us."

"Anybody else?"

No one said anything.

"Rest while we can and prepare for what tomorrow holds for us."

The group gathering broke up, but Arium took the opportunity to draw Brogan aside for a private chat. She looked at Jeren to give him a reassuring smile and a nod. Jeren nodded in return and then walked Selana back to their bedding on the far side of the camp to the other children. Darik claimed her for a child game with the twins.

Arium remained in conference with Brogan past the time Jeren and the children went to sleep. In the morning, Jeren didn't ask anything about her meeting, opting instead to get about the important business of the day.

Gensten was already mounting up to take the lead while many in the camp were still breakfasting. The day had a momentous feel to it, though some might say an ominous feel. As if adding to the feeling of dire tidings, it rained soaking everybody in a steady cold torrent of misery. There was no magic Jeren could provide to shield them from the forces of nature.

Later, they approached the border outpost. Soldiers loyal to the King eyed Brogan grimly, but let them pass to exit Cronda. Their handful of men stood no chance against this daunting force and they knew it. The entire group of the allies was in surly moods glaring at the guards. The border guards never came out of their building.

It felt like entering a bad dream as they crossed the border. The rain did not relent, but only increased.

Across the border, there was no border station or sentries, only an abiding sense of dread, like they'd made the mistake of their lifetimes. Selana's perception of something amorphous ahead was now at hand. It did feel dark and sinister to the magicians.

Selana looked a little frightened.

"Perhaps we should raise our defenses," Arium whispered.

The group linked magically and all of them exuded the aura and blue glow of the power of the light. However, for the first time he'd ever seen, Jeren noticed Selana's long dormant ruby gem worn around her neck started to glow, but with a red light. It was alarming, especially when they all 'felt' it magically in a disconcerting way. The jarring effect threatened their normal communion and link. Selana seemed suddenly disoriented and confused. Her blue aura sputtered and intermittently flickered red. That transmitted into the five others leaving them wobbly, magically speaking.

The feeling of being surrounded, sinking into an ocean of blackness, sucked at their spirits and tested their resolve. The impulse to race away to hide was overwhelming and pervasive. Even trying to maintain contact with each other became difficult.

Why am I doing this? It's a hopeless task.

The disabling thought transmitted filtered through the whole group as each felt cut off, isolated, and inadequate.

Physically, they were still riding ahead, but they had lost the sense of it. In a daze, blinded to the external sense of their surroundings and circumstances, they weren't aware of being taken off their horses into the rough hands of crude warriors and hauled away into the deep forest. There was no fight against this enemy as none had the consciousness to realize their jeopardy or the loss of use of their bodies to respond.

How long they were unaware, how far they traveled and to where, no one had any sense of it. The blackness held them firm.

It was a bloodless defeat against a force they couldn't even comprehend, locked in a stupor.

Awakening later from the fog, instantly they all felt consuming despair. Trussed up in a mammoth cave, the acrid smoke from ceremonial pyres stung the eyes and made them cough. Whatever was being burned was not conducive to humans.

The effect lasted for a time before it dissipated. Looking around, taking stock of the situation, it was challenging as the dread had never left them. Sapping their courage, none could utter a sound.

In the distance, a large figure emerged from the fog, moving slowly toward them. His aura was appalling. None felt anything but fear with the thought he could be nothing but a horror to face.

As he neared, he chuckled, a deep rumbling sound that had no humor in it, just triumph.

"See what has fallen into our laps, my children. This is the mighty quest riding to save their world."

The group realized how vast was this underground cavern and how equally vast was the assemblage all around them. The deafening shout echoed throughout the cave, chilling their blood.

The sense the end was at hand throttled them all. All hope was gone.

"I'm Mobokta the Great."

Their host roared again.

"Welcome to my home."

He moved along their entire rank, eyeing them closely. They were situated in a long file helpless in restraints of a manner none discerned or could challenge. They were his puppets.

When he got to Jeren, the probe coursing through his body was painful, engendering feelings of illness, nausea, and of course, total defeat in him. He'd never felt so inadequate and worthless.

Arium gasped when it was her turn for Mobokta's examination. With her moaning in agony, seeing her writhing to escape the discomfort, Jeren could only watch frustrated in helplessness. Mobokta took his time like he savored his cruelty, and he was no less gentle with the children. The last target was Selana. When he entered her mind, he looked astonished.

"What is this?" he exclaimed.

Her examination took on the appearance of a struggle and a contest of might. For the first time, Mobokta's absolute control seemed in question.

That transmitted into the group as suddenly, imminent death, and the worse things of a living hell Mobokta had put into their minds, receded and the memory of resistance awakened.

They still could not break out of the force holding them captive, but the knowledge of the tome gave them an idea to form a sanctuary within their minds to shield their spirits in a protective cocoon, safe from Mobokta's designs. Jeren, Arium, Darik, Amik, and Sari were quick to save their souls from Mobokta.

Meanwhile, the contest continued as Mobokta attempted to subdue Selana. But her vast well of power thwarted him and tangentially, her companions.

Mobokta's considerable attack should have been unstoppable, but it wasn't.

At long last, he relented, staring at his prize, puzzled.

"What manner of creature are you? You're an enigma in every way. How can that be, and how can such a creature as you…be? How can you not be at war within yourself?"

Selana said nothing, merely eyeing him impassively.

"There's a familiar taste to your aura, actually a number of familiar tastes. That's impossible."

Again, she remained mute.

"Know this, child. You will suffer the same fate as all who have entered my home. I will consume you, and these pitiful companions of yours. The power of the light will be gone forever."

Selana's amused smile irked him.

"You think you can overcome me? I'm older than this world. I'll stand until the end of days and shout at creation itself. I am the Mobokta, the guardian and protector of the entrance. Do you think to pass by me to enter your goal?"

"I think nothing about you, braggart. Bask in your delusions, for I care not. Test me again if you wish."

"I will find a way. What if I extinguish this child body of yours? What becomes of you without a host?"

Selana smirked. "You may try."

With a sudden attack, Mobokta leveled a withering torrent of red power so strong it incinerated masses of his followers. However, it could not touch Selana, and could not break her protection of the quest members.

When he stopped, he looked dumbfounded. "This is not possible."

"Clearly it is possible for here we both stand. Do you wish further schooling in reality?"

"What do you want? I realize you could have avoided my trap, but chose to enter here."

"Isn't it obvious? We're not here for you or yours. We've come for Evanshard Glade. You're the gate guard."

Now Mobokta acted amused.

"You have no idea of what you'll find, or you wouldn't want to go there. Rare are the select few those who enter Evanshard Glade and none ever return for I am here to consume them, whatever is left of them at that point. It's a meal I've never had, but in your case I'd love to have."

"You've given me a great boon, though you don't realize it," Selana explained. "With your assault, you've allowed me to take a great step in my evolution and made me into a much greater being."

Mobokta eyed her thoughtfully. "I think perhaps you have your limits too. Your arrogance can be a weakness and an avenue for attack for your enemies. If you think you're invincible against them, or any others in this world, you could cost your quest in the end. There is a reckoning, even for you."

"Duly noted. Are you going to release us, or must I do it?"

Suddenly, the restraint was gone. The quest members stared at each other. Although incapacitated, they'd all shared in the communion between Selana and Mobokta, witnessing the battle of titans.

He had a calculating look.

"You wish to enter a new realm? Do you think it is done now, our contest?"

"Enough," said Selana sternly.

"As you wish."

Following Selana, the rest of the troop was in a daze. What Selana had done was beyond mind-boggling. Mobokta's revelations about her only opened more questions.

Mobokta was oblivious to the carnage he'd wrought on his own followers as bodies were strewn everywhere as they walked ahead.

Darik, Amik, and Sari looked intimated by their 'sister'. She was left to walk alone, trailing Mobokta.

They reached a fork of two caves tunnels. Mobokta led them to the right. It sloped downwards and it was a lengthy trek. Ahead they could see a glowing light; it was a glow of red.

As they neared, all in the quest group felt sickened, their bodies rebelling against the noisome power of darkness.

Mobokta laughed. "Do you still think your goal is a wise choice?"

Selana scowled, concentrating on what was before them. With a wave of his hand, Mobokta brought up a roiling vortex. It looked deadly and dangerous even to try to approach.

"Here is your doorway." Mobokta said, with an evil grin.

Selana started forward, chanting ancient magic as she went. Grasping control of the other five in the process, she formed a new union where they were like a six-sided single being of which Selana was the brain. Moving in concert, the barrier sizzled and crackled dangerously at the approach of competing power. Their blue auras blazed to life setting off a corresponding reaction of red in the barrier. However, it wasn't an apocalyptic showdown and world-ending war of magic they anticipated. Selana's gem awakened, blazing equally strong in an impossible fusion of the power of darkness and light. It was like a key had been inserted in the lock of time which was the barrier before them. That barrier transformed into an open passageway into the beyond.

Selana led the quest into their original destination of entering Evanshard Glade. What they saw on the other side was incredible.

Their Garden of Eden, it was lush with exotic vegetation, wondrous scents, nearby were pure clear lakes with a gentle stream directly ahead, and a feel of peace and serenity.

That proved temporary, because once they started to walk, the idyllic scene transformed dramatically, like a false barrier was ripped away and what was real became clear. It was a dark threatening sky, rumbling thunder, jagged bolts of lightning, and the terrain was transformed into a wasteland of rotting dying vegetation, polluted waters, and a return of the feelings of despair.

The pleasant fragrances were gone replaced by the charnel stench of death.

Selana led them unerringly toward whatever would be their fate. It was a fearful prospect as they looked around.

Jeren pondered ruefully, *Will courage and strength of arms serve any purpose here? Or will we suffer meaningless wasted deaths for no reason?*

It was a chilling prospect.

Entering the dying remains of the forest, they walked a path for some distant before seeing a structure in the distance. The fact it was still intact amongst the devastation was curious. Whether it should be seen as hopeful or dangerous, they weren't sure.

Chapter 13

Truths Revealed

The closer they got, the more foreboding the structure seemed.

What was even more frightening to the quest members was the emergence of Selana's dual parts, one of the blue and one of the red. They'd started to divide with the red gradually ascending over the blue.

Her face was rapt staring at the arches and into the structure.

"Come, we must hurry," she said, but in a voice with vast overtones, like she was suddenly multiple persons.

Drawing near to the entrance, huge doors opened and a voice called out in their minds.

"Come forth and enter, brave members of the quest, for you have done well. We are well pleased."

Selana took the first step inside. Although reluctant, the others followed her.

The normal throbbing pulse of her red gem was a solid illumination now.

Ahead was a vast amphitheater, but empty except for two beings seated on thrones.

As Selana increased her pace, anxious to reach the duo, her gem flamed to a beam so intense, none could look at it.

"Come forth, my daughter," said the female. "Welcome home."

"You are my real mother, and father," she said rhetorically.

"We are. My name of Sindora, and his name is Arcuron. We are the high priest and priestess of darkness, leaders of the order of dark mages. You are our final achievement and the culmination of ages of carefully crafted plans. Over eons of time since the beginning, we've had one goal and you are the instrument of that goal, child."

"I see it now. I understand."

It was terrifying to behold as she blazed brighter in a crackling cocoon of red power. Her eyes looked like a mirror of the immense being she was.

The High Priestess, Sindora, looked down at Arium and Jeren.

"I placed my baby in your care because you gave her what I could not. As she grew in your way subscribing to the power of the light, something I could not touch and give to her, we could mold her into the unique creature she's become. She can broach any barrier. There's no limit to her abilities with a foot in each realm. You knew nothing of this. I placed a word for you when she was given into your care, Selana. You gave her that as a name.

"That word in our ancient language means destroyer, for now she is perfected into the greatest weapon of all time, a living avatar of darkness. What will happen now cannot be stopped. You've enabled your doom and that of all others in this world as well."

When Selana turned her head to behold them, they were all shaking in terror. There was nothing they could see or sense in her to give them any hope at all. It seemed her real mother was speaking the undeniable truth.

The transformed child they now saw before them was not the child they'd raised. This newly created being crackled with incalculable power and potency, like they were standing near to a blazing star from space. Whatever life they'd had as a family, it was gone. As she gazed on them, they felt like they were less significant than insects crawling on the ground at her feet.

Sindora continued, "Arium, do you judge me? Do you imagine you're morally superior as a follower of the light? You saw my growing child for all of these years and what she was become within your care. Is it so hard to imagine that I'm so different from you? With other choices, I could have been you. My husband and I came to that fork in our road previously in life and made a selection to travel a new path.

"It was a conscious choice with our full knowledge and acceptance. We realized your path was the lesser option. Following a doctrine and tenets unrealistic and doomed to fail, it shocked us we'd even considered it. Your religion, if you want to call it that, it is obsolete, *passé,* fodder for the pyre of progress.

"You've never experienced the pure joy and freedom of the dark way. Don't think I don't know what percolates secretly within you, the lusts you still harbor in your heart for another while you lie to your husband. Is this the goodness you tout? I laugh at the preposterous ruse. He is too weak to hold you accountable. We used yours flaws to great effect, don't you agree?"

Arium felt shame on a scale only this forum could muster, exposing the ugly truth for all to hear. There was no defense, rationalization, or explanation possible. What Sindora spoke was true. As if to reinforce her damning accusation, Sindora evoked a powerful reaction in Arium leaving her panting and gasping from Sindora's red power. Flooded with seamy passions and lust, she yearned to rush over to Brogan, but she was still frozen in Sindora's control, unable to move.

"With our side, such silly distinctions and niceties no longer matter. From our perspective, they never did. If I was in your position craving another, I have any choices available that I wish, including any indulgences. You can see the vast possibilities coming for the new world we can shape. Your side never properly accounted for the weaknesses inherent in all of us. That is a fatal mistake. It's how the seeds of your undoing could be planted to grow and dominate you to the exclusion of all else. You never stood a chance in restraining your hungers."

Suddenly, Sindora ended the dark stimulus. Arium gasped and shuddered, feeling innately unclean.

"Come friends, there is a sight you must see."

The couple got up from their thrones and led the quest troop to a different place in the vast building, like pets on a leash.

"Jeren, you'll now see the answers to your questions. What happened to your order, your pathetic force purporting to champion the light? The mystery that has driven you to pursue this epic journey has simple explanations. Behold."

Walking into a large chamber, the entire staff was there, including the High Council members and the High Mage. It was a shock, but what was more shocking was they were performing a ritual of the dark mages. There was no blue light anywhere among them.

"See what I've told you. Turning them to our will was the easiest of our tasks. Your supposed High Mage was not high in any way. He was a seriously flawed man. His fall to his glaring weaknesses opened a door for us to infect the entire host of your brethren. You have the opportunity to join them, if you so choose. In your case, due to what you've done and provided for my daughter, protecting and loving her, I will not compel you. Instead, I'll give you free choice about the path of your future."

He struggled against the restraint, but it was useless. His link to his power was impeded.

"Now you can truly understand the depth of my revelations. Your order has ended, your wife is revealed for the harlot in spirit that she is, and your daughter is no longer yours. She was always mine with her ultimate purpose undeniable. There was never anything you could have done about any of it. This was your sad destiny."

Selana walked at her birth mother's side. Her ruby gem glowed brightly. The entire room had a pervasive feel of wrongness, the vileness assailing them. Walking along, the crush of red power was like an attack on their bodies by stinging insects, painful to the extreme. Breathing the air was like breathing in heat from a blast furnace.

Sindora turned to Arcuron, her husband. "Did I not foresee this great triumph? It is exactly as I dreamed it. At last the world can be freed from their stodgy dictates and judging ways. These last survivors of a doomed belief system will be appropriate sacrifices to the power and majesty we will install. All will bow down for us, and to us."

"Yes, dearest, it is as you say."

"You doubted, and had reservations when we chose our path so long ago, but as you see, they were groundless worries. There will never again be any outcome allowed other than what we choose."

As a further gesture to punish Jeren, she moved Arium away to stand at Brogan's side. It was mortifying and nearly toppled him. Added to the other measures, it took him to his limits of endurance physically and emotionally.

Within his mind, he struggled. *Is this my end? Am I already in hell to suffer for all eternity? What sins have I done to deserve this terrible fate?*

Like watching a performance of Sindora's puppets, Arium and Brogan embraced romantically like long-lost lovers, freed at last to share their mutual love. Jeren wasn't allowed to look away. He had no ability to affect this dilemma, no control of any kind. Meanwhile, the sickening drone of the vile chants of the brethren of his former order drilled into his head. It was like their new purpose was solely for turning him to darkness.

Whatever happened next, Jeren couldn't remember as everything for him went dark in unconsciousness. Awakening later, he was lying on a bed in a sleeping room. How he got there was totally a mystery. The aegis of pain was lifted. He could breathe normally and move about. Sitting up, he looked around at the small room. Checking himself, he didn't seem to have any residual injuries.

There was nothing but the bed in the room, a small table and chair. Walking to the door, it was locked which didn't surprise him. Getting out of the room would have been useless here. *Where would I go and what would I do?* He mused at his helplessness. The life he knew and the dear people in it were gone. Of that, he had no doubt. Whether they had already converted to darkness, he had no way to know. That assault on his spirit in the dark ceremony by the people of his order that he'd revered was as galling as his wife cleaving to Brogan for all to see.

However, within the deepest parts of his mind, something remained of his fighting spirit rejecting this, all of it. Rebellion survived though he had no practical means to respond. Changing the script they intended for him seemed impossible. At the same time, he made a choice.

I will never bow down to them and their ways. If I'm meant to be the last believer in the light, that is how I will meet my end.

However, rather than a noble sacrifice, he 'felt' impotent, like total of it was merely an expression of his helplessness, incompetence, and avoidance of the truths of his life and marriage, too insignificant a person to warrant real attention or concern.

Over time, their enemies isolating him, and also the others of the quest, it added to the malaise and the continuing assault on their spirits. Trying to blank his mind to the ongoing attack was proving problematic as thoughts, impulses, and images haunted his nights rendering restful sleep virtually impossible. Realizing this dark magic came from their captors meant nothing for him. Since he could do nothing to counter the onslaught, it gave him no peace to help him cope.

However, the continuing passage of time confused him. *They have total control, what are they waiting for? End us and be done with it.*

Moving ahead to implement their dire plans, logically it seemed to him their best option at this point. This delay made no sense at all. *Whatever occurs after death, I'm ready to face it as it couldn't be worse than this life as helpless prey for the predator to toy with before the release of death came for him.*

Sindora came to visit him in his room after a month, or at least that was his guess about the time. He had no way to be sure if it was less or more elapsed time.

"I'll dispense with the formality of pleasantries. You deserve that."

She eyed him intently before continuing, "Will you believe me when I tell you that I and my husband respect you, at least on certain levels? From where you started fresh out of your wizard training academy, to accomplish what you've done, to hold together that mixed collection of military brutes, endure the emotional ravages of a worthless wife, and still love my precious child as you did, it amazes us still."

"Am I supposed to exclaim over your compliment?"

She chuckled. "Long ago before this incarnation of me, I would have found you very intriguing. Sadly that chapter is closed for me to be the kind of woman you would be drawn to. I know it's a waste now to offer you alternatives in that vein. However, remember that your old rules are gone; therefore, you have the freedom to make new choices. I say at this point, why not?"

"You mean, like a proverbial last meal, but instead by acting out with you in the intimate arena?"

"I'm still a beautiful woman, where do you think Selana gets her looks? What do you think your former wife does with her time now that she's finally rid of you? I guarantee there isn't one second of any of her busy days where she thinks about you. Her heart belongs to him, undeniably and irrevocably. Truthfully, it's belonged to him since they first met. That stain of her desire for him bled into her soul and has changed her. Choices have consequences for her and those associated with her. That's what you are now, her associate, a former acquaintance."

"This seems to give you great pleasure telling me these things and making spurious claims about my wife. Sitting here, how could I know the real truth?"

"That's easy enough to provide. Have you not yet realized those strong dreams are more than just dreams?"

"So, you wish for me to collapse at your feet, broken in spirit, because you've filled the mind of your captive with these galling nightmares. I give no more credence to them than I give credence to your tenets and your ambitions.

Seemingly you think eventually the members of this quest will succumb to your subterfuge and misinformation."

"Hah!" she shouted. "Fool, I need no schemes to trick your mind. This strength of character you purport, where is it? I've seen none of it in your cohorts, and your wife seems bent on proving her true calling being a—"

"Stop! I don't need to hear more of your lies. You've made the statement that choices have consequences. That doesn't apply to only the members of the quest. We all face a reckoning for our actions, and in your case, I shudder to think of what awaits you in the afterlife."

For the first time, he'd managed to shake her. The look on her face, although only momentary, was human, not the imperious queen of darkness. Doubt crossed her face before she regained her footing.

"Clever, Jeren, very clever. I may never have met a person of your stature. Certainly, you move me. Honestly, I can't comprehend your wife and her wavering heart. She's the biggest fool of all. Yes, you make a valid point. My husband and I have made a conscious choice. We committed to this path regardless of any future consequences."

"That's all well and good for you, but what about Selana? What choice did she have in this? You're condemning her to damnation for the choices of your hardened heart. I've seen who she is and who she could become. Warping her into the dark creature you wish for her to be, it's an abomination. I say again, for all of us who live and breathe, there is a final accounting. There are those greater than us, I know this for a fact. I suspect you will know it too soon enough."

"Those are brave words, Jeren, but to what purpose? Can you show me proof of whatever you mean? Your paltry magic was extinguished easily enough. Your High Mage was a sham. These days, he is the least of you. Embracing the darkness fully, he looks to rise in our ranks, and he revels in our delights. He discarded your order with no more thought than removing a cloak."

"Say what you will. My feet are planted in defense of the light. That will always be so."

"Your feet are planted in quicksand."

"I don't deny you can take away my life."

"Good, at least you acknowledge the obvious. Perhaps you can accomplish more realizations. As I think about it, perhaps we should arrange dinner. You can meet the happy new couple and see if I'm deluding you. Ask them both about their feelings, close relationship, and even about their actions, if you can cope with very difficult answers."

"Again, do you think this concocted creation of yours defeats me? Even if the worst had happened…well…"

"You're not immune. I can feel your inner turmoil."

Jeren paused and then spoke, "Can I ask you some questions? I don't think it's any threat to you telling me anything. Do you agree? You're capable of ending my life at any time."

"What would you like to know?"

"I don't understand why you as a woman, having your husband's child, would birth a being so remarkable as Selana? Why is she different than any other child?"

"Excellent point, Jeren. Our bodies and the heritage we pass on are the same as you. For eons, our dark mages have tediously toiled toward a goal to recreate a world of our choosing. Merely sharing a bed together can impregnate, but this was a carefully orchestrated ritual. We employed dark magic to imbue her with more than the spark of life. She hosts an expanded consciousness not possible in the normal propagation of our kind.

"We altered her beginning on the first day and augmented her growth along the way. You can see the result. She has a child body, but her intellect and magical powers exceed most of us. There will soon come a time to take a big step that will transform her utterly into a new creature, a higher form of life."

He eyed her in silence, pondering her disturbing explanation.

"I can see you're highly skeptical of this truth, just as you are about what I tell you about Arium."

"I'm not judging anything. I have no basis to separate truth from fiction."

"You feel pleased with yourself, thinking your verbal jousting puts us on an equal footing. It does not."

"I didn't say that. You're doing all of the talking."

"I'll admit, you intrigue me when there is little else which can."

"By saying you used dark powers; I don't know what you mean? We have no teachings about such things, altering nature and natural processes. What you describe seems impossible, yet I can't deny the reality that is Selana."

"Your ancestors limited their studies long ago for your order and then codified it so none would ever explore daring topics and ideas. We all descended from common progenitors. That's no secret you don't know. We subscribe to the path to learn all there is to know. Limiting ourselves in mind, body or spirit makes no sense, so we don't do it. Literally for us, there is no final barrier or topic deemed inviolate. I'll admit, I tampered with Arium during this quest. Some of her misadventures weren't of her own making. However, once I gave her a little nudge, she rushed to embrace a different path." Sindora laughed heartily.

"I won't ask what that's supposed to mean. I don't care. Coming back to the topic at hand, I find it hard to believe the power of evil could accomplish this. Your mantra is destruction, not creation."

"To create the perfect person, our daunting task was to find a way to meld both disciplines into her. She needed the dark powers we could give her, but to receive the light, there had to be a new path, one fraught with risk for us."

"Why did you pick me, of all the wizards, I don't understand?"

"We didn't pick you. Your High Mage picked you. He was already in league with us and was present on the night of the consummation to make Selana. It was he providing the power of the light to blend into her. The result was a hybrid child with a foot in both realms. He reasoned you were the best choice for this task of taking on an unknown child.

"Your loneliness, decency, and tendency to care about strays, we banked on you bonding quickly. Once you saw her as your daughter, it was easy. Pairing you up with Arium completed the puzzle. A stunning woman suddenly enamored with you, it was farcical, but it worked. Would she have noticed you otherwise? What do you think?"

She smiled as the hurtful barb landed painfully. Jeren concentrated to fend off the inferiority feelings Sindora was trying to foster in him.

"Does helping you see the truth at last constitute gloating? That's what you think; I can sense it in you. I have no need to gloat. As you've already said, we have complete control. There can be no outcome but what we allow."

For the moment, he said nothing.

"With Arium and her errant ways, you wonder about my tampering? I didn't make her choices, but I did facilitate her opportunities to act. She met you as a simple village wife, but look at what she has become now. I augmented her native desire to become a person of import. When her energy flagged in her initial physical training, I gave her subtle boosts. Crafting her body into physical perfection, it served our purposes and opened her potential to developing into potent realities. Thereafter, she was seen as the supreme temptress, irresistible and a universal lure for all. It made the marital strife piece an easy step, and with your innate self-doubts, an incredibly successful one.

"I considered Brek and Drake for the role, both are handsome, but they weren't roguish enough as my final choice of Brogan. He was a man act to on his impulses, and a man to have strong impulses. She swooned at him instantly and he was agog with her. Manipulating scenes and circumstances to punish you with uncertainty, it was an entertaining game. You fell for everything."

She eyed him closely. "You want to ask if he did act on his impulses." She grinned in perverse satisfaction.

"No, I don't."

"That is a lie, sir. There were certainly plenty of opportunities, some you're aware of, and some you were not. As a gesture to you, I'll honor your need and desire to hide your head in the sand, but it would be better to lance the boil, to use an analogy I say face the truth and be done with it."

This was the most difficult moment, trying to avert an outward reaction. Steeling his resolve, he fought off the myriad of roiling negative emotions. Opening his eyes again, she had a smirk on her face.

"Just so you know, if I was your wife, there would be no other persons lifting my dress."

"Good to know," he replied flippantly.

She laughed heartily. "I think your plan is for me to fall in love with you. I haven't been this entertained in…well, forever."

"Well, that makes one of us."

Again, she laughed.

"I wish I could say reassuring things, but reality is what it is. If you wish for me, call at any time and I will come to you. I've told you the truth, we have none of your arcane restrictions, so if you wish for…companionship. There is no wrong in it other than what your faulty order concocted to make you misbelieve. We are meant to live our lives to the fullest."

"Thank you, but no. I prefer going to the next life without creating new mistakes and sins to drag along."

Again, it stopped her. She frowned and turned. Walking away, she said, "Remember all that I've told you."

Returning to her quarters, she was irked. *How can that man rile and upset me so?* She stormed about her room wallowing in her foul mood.

Do you think you've seen the worst, Jeren? I can make it so much worse.

Pondering various means of revenge, afflicting him wouldn't have the effect she wanted. He was already convinced of a fatal fate. Only those he cared about offered her the leverage she needed.

Pairing the soldiers to fight to the death against each other, it would devastate him, but, she wanted worse. The obvious, putting Brogan and Arium together in that way seemingly to maximize punishing him, on the surface it seemed the greatest weapon, but after being near him over a period of time, talking to and gauging him, even infidelity may not topple Jeren.

The contrived acts of performing puppets on her strings would strike him as false. He could seem to see through her ruses, too much so. Expecting that sorry scene to be paraded out before him sooner or later, even there he may have prepared himself to deflect the emotional impact. Down deep, he felt it was already the case so the probability it would have the desired effect was questionable.

Thinking hard, an idea surfaced. One of her past interferences had netted a surprising impact both on him and her at that time. Sindora considered how she could craft this into a weapon to use against Jeren.

"Perhaps…" she muttered. "He will be defeated, I swear it."

For his part, Jeren was pondering also, not about what might be coming his way, but about more puzzling questions. *How did Arcuron and Sindora get past Mobokta, the guardian of the gates into Evanshard Glade? What happened to cause that radical change from the idyllic paradise into the rotting nightmare it is now? Is their power so all pervasive now that they control all things? They managed to bring the former wizards of the light here and infect them with darkness. What other impossible things could they do, and have already done? Have they warped Selana into this frightening avatar, or was it always in there and they merely released it from within her.*

He had no answers and as he sat, it felt to be an exercise in futility. Regardless of anything he was mulling over, there was nothing he could do about it. Something was stopping Sindora from enacting the final solution, but did it matter to him? His fate was sealed and was only a matter of time.

Sindora's 'dinner' idea came to pass as Jeren was brought to join the collection of his colleagues. The entire assemblage of the quest gathered to break bread, but it was no joyous occasion. As Jeren looked around, none of them looked to be harmed physically, but every face was sullen and downcast. None escaped her kind of torment.

With Sindora placing Arium and Brogan side by side directly across the table from Jeren, their romantic antics had virtually no effect on him. Instead, he paid momentary attention to the look on Sindora's face, and then stared mostly at Selana, seated with the other children.

"Jeren, come and take a seat, welcome to our little *soiree.*" Sindora had uttered the invitation pleasantly like it was a respectable social event, but with a smirk. She had seated him directly beside her, patting her hand on his knee. "Are you not happy to see your wife and friends are unharmed?"

"Unharmed? Why do I not believe you?"

"Our little contest goes on, my darling man, but regardless, let us enjoy a sumptuous feast. I personally picked the dishes for the height of luxury."

He ate the food and drank the wine. After all, there was no reason to starve himself. Keeping up his strength might be another exercise in futility, but he would do it for the time being.

During the meal, he paid attention to Selana. It was like she was a complete new person, but even with that, there was something niggling within him. His hope refused to die.

Sindora watched him as closely as he watched Selana.

"You are certainly predictable, Jeren. I can say it's commendable, but we both know you're hanging onto your pointless resistance by a thread. You can have a high place in the new order which is coming. It's quaint of you harkening back to the past, but useless. Look around you."

Sindora laughed. "Can you not see that refusing the truth of the inevitable accomplishes nothing?"

"Apparently, it does. Why else are we all sitting here, still among the living?"

Sindora scowled. Arcuron chuckled. "That is an excellent question, my dear."

"Shut up," she snapped.

His tiny rebellion caused Selana to turn her face to him. As usual, her eyes were frightening to behold, but her expression took on a look of puzzlement. Whatever she was thinking, he couldn't say, but maybe...

"That shows you how deluded you are," Sindora snarled. "You think this is hopeful seeing Selana's little reaction? It's the smallest of things. Is she about to revert back into your mewling daughter any second now? Hah, you're beyond deluded."

"I have no aspirations for her. I'm just waiting for your machinations to end. The meal is ended, so is there something else you need or may I return to my prison cell?"

Sindora caused all of the people to cry out in pain, irked by Jeren's continuing resistance.

"You think you are greater than me! You have no idea what I can do."

"Sindora, why can't you grasp the simple fact that at this point, I don't care. What is it you strive to accomplish with me?"

"Well said," Arcuron added.

Sindora turned her head to her husband replying in an acid tone, "Take care what you say to me."

"Or what, what will you do? I am as you. Do you think you can throw me down like these helpless pawns?"

"I think perhaps I no longer have need of you. Calling you husband, that no longer suffices. Marriage is antiquated anyway. We haven't been spouses in a long time. I disclaim you."

"And I disclaim you. Your barbs hurt me no more than they hurt him. Marry him if you like. He seems to be your latest romantic interest. There is no other explanation for why you perpetuate this needless comedy. I think he doesn't want you, dearest."

Sindora seethed and arose from the table. Her red aura flamed to life. Arcuron raised up his own defense instantly.

Jeren expected a battle, but suddenly, Sindora got a calculating look and dropped her threatening stance, and her power.

"Arcuron, we will see what I can accomplish."

Jeren was looking at Selana. Her puzzlement seemed to be growing.

What are you wrestling with, little girl?

Sindora sent everyone back to their rooms. Her event was a failure, but she'd expected that. However, Arcuron vocalizing his theory that she wanted Jeren as her new replacement companion? It irked her.

That's preposterous. Yes, it is compelling to be around him. His inner goodness and strength of character evoke me. I know he will never answer the dark call. Nothing I can do will compel him. Why do I care? I put away the last vestiges of the light from my heart and soul when I made my choice. I freely seek that state of complete surrender to the darkness. It cannot be possible I have any vestige of light still living within me. Placing my daughter with him in the light, it was a calculation and a strategy, not a protective act of motherhood.

Her inner argument didn't solve her dilemma. Arcuron's allegation it was her weakness in question delaying the final act of obliteration. Her kicking Arcuron to the curb impacted him in no way at all. Their love was dead, banished from existence in the new world, just like marriages. All that would remain would be meaningless random indulgences with other people. Sindora felt uneasy.

Why does that leave me feeling unsettled? This is the world we wanted, isn't it?

Factoring in also in her thinking was Jeren's little barbs about her afterlife. Whatever dire fate she would face, that fear had taken root. He had no fear of dying with his spirit moving on to a different plane of existence. *Why is that? What does he know that I do not?*

Grappling with issues was an uncomfortable development she never anticipated. Supposedly in complete control, Jeren was proving too slippery a quarry and annoyingly stubborn to boot.

Rather than the "Goddess" she'd imagined herself to be, acting peevish, childish, reactive, petulant, these were becoming her daily behaviors. It angered her toward the need of changing this experiment.

****

Outside of Evanshard Glade, back in the world, time moved on. Old foes were befuddled that their quarry had suddenly disappeared. It was as great a mystery as the disappearance of their leaders, Arcuron and Sindora.

Gueldar was a child, but ascended into the leadership vacuum by acclamation. No longer having any foes with the absence of the wizards of the light, the dark cause foundered without a plan and purpose. Merely tormenting the helpless populace served no purpose. Attacking the remaining bastions of resistance, like Grecia and Warmark, they could be conquered at any time.

Gueldar was fixated on finding the quest, and in particular Selana, his imagined future soul mate.

At the same time, Antith was not idle either. Unlike Gueldar, his knowledge and therefore his goals were much different. He knew of Evanshard Glade, but finding it had been denied to him going all the way back to his ancient beginning.

He hungered for his own confrontation, but one of a much different sort and with far different opponents.

Racing about in random searches no longer served any purpose. If they were anywhere to be found, he would have sensed it.

Where they had been going, he moved that way to seek out signs of them.

I am not defeated. I will find you. We will see the fruits of your crimes against me recoil upon you. In my wrath, I will give you my answer.

Elsewhere, on the other side of the fence, Kings Tarkan and Argost, prepared for war. The feelings of dread sweeping every country did not miss these two bastions of the light. The champions, the corps of wizard were gone without explanation, and the quest seemingly was lost without word of their fate. It was unsettling, but these were not weak people to cower in fear. Grecia especially intended to rise up against any threat.

The two Kings agreed to a mutual defense pact in case either was attacked.

Gerak, the legendary Grecian general, kept his daunting forces drilled and practiced even more, honed to a fine edge. Whatever could take out the wizards, and brave skilled people like those in the quest, would be a supreme foe. Grecia would give them the fight of all time if they came into the realm.

Remembering Arium, she stuck in his mind and that was a great departure for him. Being the ultimate warrior left no time or any room for considerations of women, marriage, and children. It annoyed him how persistent was this fascination.

He mused, *She was the finest opponent I ever faced, and the only one I personally trained.*

Such perfection as she'd accomplished still dazzled him. Imagining her eschewing the quest in favor of remaining back in Grecia, with him, it was a pleasant thought. A life with her in it, the appeal called to him still, even after all of this time and the many years they'd been gone.

If any of them were still alive, he could not ascertain. It was out of his hands. They knew the risks, but that didn't mollify his feelings.

"Arium," he muttered sadly. "What could have been, my darling. That foolish quest of yours was doomed from the start. I should have prevented you from leaving. I will never meet another woman like you."

The many plates of intrigue continued to spin as each independent issue added up to a unified picture, though none of the players could see it as a whole. The ripple of every action caused a reaction in the grand scheme of things. Fate was inevitable, but what that would mean remained to be seen.

Each participant imagined their own version of a happy ending and those versions were wildly divergent, in many case polar opposites.

Against this backdrop, Sindora brooded at her continuing failures. Subduing the quest could never be complete if even just one of them remained standing to defy her. Allowing Jeren to thwart her glory, avoiding her snares, failing to buckle to her enticements and lures, it infuriated her. Rejecting the illusions and falsehoods was difficult to stomach, but when he dismissed the opportunity she offered to be with her as the new consort, that went too far. She would no longer tolerate it. In spite of her reluctance, Sindora made the fateful decision.

The time has come, Jeren. You could have had it all seated at my side to rule the world. Now, I will grant you your wish to end this captivity in the only way you can be released. You're anxious for the next life... So be it.

Sending out the fateful word at last, Arcuron was surprised.

Perhaps you can learn from your mistakes, darling. Now we shall see what will be wrought.

Jeren felt queasy. Although he'd portrayed utter disdain for Sindora and her threats, now it seemed she was prepared to follow through. Life is precious and all living creatures fight to survive. He was no different. The end wasn't something he relished, but he would not go out as a coward. Whatever form she chose to take his life, he would not waver.

Chapter 14

The Destroyer

Being escorted from his cell back to the throne room, Jeren walked solemnly, replaying the decisions of his life that had brought him to this moment and what he could have done differently. His conclusion, he would make the same choices again. He mused, *A person does not choose their fate. Rather, it's put upon them.*

It was amazing to him how vivid were those memories and it wasn't just the decisions and strategies. He remembered childhood, his parents, the love of a mother and her gentle care, the later years coping with aloneness once they were gone, lost to illness. The shock of awakening one day to find the order vanished and Selana placed in his room. The fear he felt fleeing feral pursuit, and all of the subsequent events which transpired because of it. Meeting Arium, experiencing love for the first time, marriage and companionship with a woman, it had been a marvel.

All of it greatly moved him to profound sadness as he walked toward his ending. The travesty of the quest, the hopelessness after all of their dreams were shattered, it punished him. The noble aspirations, what did they mean now? His life was going to be cut too short for that of a young man. The unfairness of it screamed at him as much as any thoughts of the end of the world and the life he knew.

What a fool you are, Jeren. A great man they called you? What a joke.

His spirits were at their lowest ebb. There was no avoiding this final act in his misbegotten life. Now he would pay his ultimate price.

Why was I born if this was to be my ending? Were my sins so much greater than any other person?

The guards could have hurried him along, but seemed content to allow him to wallow in self-pity.

His resolutions about standing up proudly, facing the grim reaper without flinching, it had seemed an inspiring dream, but now in reality, he felt sick, weak in the knees. With sudden rubbery leg muscles, he wondered, *Can I even walk into that death chamber without collapsing?*

The doors opened and his emotions escalated. Peering inside, he was momentarily frozen in place. They were all there, his former wizard brethren, his quest companions, and a small army of Sindora's apostates.

Arcuron and Sindora were seated on their thrones. Arium stood to her right, her arms wrapped around Brogan.

All faces were staring at him as he recoiled from the shame of his utter failure. They would witness his execution.

Unbidden, his mind added to his misery. *Arium, you will finally be rid of me, the worst mistake of your life.*

He felt like screaming and running away, but that was no option. Sindora controlled him and his movements.

Prodding him back into motion, the guards each took an arm since he was faltering. His bravery and resolve had evaporated leaving a pathetic wretch limping along instead.

Each one of those tormented steps brought him closer to the moment of ultimate shame, disgrace, and aloneness. There were none left to comfort him.

Sindora loosened her restrains, adjusting it to the moment. The assembled started to hiss and boo at Jeren. Some shouted taunts and accusations blaming all failures on him. Others touted Arium's rejection of their marriage and choice of mighty Brogan to be her new partner in her life, and in all other ways. She would be a happy wife at last, fulfilled finally with a capable consort at her side. The punishing taunts were relentless and painful.

Brogan smiled disdainfully, stroking her luscious long hair possessively while she stared at Jeren, smirking with utter contempt.

Too much came at him from too many sources, his body was flooded with more torment than it could handle, so it responded automatically, defensively. His awareness of the din and the discord shifted, like he was no longer a part of this scene but watching from above, a mere spectator of spirit.

Taking those last few steps and stopping before the thrones, Jeren couldn't suppress his body shuddering involuntarily.

Sindora arose and began speaking in a loud voice, augmented by her power.

"And now we have come to it, the end of the folly of the light, for all else has been snuffed out but this last one. Yes, here stands the last of them, the only remaining believer. I give you Jeren, the lesser, for he has earned that shameful title with his weakness, his litany of errors and personal flaws. None can say I did not offer every opportunity for him to cast aside the past and join us going into our glorious future, but he was foolish and stubborn, refusing to acknowledge the truth."

She looked around the room as she brought back the jeers and taunts louder than before.

"Do you recognize it, what he offered you? His pride, as if he had all answers to all things? What do you think now?"

After a loud crowd reaction with more insults and recriminations, she continued.

"However, as significant as putting him down might be, the more important reason we are gathered here is the presentation of my daughter to meet her destiny."

Selana walked out from behind the thrones, clad in a black dress of shimmering raiment, a necklace of jewels decorating her neck, jeweled bracelets on her wrists, and jewels also used in pinning her long hair up in a formal sweep making her look like a miniature woman rather than a child.

Her expression was imperious, like her mother.

Walking to stand between her birth parents, she gazed away like she could see things in the distance others could not.

"Selana, my beloved child, we have brought you here at the crossroads of your life, the pinnacle. We came to this same place in our past and made the choice to cast aside their way and surrender our lives to darkness. You stand here now with your choice before you, but with so much more. You are unique, the beginning of a higher race meant to supersede these flawed beings you see around you. I smile with pride I could have a hand in it."

The crowd cheered wildly.

Selana looked to be oblivious, locked onto whatever distant phenomenon only she could see.

"The time has come at last, your time. Return to us now. Fix your countenance upon this flawed man standing before you for your judgment and reckoning. He richly deserves this fate, his impending and inevitable doom."

Her eyes blinked and then she looked down at him.

For him, it wasn't a person examining him. Whatever she was now, it bore no resemblance to the child he'd reared and loved.

"Embrace your true nature, my darling; accept the mantle of dominion over this realm, for you are aptly named, Selana. Become now that Selana, destroyer of worlds."

What he saw in her eyes was terrifying. Desolation lived there now, readying to spring forth upon the weak and the innocent, and he would be her first kill.

Sindora spoke, "Death of Father, death of love, death of the light."

Selana repeated it, but in a commanding chant full of overtones summoning her vast powers, "*Mortis patris, mortis amoris, mortis lux!*"

The fathomless well of that power gathered as she prepared to strike. She started to raise her arms to unleash death and hell upon him.

Jeren felt the desolation he saw in her eyes to the depths of his soul, not for his own imminent passing, but for what had been done to this precious child. His abiding love for her, it suddenly welled up to become a cry of anguish echoing across space and time. An unknowing plea on his part, it was heard in hallowed places and a door opened. Again, suspended in those nanoseconds in between the passage of time, he saw those great beings of the light. This time, it wasn't a passing glimpse as they forcefully reacted to the horror of what he faced.

The final abomination, the hope of the dark mages to corrupt and claim the innocent, her choice to accept that role to bring about ultimate horror to the universe, it did not happen. Within Selana was equal of light and that half flamed to life at the intervention of mighty beings. The seemingly invincible power contained in her blazing ruby red gem exploded, shattered like a mere glass trinket, and her innate power of blue light erupted so brightly, none could look at her. The sound of it was deafening, like the roar of a storm of such magnitude as never had been seen before in the world. The righteous indignation from beyond transmitted through Selana into the titanic conflagration of might.

In the midst of the pandemonium, Jeren felt her gentle touch in his mind. "Father," she whispered. "Fear not, I am returned to you."

Like a helpless bystander, he could do nothing, but he was aware of what happened next.

When Selana spoke in the ancient language, words of great power, everything changed.

Sindora was so lost in her reverie, she didn't immediately realize something had gone wrong.

The power of the blazing blue light grew, sweeping back the red power everywhere. Not only within the building, but outside in the land, it was unstoppable wiping away the scourge and damage of the red carnage. Death and decay was replaced in an instant by the return of health and vitality. The pristine garden was returned to perfection with her words and a sweep of Selana's arm.

Standing as a titan impervious to Sindora, raising both fists upwards, she orchestrated the internal cleansing of the once hallowed hall. Great chords sounded of stunning music so pure, noble, and holy, that echoing throughout the building and throughout the countryside, it signaled blue power ascending to preeminence and instantly the shackles on the quest captives were burned away. They were utterly moved, down to the essence of their beings, crying out in thankfulness, for deliverance from damnation.

The stunned followers of darkness had no answer to this sudden reversal and the untouchable power of Selana. They could only respond flocking together in a defensive array to protect Sindora and Arcuron, fleeing for their lives. However, when the brave allied soldiers came for them, the apostates made no stand to fight but merely fled away to escape.

The return of blue power not only allowed Jeren, Arium, and the three other children to attack, but the former wizards of the light joined the effort, shielding the allied soldiers from deadly attacks of red magic of the fleeing enemy.

Red power still existed in the world, but it no longer ruled over all. As galling as was this defeat for them, the eternal battle was not over. They had no choice but to flee to fight another day. It was a short battle.

After the conflict, the brotherhood that had been the wizards for goodness, they were frozen in place with indecision, unsure what to do next. Beforehand in the grip of evil, their galling sins complying with Sindora's dictates were fresh in their minds, but here had been an opportunity to get revenge on those who shamed them. Attacking instinctively along with Jeren had been a matter of reflex against their ancient foes.

In the initial throes of the brief fight when Jeren awoke, released after Selana's touch, blazing with blue power and his own righteous indignation, he had reformed the communion with Arium and the other three children. Enraged at the reversal, Sindora tried to take her revenge, but Jeren was helpless no longer.

"*Flammis*," he shouted in a booming voice. No longer shackled, the ferocity of his feral blue blast more than offset the effect of Sindora's counterattack.

Driving her back caused the others of her side to begin the retreat that never stopped until they were ejected from Evanshard Glade. Selana didn't participate in that battle. These were still her birth parents.

Only the High Mage had chosen to follow Sindora in leaving paradise. The brethren stayed back, but now looked at Jeren, expecting the worst.

"We have no words to excuse what happened here. The abomination of them wresting control of us and of this holy place, the shame we brought upon ourselves and to our way is unforgiveable. We can only offer to you the mantle of leadership as a worthy and true High Mage, one you have earned with your deeds where we all failed. If you permit us to follow you, we will. Whatever penance you require, we will pay without question. If you want to ban us forever, we understand completely."

"I don't know what to say to you. I'm no better a man than any of you. As you saw, it was no magic or power of mine that saved you, or my daughter."

"What?" They looked at each other in confusion. "What other power do you mean? We saw only you and her restoring and wielding the holy blue flame."

He paused in puzzlement. *Was that connection to those great beings shielded from everybody but me?*

He made a command decision.

"I can forgive all things," said Jeren. "I'm no worthy judge of others, nor would I want to be. If we restore our brotherhood and bring in new adherents to the academy, I see that as a good thing."

Balderon, a man who had been a prime teacher to Jeren, someone he'd admired and respected continued speaking for the host.

"Thank you. Your compassion and generosity are wonders for us. Emulating you will be a new mission for us all to guard against such a horror ever happening again."

Jeren turned to Selana, she smiled. It was the face he'd so longed to see, his daughter returned to him.

"You are such a miracle, precious one."

"Don't say that, Father. I was the blackest being possible before the intervention. There is no power on this planet that could have deterred me from the carnage Sindora wanted to bring about. I accept the fact that she birthed me, but I'm not her daughter. You are my father, and Arium is my mother. For me, parents of spirit are greater than any parentage of the body."

"Arium," he muttered thoughtfully.

"Can you open your mind there too?" asked Selana. "How was her shaming different than the rest of us? She had no more hand in it than anybody else."

"I have no excuse for my poor responses. I was sorely wounded and recoiled within myself when she needed me most to step up and give her aid. That was Sindora's main attack because she knew I was useless, and how to best use me for her purposes. I'm sorry I'm such a weak man."

"You're not weak. You stood alone against the storm when all others failed, including me."

Jeren glanced around. Arium was talking with her old friends. Brek, Grakar, Gensten, Drake, and of course Brogan, they were all there. The outward signs of the behaviors of her fascination for Brogan were gone. She sensed his gaze and turned her head. Her look of shame and sadness hurt his heart.

Grabbing Selana's hand, he hurried them over to where they both embraced her.

"It's over now, wife."

"I'm so sorry—"

He cut her off. "The matter is closed. Let's agree to speak no more about it."

Exiting the building, they were stunned with the flourishing revived land, truly paradise reborn at its best. All signs of the destruction were gone.

"What should we do now?" asked Grakar after a time. "We've been focused solely on the quest, so now that it's over, I feel empty. What other purpose could ever match this?"

"Well, Sindora and the dark mages are still out there, Gueldar, and of course, Antith. Our task is not finished."

Drake asked, "Selana, now that you understand the true meaning of your name, do you want to change it?"

"It's been my name all of my life, so I will keep it. Sindora was right when she said I was aptly named. I could have done all those horrible things she wanted. I was about to. The dark side of me that you saw, it's still alive and a part of me. How I can be this Selana or that Selana so easily, you can see my great challenge. I have no doubt they will go back to finding ways to flip me back to their side. I must be vigilant always. I think I might like to enter this academy of wizards of yours. Will you be my teachers, Father, and Mother?"

He chuckled. "There have never been females admitted there, though I can't say I know why that was."

Selana smirked. "It's time for a new way, and more females, plenty of them. Sari is a perfect example. She's the equal of her brother Amik."

All of the members of the brotherhood of wizards were staring at Jeren.

He didn't hesitate. "I agree with her. Would any of you like to take the opposite approach and try to dissuade her?"

"No," they replied quickly and in unison.

"So be it. Ladies, you are now welcome."

"How do we get home?" asked Sari.

"That is a good question. Facing Mobokta again will not be pleasant."

Selana answered, "I do not believe it will be a problem. I have an idea for a solution."

"Good, I don't relish another fight so soon after that battle with Sindora and her ilk."

"I guess there's no reason to wait. Lead the way, Selana. Let's get to this."

"Yes, Father."

Arium stepped to his side. He took her hand, causing her to smile warmly at the thoughtful gesture.

She whispered, "I think I already said, you didn't get the best in this marriage. I fail you so much, how could you ever believe anything I say?"

"Being manipulated by Sindora, that's not right to take blame where there is none. Honestly, I hold nothing against you."

"I wish I could just wash it away, but the memories are still there."

"For me also, but they will fade in time, as all memories do."

"What a lucky wife I am. What other man could show such compassion and forgiveness through that nightmare. You stood up and kept fighting."

"I wouldn't deify me. I did far less than what you imagine. Regardless, I don't want to talk about the past any longer. I suspect the future will hold challenge enough."

"You're probably right about that."

Selana's expanded personhood included access to her immense power. With a wave of her hand, a vortex appeared and they walked through it to find Mobokta waiting. He was puzzled.

"First, that dark horde races out apparently defeated at your hands, and now here you come. I have no directive regarding people leaving the garden."

"We didn't come to battle with you before and we have no malice against you now, Mobokta," Jeren replied evenly.

"Then you may go in peace."

"Thank you, but I think my daughter wishes to speak with you."

Selana walk up to him, as close as any living entity had ever come.

"My, my, you are a precocious little child, are you not?"

"Precocious?" Selana laughed heartily. "That is an interesting word choice. However, I'd like to offer a change for your life. You've stood here over the countless eons apparently with no end in sight."

"I'm well aware of that, child."

"I don't presume to know the minds of them who put this onus upon you, or the reasons for this sad state."

"Sympathy, for me? That is a refreshing change in itself."

"Were you told why you could not gain admittance into that paradise garden?"

"I was not. What I was given was the ironclad mandate to guard this entrance against all who attempted to enter."

"That strikes me as an indictment rather than a mandate. I don't like it."

Mobokta chuckled, but with his deep voice, it sounded like two massive boulders grinding together.

"I have not laughed since I was put here. I'd nearly forgotten how."

"Does your mandate require you guard the entrance from out here?"

"I never considered that. The thought to enter the Glade never occurred to me."

"It seems your guardian efforts could happen in there as easily as out here. Who can open the vortex, there are precious few. Merely having the use of magic doesn't suffice."

"You are a crafty creature wearing the garb of childhood. There is no child like you. The dual nature which defines you is the most dangerous part of all. While you can be the savior, you can just as easily be the destroyer. I see that you now know the meaning of your name. Does it distress you, because it should? I haven't seen such power as dwells within you since the beginning, when the true titans walked this world."

"I don't consider that fact lightly, and yes I'm terrified of that other path."

"The vulnerabilities I saw in you are gone, but you're not safe from peril. The nature of the risk is much different now. As a matter of fact, the precarious state of your quest, the glaring personal weaknesses, they are alleviated too, but all of you have threats of different sorts now."

Turning his head, he spoke, "I would say to you, Jeren, stop selling yourself short. You were the lynchpin in there, Sindora knew it from the start and attacked you on every level that she could. She was a breath away from her goal, although that in itself was a colossal travesty. Molded from the same clay as you, she was deceived far worse than any of you into craving a world of such horror, it could never have stood. Destruction would not have been reserved only for her opponents, the followers of the light. Her torment would have been equal to yours in the grasp of the demonic who wrested her mind and soul away from her."

The revelation was daunting.

"Do you see? She's made herself and her ilk believe they're your mortal enemies without realizing she is her own mortal enemy too. What waits for her beyond the end of this life, I can't manage to ponder it. Even I feel fear."

No one of the quest could respond. Such a nightmare that could daunt Mobokta couldn't be allowed to prevail.

Selana raised her arms and evoked her power. The vortex appeared.

"The way to paradise is open to you."

He stared through. "I've seen this sight, the perfect garden, from out here. Strangely, the chance to go there is frightening to me."

"It is your choice," Selana replied.

Just as he was about to take a step into the roiling magic, there was a loud sound like an explosion behind them. They all turned to see red power roiling in a cloud coming toward them.

The allied troops drew their weapons and deployed into battle formations. Jeren attempted to link his family into their magical cocoon.

"Wait!" Selana shouted. Everybody looked back, but she wasn't talking to them.

"What?" asked Mobokta. He looked confused.

The red cloud dissipated and out stepped Antith, sweating and gasping at the effort it took to enter Mobokta's realm.

"Brother," he shouted.

"Antith, how are you alive?"

"How could I die with how things were?"

"Antith is your brother?" asked Arium, incredulous.

"We're ancient beings," Mobokta answered. "I told you the truth that we were here at the beginning."

"That's why you could so easily enslave us, and render our magical defenses useless," Arium whispered as it dawned on her.

Looking at Antith, she continued, "We understand what plans Sindora had for us, but I assumed the same was true for you. I was wrong."

"Yes. My goal was never anything of this feeble world. Your vanity that I lusted after you as a woman was foolish. I've known multitudes of lovers over the vast span of my life. None were any different than the rest. I've had all manner of possible life; there is no unanswered question or unexplored experience for me. I could have only one goal, to shake my fist in the faces of those who damned me to imprisonment here for all eternity.

"If you had a purpose other than as a means to enter Evanshard Glade, I briefly pondered a special child I could create for you to birth, but a special child is already made, standing here before me. You are a marvel, child, Selana the destroyer."

She said nothing.

"Will you bar me from entering the Glade with my brother?"

"No. Do you believe it will avail you some manner of revenge?"

"It will offer me what I want, release from the misery which has been my life, and yes, confronting them will vent my feelings. At the very least, I'm reunited with my brother for a time. If the end of this is my demise, I welcome it. Living without the chance of dying is not a blessing, it's a curse."

They looked at Mobokta. "I cannot disagree with Antith. I've lived in this plane of existence far longer than I should have. If we sinned in their eyes, this punishment goes too far. We should be allowed our eternal rest."

"I'm sorry, I misjudged you," said Arium. "You're right. I thought you had seamy designs for me. Perhaps you're right that vanity is one of my glaring flaws."

Antith added, "Let me say this to you all. Taking me out of the picture as one of your pursuers does not lessen your need for caution and constant preparedness. Those others of your foes are very dangerous and can still achieve their dire plans for the world. This is no time to glory in your momentary victory or to rest on your laurels.

"As you are now aware, Selana the Destroyer must walk a fine line in her life. The call from the dark side will haunt her for as long as she lives. That is not a small thing. My brother and I know how alluring that is. It's part of why we're in our predicament. You have noticed I evoke red power. It isn't by my choice but a part of the curse upon me.

"Heed my words because the smallest of openings is all they need to wreak havoc. Don't think the trials you've gone through are over. Where you were in Sindora's grasp not so long ago, understand that can happen again. You must build your powers to match their daunting force. If she gets control of you again, she won't toy with you this time. She will be feral."

Jeren spoke, "Antith, I never thought I would say this, but thank you, and I hope all goes well for you and for Mobokta. We're all sorry to find out this terrible state you've been forced to live in for all of this time. Good luck."

Antith nodded and then turned to Mobokta. "Are you ready, brother?"

"I am."

The two stepped through the vortex and into Evanshard Glade for the first time. The vortex closed so whatever happened next to them, the quest members did not see.

Arium took Jeren's hand. "As Antith just asked, are you ready for this?"

"I am."

"Where do we go?" asked Gensten.

"For some reason, I feel we should finish the trek to your home. If I understand correctly, it isn't far."

"Yes, you're right. I can't promise much. My country is like these lands we've traveled through with plenty of petty jealousy amongst the rulers and the noble class. The secretive group which sent you the tome, I can't say if they wield power. If they do, I don't know if it is blue or red."

"We'll deal with whatever we find. If you wish to return to your former life there, we will understand."

"Honestly, there's nothing for me back home. My parents have passed over, and my status in society was low level and unremarkable. I believe no one expected me to succeed in this task or to survive. I've come to think of all of you as my family."

"We are your family," said Arium warmly. She gave him a firm hug.

"Then it's settled," Jeren added. "There's no reason to delay."

The troop mounted up and rode away eastward. The tales of their adventures were known only to themselves and their enemies. No historians or scribes were immortalizing the story for posterity.

Selana and Darik were approaching an eighth birthday and the twins, Amik and Sari, were unrecognizable from the terrified cowering tiny survivors they'd been. Four miniature wizards posed a genuine threat against any potential foes.

Grakar, Drake, and Brogan were far different soldiers too. They'd experienced the highest and the lowest in defeating the seemingly invincible while having experienced the shame of abject captivity as Sindora's pawns. Brogan in particular would never forget the connection with Arium, even with the contrived and manipulative start from Sindora. These feelings were actual, genuine and they would never go away. Fighting them down to try to function without her as his mate was a task which nearly drove him mad.

Brek was no less enamored with Arium, but he'd never had that same situation as Brogan where she was his briefly. Drake too was a thwarted suitor forced to accept defeat about her.

In truth, not a single soldier in the quest didn't dream of Arium and entertain fantasies of her being their wife.

Arium had her own issues coping with the residual aftermath of the travesty of captivity, helpless before Sindora. The residual strong feelings for Brogan worried her a great deal, about as much as she worried about Selana's dilemma fighting off her dark side. Arium realized, she had her own equivalent of a dark side and it humbled her. Her punishing thoughts were not easily dismissed.

Jeren is the worthiest of husband's standing firm through all manner of assault, but can I expect him to continue if my weakness proves too strong, again. What if I fall?

While Arium suffered self-recriminations, she wasn't alone with inner turmoil.

Added to the traveling group were all of the brothers, the restored wizards of the light. They'd followed Jeren without question, humbled too, just like the allies.

As Antith had said, revamping and rebuilding their ranks, becoming strong enough as the proper countermeasure to Sindora and her forces, it was a vital task and one which shouldn't be delayed, but none would dispute Jeren's choices. He was their High Mage and that decision was irrefutable.

Gensten took the lead, his normal place, directing this potent force where to go. Leading them to his home country was an easy enough task but whether they should be going there was the issue. Even he had a question about Jeren's pick for their first destination.

The place he occupied in this august company, included as one of the leaders, it was a condition Gensten could never have imagined, or aspired to. What waited for him back home was a return to irrelevance and ignominious servitude. That, he did not relish. The high place and the respect he'd earned fighting alongside these incredible companions had changed him into a new man, one that would not be content any longer as a lackey.

Riding forward at Jeren's directive didn't alleviate his queasy feeling he was leading them into trouble.

Glancing to his right, Selana was approaching. When she rode to his side, she smiled.

"May I ride with you?"

"Of course you may. Is there trouble ahead?"

"There is always trouble ahead for us, but it doesn't matter which way we go. Do not fear. I can sense you worry about taking us to your home. We are all here with you."

"Thank you, I did feel responsibility for whatever we face there. In my land there can be troubles as much as we've already passed through and perhaps more. I worry a great deal about those secretive fellows. What if they're purveyors of darkness in league with Sindora?"

"If that is the case, I think it is they who should worry, wouldn't you say?"

"I didn't look at it that way. You're right, Selana. What greater force can there be than us? I feel better already."

"Good, however I would still like to ride at your side, if you're agreeable."

"How could I not be agreeable to that? We are all interwoven now into a single fabric."

"I like that."

"That is my great philosophical idea of my lifetime as I'm no great scholar."

Selana laughed.

She smiled at him again. "You're a good man, Gensten. It may surprise you to hear this, but when I look for relief from my burdens and need comforting; I enjoy spending time with you. Does that displease you?"

"Of course not, I'm flattered. Can I ask though is it my dull brain which you find intriguing, where you have no worries about hearing challenging ideas come out of my mouth?"

Again she laughed, heartily.

"As you just said, I feel better already. Thank you, Gensten, my dear friend."

"Selana, I'm sorry about this unfair onus you carry. I wish I could do something for you."

"You have, you calmed my spirit. What I face only I can deal with it. I accept it, but having anchors like you in my life are essential. Do you see?"

"In that, I hope I never fail you. I feel inadequate so much of the time."

"You're not inadequate. Look at all that you've done that no other could have."

"Well…maybe I've done a couple of little things."

They both laughed this time.

The world continued to rotate on its axis. Days and nights passed, plots thickened and schemes were hatched as the new quest endeavored to prepare for any challenge. Each individual was a microcosm of the world around them as they coped with their inner demons to greater or lesser extent.

In essentially a male-dominant society, two females were the center and the focal point of so much—Arium and Selana. Whatever the future would be, they would be prime factors.

The End

CPSIA information can be obtained
at www.ICGtesting.com
Printed in the USA
BVHW042004200721
612415BV00014B/1281